A PLACE CALLED DESTINY

The Destiny Series Book 1

EMMA EASTER

A Place Called Destiny
by Emma Easter

Paperback Edition

CKN Christian Publishing
An Imprint of Wolfpack Publishing

6032 Wheat Penny Avenue
Las Vegas, NV 89122

Paperback ISBN: 978-1-64734-703-1
Ebook ISBN: 978-1-64734-702-4

A PLACE CALLED
DESTINY

ONE

Rachel opened her eyes when she heard Mike's heavy breathing.

Good, he's asleep, she thought, and then heaved a sigh of relief. She slowly extricated herself from Mike's grasp and put her feet on the ground. She slipped on the sandals she'd placed beside the bed and prayed that Mike would not wake up.

For a brief moment, she sat waiting for her eyes to adjust to the darkness of the bedroom. When she could finally make out the shape of the blue sofa she'd tossed her dress onto some hours ago, she stood up from the bed and soundlessly went to pick up the dress. She hurriedly put it on, tied back her dark, waist-length hair, and tiptoed to the closet. A cry escaped her when she hit her leg on her purse stand, and she immediately clamped a hand over her mouth. Her heart began to beat wildly in fear and she silently scolded herself. *You clumsy girl. What have you done?*

She didn't dare turn her face toward the bed. If only she didn't have to sneak around in the darkness. But she couldn't afford to turn the light on and risk waking Mike up. She stood unmoving, tears in her eyes, not just from the pain radiating in her leg, but also from the fear that Mike would wake up. If he did, all would be lost, and she would continue living in this hell on earth.

She put her hand on her growing belly and whispered, "Lord, please help me escape, not just for my sake, but my baby's." She sighed. There was no way she was going to raise her child in a place like Fallow Creek or with a man like Mike. She planned to go to Phoenix as she had a cousin who lived there. True, she hadn't spoken to her cousin in years, but she was hoping for the best — just a place to stay and some food to eat until she could find her feet.

After what seemed like an eternity of waiting and praying that Mike would not awaken, she exhaled. Weak with relief, she went quickly to the closet and opened it, less careful now about not making noise. All she wanted to do was leave quickly. The more time she stayed here, the higher the chance that Mike would wake up and find her trying to leave him.

She picked up the sole purse from the stand, opened it, and brought out her phone. Pressing a button on it, she used the dim light to search for her duffel bag. She had packed the bag last night and hidden it at the back of the closet.

She found the bag, brought it out, and then grabbed the keys to Mike's truck on the bedside table. Her conscience pricked her as she dropped the keys into her purse, but she brushed the guilt aside. He had five other cars.

She once again tiptoed toward the door, still praying that Mike wouldn't wake up. She got to the door and just as she put her hand on the doorknob, Mike grunted, "What have you done?"

She froze and her heart began to pound in terror. *Oh Lord, why?*

Even though the room was dark and she was sure Mike couldn't see her, he had probably heard her skulking about the room. In his usual annoyingly perceptive way, he had probably guessed what she was trying to do. Any minute now, light would flood the room and she would be found out.

She turned around slowly, already knowing what Mike would say, what he would do. Shivers went down her spine.

"We have been through this before," Mike said.

Rachel's mouth felt dry and her stomach churned. She opened her mouth to tell Mike that she was just going to get something to eat because she could not sleep, and then raised her brows when Mike began to mumble gibberish. After a while, silence reigned again and it finally occurred to her that he wasn't really awake. Once in a while, he talked in his sleep, which was what had happened now. Again, overwhelming relief flooded her as she silently left the room.

As she walked past Olivia's room, she resisted the urge to enter and tell the woman she was leaving. In spite of how Mike had tried to pit them against each other, and despite the fact that they were rivals, she liked Olivia. But more than that, she felt sorry for Olivia and never stopped blaming herself for being the cause of the woman's constant sadness. *If not for me, Olivia would have her husband all to herself,* Rachel thought.

She wanted to tell Olivia that they could leave Mike together with her two children, but knowing Olivia, she would never agree. Mike was like a god to her, the way many husbands in Fallow Creek were to their wives. Olivia's two children occupied the bedrooms next to hers and if it weren't so dangerous, Rachel would take those dear ones away from this place.

She tiptoed down the stairs and got to the living room. Turning on the light, she took the keys to the front door from the TV stand, and then went to unlock the door. Taking a deep breath, she looked back at the living room and the house she'd lived in for four years; four torturous years. The living room, like the rest of the house, was furnished lavishly. Mike was the second richest man in Fallow Creek, and he'd never been afraid to spend his money on luxuries that had sometimes raised a few eyebrows, like the half-dozen cars parked outside their large five-bedroom home. She turned around again and stepped out into the night. She ran to the red truck, opened it, and got in.

For the first time, she was grateful that the houses in Fallow Creek, the religious community — or polygamous cult, depending on who you asked — that she'd lived in for most of her life didn't have gates or barricades. She could drive away from the house without needing to first open a gate. However, there was something worse than a barricade that she was worried about. The security squad, a group of young men who patrolled Fallow Creek twenty-four hours a day, would be out tonight. She had already concocted a story to tell them. She only hoped they would believe it. If not, she would try to bluff her way out of the community.

Her heart hammered as she started the truck. If the sound of the vehicle roused Mike or anyone in the house, her leaving would be in jeopardy. Even if they got down here after she'd driven off, they would definitely call the patrollers at the edge of the community and she would be prevented from leaving. And then her plight would be worse than it had been before. The punishments for trying to leave the community, especially for women, were varied and severe. No woman was to leave her husband's house without his express permission. As for the security squad, they could probably hear the roar of her truck now. They would be expecting her.

Over the years, she had marveled time and time again at how the polygamous community had been able to exist mostly under the government's radar. The community was a very small town in Arizona made up of roughly three hundred people, most of whom she'd grown up with. It was peaceful, mostly due to the fact that all the inhabitants obeyed the strict religious rules. The other "wives" the men in the community married were not legal, but "spiritual wives", and in that way, they escaped prosecution for practicing polygamy. Only a few people had ever successfully moved away from the town. Rachel planned to be one of them.

"Lord, please help me," she muttered as she backed out of the driveway.

She drove away from the house, thanking the Lord that no one had woken up and rushed downstairs to try to stop her. But she was still afraid. The security squad was ahead.

She drove fast, driving by the houses in the community. Some of them were as tiny as the living and dining rooms in Mike's house. Others were bigger homes, but none as big as Mike's. So far, no one had seen her, for which she was grateful.

The stars seemed to shine brighter tonight than ever before, but maybe it was just because she was beginning to feel excited about the prospect of finally leaving Fallow Creek. She began to approach the edge of the community, and then blinked in surprise. She didn't see any security squad members.

Just before the edge of Fallow Creek, on the left side of the road, stood the home of Dennis Hamilton, the leader of the community who was also their spiritual leader. The man had as many wives as he had children, all of them living in his four-bedroom house.

Rachel's heart began to pound with excitement as she passed the house. She still hadn't seen any of the men in the security squad. And then she sucked in her breath. A short distance away was a group of armed security squad members in fatigues, their faces and forms illuminated by the headlights of the SUVs around them. It was as if the whole security team had gathered at the edge of the community; as if someone had tipped them off about her plan to flee Fallow Creek. They were all looking in her direction, their cars barricading the road.

She reduced her speed, her heart racing faster than she could ever imagine, while praying fervently for help. She had told no one of her plans, so how was it that they were all gathered here now, about to stop her from her journey to freedom? The thought of remaining in the town was too much to bear.

Maybe it was time to turn around and drive back to Mike's house. Or she could keep going and try to bluff her way past the team. But her plans to do that had been based on the fact that she'd believed she would only have to deal with the one or two members of the squad who usually patrolled the border. Never had she imagined that she would have to face so many of them.

As she crawled on, she made a split decision not to turn back, the myriad of squad guards ahead notwithstanding. To continue staying in this community was, in a way, as undesirable as dying. Besides, they had already seen her, and if she went back they were sure to tell Mike she'd been there, and then not only would she get into a heap of trouble; she would be monitored constantly and would never get the chance to escape again.

With her hands dripping wet and clutching the steering wheel, she increased her speed until she reached the guards. She stopped in front of them and prayed furiously as they walked toward her truck. She could see their faces clearly now. Some of them looked curious, others bemused.

One of the men came to stand beside the truck and stared at her as she rolled her window down. She knew him really well. His name was Daniel and he had been her older brother's good friend when they were growing up. Seeing him immediately reminded her of her older brother, Taylor, who lived on the other side of Fallow Creek. She and Taylor had been quite close when they were children but had grown apart as adults. Even though Taylor lived in Fallow Creek, they had not seen each other in months.

Daniel's eyes grew wide, and he said to her, "Rachel, where on earth are you going at this ungodly hour?"

She pressed down her fear and put on a smile for him. "Dan, I haven't talked to you in a while," she said as pleasantly as she could manage. She tried to remember exactly what she had planned to say as some of the other men came to stand on the other side of the truck. She turned to give them a bright smile and then turned back to Daniel. She stopped smiling and said, "Actually, one of Olivia's children is having an asthma attack and I was sent to get his medication immediately."

One of the guards, a young man whose name she couldn't remember, said in a dubious tone, "How come you did not go to our local pharmacy? It's only a few minutes' walk from your husband's house."

Rachel stared at him with her eyebrows raised and said in a steely voice, "Do you want to be responsible for a child's death? Do you think I didn't think about going to the pharmacy? As you well know, it doesn't open at night." She glared at him. "You need to let me go. If something happens to that child, I will make sure to tell everyone that you are responsible."

Daniel said, "I think we should let her go."

Another member of the squad, who stared at Rachel with disbelief in his eyes, said, "Why didn't you go to Peter Miller's house, then? You know he owns the pharmacy. You should go there now. Since it's an emergency, I am sure he will open the pharmacy for you and give you whatever you need."

Rachel bit her lip and hastily searched through her mind for something to say. An idea came to her and she said, "The last time we went to buy the boy's asthma medication from the pharmacy, Peter told us it wasn't available. We had to ask Elder Pearson to get the medicine when he went for that brief visit to Phoenix. As I told you, it's an emergency. I didn't want to risk going to Peter's house only to be told the medicine was still not available, which would be likely considering that the pharmacy has not been restocked for a while. Now let me pass, or do you want to be held responsible for a child's death?" She glared at the three guards who were looking at her.

They looked sufficiently chastised. The one who had been interrogating her turned to the others who were standing near their SUVs. "Let her through," he yelled.

Rachel stifled a loud sigh of relief and put on a scowl instead. She tapped her fingers on the steering wheel as though she were losing her patience by the minute. Her heart kept racing and she continued to pray silently that nothing would go wrong and that no one would think to call Mike to corroborate her story.

One of the men who had been standing some distance away walked up to Daniel. "Are you sure we should let her through?" he asked.

Daniel said, "It's an emergency. One of Mike Cadwell's children is having an asthma attack and Rachel needs to get his medicine. Peter Miller does not have the medicine, so she needs to get it outside Fallow Creek. Unless you want to be blamed for whatever happens to that child, I suggest you make way for her to pass."

The guard hesitated for a minute and then nodded. He ran to the other squad members and said something to them. When they got into their vehicles and began to drive off the tarred road, Rachel pressed her lips tightly together while maintaining her scowl.

The two guards who had been questioning her nodded and moved on. Daniel smiled and told her to be careful, as it was the middle of the night. He said, "I will ask one of the men to go with you. It's not safe for a woman to be on the road at this time of night." He waved one of the men over and Rachel's heart filled with dread. *What do I do now Lord?* she silently prayed. If one of the guards followed her, she would not be able to escape. She muttered beneath her breath, "Lord, I need your help right now."

"Please just let me go, Daniel," she said. "I don't need anyone to go with me. I have a long way to drive and you wouldn't want any of the men to be away from their post for so long."

"Nonsense," Daniel said. "Billy will act as your bodyguard."

She looked at the road in front of her. All the vehicles blocking her path had cleared out. She could just speed off. She immediately put away the idea. The members of the security squad would catch up to her in no time.

Daniel was studying her face and she knew she had to do something. She recalled Mike saying something about a police station in the next town. All she had to do was outdrive the men until she could get to the police station. Once she was inside the station, the guards would not be able to get to her anymore.

As Billy began to walk toward her truck, she floored the accelerator and sped away. She heard a commotion behind her but did not look back. A few minutes later, as she raced down the road, she looked in the rearview mirror and her stomach flipped. The squad team were gaining ground. Once they overtook her, it would be all over.

She increased her speed, knowing she was now driving at a dangerous pace. Still, she had to escape, not just for her sake, but her unborn child's as well.

Her heart beat wildly as her tires ate the road. She checked her rearview mirror again and nearly passed out from fear. The squad's SUVs were now almost bumper to bumper with her truck. Soon, they would overtake her. She pushed the car even faster and then winced in pain when her chest hit the steering wheel. Someone had crashed into her from behind. She ignored the pain and drove faster and faster until someone hit her from behind again. She lost control and her truck swerved and skidded off the road. Her eyes grew wide in horror as the truck headed for an electric pole. She tried to veer it away, but it was too late.

"God, please help me," she said just before the truck crashed violently into the pole. She felt herself flying off her seat and hitting the hood of the truck and then her body dropped down again. She felt herself slipping away and whispered, "God, please let my child live," and then blacked out.

TWO

Keith Thorn slowly sat down on his sofa while clutching his phone to his ear. He couldn't believe what his older sister was telling him. When she finished talking, he said in a voice barely louder than a whisper, "What are you saying, Mary? You're trying to tell me that all the money I got from Grandma when she passed away is gone? How is that possible?"

Mary, who was also his banker, said, "You have no more money to withdraw, Keith. It's what I've been trying to tell you for some time now. You have withdrawn all your money. I warned you about this. It's not like Grandma left us millions. It was only thirty thousand dollars, which she saved for years. I still have most of my fifteen thousand while you have used up yours."

Keith put his hand on his forehead and shut his eyes briefly. He opened them again and said, "Mary, you know we needed a new church here in Destiny. No one in our small town has that kind of money."

"And so you had to use all your money?" Mary

said exasperatedly.

"You know the old church had gotten too small since church attendance doubled almost a year ago." He sighed. He had taken over as the pastor of the only church in town about two years ago. Since then, attendance and membership had grown faster than he could imagine and was still growing. As great as that was, the small church could no longer contain everyone. His dream was to see all the eight hundred or so inhabitants of Destiny attending church regularly, but it would not happen if there was no space for them. "Soon, we'll have to start turning people away," he said. "And that would be so wrong, especially as I have been praying for an increase in church attendance. I had to use the money to start building a new, bigger church."

"Are you trying to tell me that you spent all your inheritance on building a new church, Keith? And you still haven't finished building that church?"

Keith pursed his lips. All the money hadn't gone to building a new church. He said, "You know that most of the businesses in Destiny have closed and employees have been laid off. A lot of people here either don't have jobs or are poorly paid. Being the pastor of the only church, people look up to me to help them, not just spiritually, but in any other way I can."

Mary sighed loudly. "You're not God, Keith. You should stop acting like you are. Now that you have given away all your money to help those people, who is going to help you?"

"They are your people too, Mary."

"Whatever," she said. "You have no answer to my question, do you?"

He didn't. He knew exactly what she was going to say next; what she always said to him every time she called. Just before he opened his mouth to tell her he didn't want to hear it, she said, "Keith, it's really time you left Destiny. I am sure Mom and Dad would say the same thing if they were still alive. That town is dying. It's why I left a long time ago. You are only twenty-eight, Keith. You shouldn't be wasting your life there."

Keith groaned. Ever since their grandmother, who had raised him and his sister, died three years ago, Mary hadn't stopped bothering him about leaving Destiny. But he did not want to leave. This was where he'd grown up. He knew without a doubt that God wanted him here. He loved the people and he loved being the pastor of the church God had placed in his care. He would never leave. Not until the Lord told him to.

"You said Mom and Dad would have told me to leave if they were alive," Keith muttered. "Since they died when we were really young, I don't know if you are right, but I know what Grandma would say if she were still alive. She would agree with me. She would tell me to stay in Destiny and shepherd the flock that God had given me. And she would also tell me to take care of the house we grew up in. The house she loved." He looked around the living room, which his grandmother had furnished with chintz curtains and chairs. It was not his style, but he had changed nothing.

"Keith, that house is crumbling and so is Destiny. Tell me, how many people your age or younger still live there?"

"More than a few still do, Mary. Besides, it

doesn't matter if no one here is my age."

"It matters! Isn't it time for you to settle down and have a family of your own? You know there are no young eligible women in Destiny. I'm worried about you, Keith. All I want is for you to be happy. I want you to find a young woman to fall in love with, marry, and have children with. I am worried that you will stay in that town, grow old, and die alone."

Keith wanted to tell her that it wasn't going to happen, but instead he shuddered at her words. Even though he tried not to think about it, especially when he'd had so much on his plate for the past two years, from time to time he worried about exactly what his sister was saying. She was right. There were only a few single women in town and none he was interested in. He wanted what Mary had — a loving spouse and children — but he couldn't just leave Destiny because of that. He said to Mary, "God will bring me the right person when it's time."

"Listen, Keith, I trust in the Lord as much as you do, but faith without work is dead. You don't expect the Lord to mold a wife just for you from the sands of Destiny."

He chuckled in spite of himself. "The sands of Destiny! That sounds like a drama-filled daytime soap opera."

"I'm serious, Keith!" Mary sounded exasperated. "You need to get out of that town. You've given away all your money and you're planning to give away your future. I can help you find a decent job if you come to Denver. Maybe then we can work towards also finding you a bride."

"Stop it, Mary!" Keith said. He knew she was just looking out for him as his older sister, but still. He would not be forced to leave the town that God had called him to. "I'm not going anywhere. Like I said, God will provide everything I need, including a wife, if that is His will for my life."

For a long moment, there was silence on the other end of the line and Keith frowned. "Mary, are you there?"

"At least let me send you some money," Mary said. "But you have to promise that you will use it for yourself and not for that church. And don't tell me you don't want to take money from me."

"You have your kids to think of. I cannot take your money. And please don't insist."

"Keith, I can afford to send you a little money."

"No," Keith said firmly. "And any money I have now will be used for the church building and to help anyone in need here. Since you don't want me to do any of that, it would be wrong to take your money."

Mary groaned and said, "Alright, little brother. I guess I will have to keep praying that the Lord will make you leave."

"Not going to happen. God doesn't change His mind."

"Okay, then. I've told you about the state of your finances. What you do about it is up to you now. I love you. I'll call you in a few days."

"I love you too, Mary," Keith said, smiling. "Say hi to Will and the kids for me."

After the call ended, Keith leaned back against the sofa, thinking about everything his sister had said. "Lord, I need your help right now," he prayed.

"I have no money left and I believe you want me to build a church that will be big enough to hold everyone in Destiny if need be. I can't do that without any money."

He wasn't even going to think about how he would survive. He had a little cash with him, but it would barely cover his weekly groceries. He had been using money from his inheritance and the little money he made from his small store to cover his expenses. Now, the inheritance money was gone. All that would be left for his daily upkeep would be money from the store and the tiny stipend he was given as a pastor. He barely made a profit from the store and when he did, it was just a small profit. He sighed, worried. From now on, he would have to be extremely thrifty. What was most important was finishing the church and helping the needy in Destiny.

He kept worrying for a long time and then finally stood up, trying to brush aside his concerns. Worrying continuously about finances and his marital status would do no good. He went to the window and drew back the curtains. And then he blinked. He'd expected sunlight to shine through to brighten his day, as it was midday in July. Instead, the sky outside was dark and looked slightly foreboding, like a storm was gathering.

He shut the curtains once more. The weather simply reminded him of his life now. His store wasn't doing well and he'd only been fully sustained by the inheritance money. Now it was gone, what would he do? The church was only half-built. How would it be completed? Why wasn't he more like Mary, handling money carefully? He'd never liked discussing finances, and now he was going to pay for his carelessness.

He sat back down on the sofa, and even though he tried not to think about all his problems, telling himself that God would make a way, he couldn't stop worrying.

He began to ask the Lord if he was indeed supposed to remain in Destiny, but he knew the answer already. This was where he was supposed to be. Still, he couldn't stop thinking about what Mary had said, not just concerning his finances, but his chances of ever finding love if he stayed in Destiny. Strangely, that bothered him even more than his lack of finances and ability to continue with the church building project.

Maybe that is not God's will for my life, he mused. He had always been one to submit completely to God, but the thought that it might not be His will for him to ever have a wife and children felt like a tragedy.

He tried to shake his worry, but it clung to him. His head ached from worrying until at last, he scolded himself for wasting time and energy, fretting over things that he could not change, at least right now. He stood up, went into his room, and sat down at his desk. Opening his Bible, he sighed, and then began to study, preparing for his sermon at the church later in the evening.

THREE

Rachel stood holding the front door ajar while she eavesdropped on Mike and the church elders. They were arguing outside the house... because of her. She sucked in her breath and drew back as one of the elders turned his head in her direction. "Lord, I hope they haven't seen me," she whispered in panic. A few seconds later, she snuck a look. The elder had turned back to Michael. Rachel said a silent prayer of thanks to God and then continued to listen to them.

"You're not taking my wife anywhere," Mike said. "Rachel has been serving the appropriate punishment in the house. I haven't allowed her out of the house since she came back from the clinic a few days ago."

Rachel pursed her lips, annoyed. She hated being called Mike's wife. The men in this community collected wives as easily as some people collected stamps. They were never legally married to any but their first wives, just the way she and Mike were not legally husband and wife. But still, in the eyes of these wicked people, she was Mike's wife. Which meant that she was his property.

One of the elders snorted. "You cannot mete out whatever punishment you choose by yourself, Michael. You know what the rules are. Whoever tries to abandon her marriage and flee the community will be taken to the House of Restoration where she will stay until her mind has been completely renewed."

Rachel's heart began to beat with dread. She had never entered the House of Restoration, but she had heard rumors about what happened there. It was bad enough that she had been caught trying to escape and then locked up in the house by Mike. To be sent to that house where there would be more of the brainwashing she'd been subjected to since she'd come to Fallow Creek coupled with hard manual labor was something she didn't want to contemplate. And yet continuously living with Mike as a proper wife when she wasn't made her stomach turn. She was carrying his baby now and was due to deliver in a month.

In a way, she already considered the child in her belly more hers than Mike's, even though in this community a child belonged first to the father. She felt like striding out of the house and screaming at all these men who were deciding her own fate without her. They had complete power over her.

She cursed the day her mother had brought her and her brother, Taylor, to the community. She and Taylor had different fathers who were not involved when they were growing up. One day, when Rachel was eight, a strange man had come into their lives. Soon, something weird had happened to Mom.

She'd told them she had finally repented of her sins and had found God, but to Rachel she became a sort of robot. Two months later, Mom had moved her and Taylor out of their small house in Glendale so they could go live with Chris in Fallow Creek, and then she'd married him.

After that, everything about Rachel's life changed and she was no longer free to be the child that she was. She was put in a drab adult gown that she had to wear every day and was forced to act like an adult. Soon, Chris married two more wives and then had several other children whom Rachel never considered to be her siblings. Only Taylor was the one she loved. Now, Fallow Creek had swallowed him up as well. Presently, he was planning to marry his second "wife".

She, on the other hand, had never really fitted into this awful community. She was too headstrong for a woman and had continuously refused to marry anyone, dreaming constantly of the day she could run away from the community and fall in love with her prince charming. Only then did she plan to get married. She would be the only wife and be treated with love and care, the way she had never seen any of the women in Fallow Creek be treated. Unfortunately, that dream never came true. Being a single woman over twenty years old in the community opened her to all kinds of indignities. Since she had refused to get married, her mom and stepfather had decided it was time she left the house without caring where she went. It was their way to force her to get married.

Knowing she could not leave the community and with no money to take care of herself, as single women were not allowed to have paid jobs, she finally gave in when one of the wealthiest men in the community asked for her hand in marriage. Mike had inherited a great deal of money from his grandfather, which he had tripled through a variety of shrewd investments. Plus, he was well respected in Fallow Creek.

Their marriage was what the community considered a 'spiritual' marriage since Mike already had a wife. She had deceived herself into thinking that somehow, since he was wealthy and a bit more polished than most, he would treat her better, or at the very least, that his wealth would make up for whatever she suffered. She had not considered Olivia, his first wife, nor his children. It was the way of the community, after all. And she had no choice. But when she moved in with Mike, she found out that he was the same as the rest of the men in the community. Maybe even worse. He didn't think anything about forcing himself on her when she was slow in giving him what he wanted, or alienating her from Olivia.

When he stopped being intimate with Olivia and made Rachel move permanently into his bedroom, she struggled with guilt and disgust for years. She started to plan her escape from the community a week before she found out she was pregnant. She put it off to rest, especially as the severe morning sickness began, and then a month ago, she began to plan her escape again. And she would have succeeded in escaping if not for Daniel and his idiotic idea to have a bodyguard follow her out of the town.

She knew Mike and the men were still arguing

because she could see the angry expressions on their faces, but she had stopped listening to them. She placed her hand on her belly and caressed it.

"Thank you, Lord, for preserving my child," she said. She had woken up a day after the accident to find herself in Fallow Creek's sole clinic. A few minutes after she'd opened her eyes, Mike had walked into the room and stared at her with fire in his eyes. She had immediately closed her eyes again so she would not have to see how angry he was. When he'd walked out of the hospital again, she'd sighed with relief, though she'd known she would be in trouble the minute she was released from the clinic. Worrying about her baby, she had been thankful when the midwife had walked in and told her that her baby was fine. "You did a stupid thing, trying to run away," the midwife had said, with a frown of disapproval.

Now she was back in this wretched community. No matter how stupid everyone said her actions had been, how ungodly, she was already planning her escape again. Once Mike lifted this ban and she was allowed out of the house once more, she would find a way to flee the community. But if he gave in to these elders' demands and she was taken to the Restoration House, she would not be able to escape again soon, maybe never. She felt weak with fear as she held the slightly open door and listened in again to Mike's discussion with the elders.

"Rachel is pregnant," Mike said. "At least let her have my baby, and then you can take her to the Restoration House."

One of the elders shook his head and disagreed with Mike but the others said nothing for a while.

"Please," Mike begged, looking at each of them. "As I have heard, that Restoration House will be hard for a pregnant woman to bear. You know the Bible says that children are a gift from the Lord. Rachel is bringing a gift into this world. At least let her bring the baby into a familiar environment where she's comfortable. I promise that once she gives birth and is well rested, I will personally hand her over to all of you."

Rachel's heart began to race. None of the options that she'd heard were bearable to her. Staying with Mike here made her stomach turn. That Restoration House sounded like a nightmare. But it appeared that Mike planned for her to experience both options. She would stay with him until she had given birth and then be sent off to that nightmarish house.

Overwhelming dread descended on her as it occurred to her that she would not be allowed to keep her baby when she was sent off to "renew her mind." Babies were not allowed to stay there. She pressed her lips together to keep from crying out and shook her head slowly. "No, Lord, I cannot leave my baby." She suddenly felt consumed by panic. She looked up thoughtfully. There had to be a way to escape.

But she knew there was none.

The elders had decided to place members of the security team around the house continuously because of her attempt to escape. Plus, Mike watched her every single day like a hawk.

She could not contain her anguish anymore and silently cried out, "Lord, please help me. I cannot leave my baby here. Even if I am sent away to the repentant house, please let me be able to take my baby with me."

She sighed with sorrow, knowing that would never happen unless the Lord worked a miracle for her. She began to pray even more fervently. She could bear Mike's presence if only she was allowed to take her baby with her once she was sent off to the Restoration House.

Someone suddenly pushed the door wide open and she stumbled back. Mike came into the living room and stared at her. "I see you have been eavesdropping."

She shrunk away from him, not sure what he would do to her. He had never hit her, but he had done other things that were just as despicable, if not more. When he sat down on the couch and told her in a gentle voice to sit beside him, she blinked in surprise. *What is he up to now?*

She sat on the edge of the couch.

"Come closer," Mike whispered, and then looked around as though there was a stranger in the house he was afraid of. She narrowed her eyes and then reluctantly shifted closer, but not close enough for their bodies to touch.

He looked into her eyes and said in a hushed tone, "There's something important I have to tell you."

Her heart sank to her feet. Surely he knew that she'd heard everything he and the elders had discussed. He was going to tell her that she would be sent away to renew her mind once she gave birth to her baby; that she would have to leave without her child.

She would not go easily. She would fight it,

though she knew there would be no use. She said to him, "I know what you want to tell me. Once I give birth, I will have to…" but she could not go on. Tears welled up in her eyes and she couldn't speak. She finally forced herself to talk. "The elders want me to go to the Restoration House after I give birth to my baby." She pleaded with him. "Please, Mike, don't let them send me away without my baby." She knew he didn't have the power to go against what the elders ordered. Still, she pleaded with him.

He put his hand on her shoulder and said, "Keep quiet, Rachel. Let me speak."

She bit her lip and stopped speaking. She would have to try to escape again before she gave birth to her child. She would not willingly allow anyone to separate her from her baby. The chance that she would succeed when there were so many security guards around the house were slim, if not nonexistent, but she would try. She had to, for her child's sake. She frowned as Mike stared at her without saying anything.

He finally spoke. "Listen, Rachel," he whispered. "We need to leave this community as soon as possible. That Restoration House is not somewhere I want you to go. You are very delicate. I am not sure you will survive the house and I want you by my side always." He looked up with a thoughtful expression. "Nobody is going to take my wife away from me."

She stared at him in astonishment. Did he just tell her that he wanted them to leave the community? That could not be. He was dedicated to everything in Fallow Creek. She said to him, "I'm sorry, did I hear you wrong or did you really say you want us to leave this community?"

"Sshh... lower your voice, Rachel," he ordered.

Rachel raised her brows. Olivia was upstairs in her room and her kids were still at school. There was no one around to hear what they were saying, so why was he being so secretive? Unless he really meant what he said about them leaving the community. Her eyes grew wide.

"You heard right," Mike said. "We have to leave before you have the baby. I need to put some things together before we go, but we will leave before the end of this week."

Rachel's heart began to race with anxiety and excitement. Did he really mean it? Would they really leave this awful place? Maybe if they succeeded in leaving, she would be able to eventually leave Mike as well. However, the chances of them packing up all their things and successfully leaving the community was unlikely. She shared her concerns with Mike.

"I know it's going to be extremely difficult to leave," he said. "But I think I have a plan that might succeed."

"Do you?" she asked. "And what is your plan?"

"Don't worry about it," he said. "This is what I want you to do: Start packing your things, but very discreetly. Tell no one about what I told you, though since you are not allowed to leave this house, I doubt you could anyway. I will let Olivia know that she is to do the same for herself and the children."

Rachel could not believe it. Michael Cadwell was actually serious about leaving Fallow Creek. She did not know whether to jump for joy or to cry out in fear. Because if they were caught trying to leave, especially her since she had tried before, being sent off to the Restoration House would be the least of her problems. And yet, in spite of the risks, she could not hold down her excitement.

Mike clapped his hands and said, "Now go and start packing, Rachel. You will also pack my clothes."

She nodded and got up from the couch. Slowly, she made her way up the stairs, cradling her belly. Her excitement increased with each step she took. She was finally going to leave this community that had taken so much from her. And then, soon, she would leave Mike.

The risk they were going to take in trying to escape and the consequences they would suffer if they were caught occupied her mind once again, but she pressed it away. Mike had said he had a plan. Knowing Mike, if he said he had a plan, it would be a good one. He had enough money to make whatever he wanted come true. He was a fastidious and detailed person. He would not rest until he had fine-tuned his plan and it was perfect. The only thing she could do now, apart from pack her things and Mike's, was pray fervently that Mike's plan would succeed.

She went to the bedroom that she shared with Mike and immediately brought out the large suitcase that had been unused in Mike's walk-in closet for years. She brought out another bag to pack her things separately from Mike's, in case she would be able to escape him immediately after they left Fallow Creek. But she soon changed her mind. Mike would be angry if he found out that she had packed her things separately and then he would be suspicious. Also, the chances of escaping Mike immediately after they left follow Creek were slim. She would have to wait and bide her time until the perfect moment when she could leave.

She began to pull her clothes out of the closet and fold them into the suitcase. After that, she sat down on the bed, exhausted, and looked at Mike's clothes in the open closet. Neither of them owned a lot of clothes, but for some reason, just packing only her stuff had completely worn her out. She did not know how she would find the strength to pack Mike's things.

Feeling a little light-headed, she sucked in huge gulps of air and forced herself to stand up. She suddenly felt a sharp pain in her stomach and cried out. Once again she cradled her stomach and shut her eyes as waves of pain coursed through her body.

What is wrong with me? She blinked. Something wet was running down her legs. She looked down and her mouth dropped open. Her water had just broken. She was in labor! But how could that be? She was due next month. At least that was what the midwife had told her.

She sat down slowly as waves of pain hit her. And then she felt excited at the fact that she was soon going to welcome her baby, the life that had been growing in her for months. She opened her mouth to call for Mike and tell him that she was in labor when she suddenly remembered the elders' discussion with Mike and what he had promised them.

"No, no, no, Lord. Please, I can't have my baby now!" she cried out. They were supposed to leave this town before the baby came. She put her hand on her stomach and began to slowly rub it as though that could stop her baby from coming out. She shut her eyes as contractions hit her. When she felt a strong urge to push, she knew there would be no delay. Her baby was determined to come into the world now.

Tears fell down her cheeks; not tears from the pain of labor, but from desperation and despair. If she gave birth now, there was no escaping Fallow Creek. The elders would come and take her away before she knew it and she would be separated from her baby. "Oh, Lord, please!" she begged, but all she felt was more pain and a stronger urge to push the baby out. At last, she screamed Mike's name, gritting her teeth in pain.

He burst into the bedroom a moment later. "What is it?" he asked, looking at her.

She wiped away the sweat on her brow and said, "I think the baby's coming."

His eyes grew round and he shook his head. "Rachel, the baby cannot come now! Is there no way to delay the birth?"

She screamed at him. "There's no way, Mike! You have to take me to the clinic right now!"

Mike began to run around the room like a headless chicken. "Let me go and tell Olivia to prepare so we can all go to the clinic together. I will call her mother to come watch the children." He left the room quickly and came back almost immediately. He picked up the bag that she had packed some time ago in preparation of her childbirth and came to put his arm around her. He slowly lifted her up from the bed and led her out of the room.

Getting down the stairs was excruciating and tiring for Rachel, but she made it at last with Mike's help. Olivia was already waiting near the black SUV when Rachel and Mike stepped out of the house. They all got in and Mike began to drive to the clinic while Rachel sat in the back of the car, breathing fast. This was not how she wanted her baby to come into the world. She wanted her baby to come into a world where both parents would celebrate her arrival. But her baby was coming now, at a time when Rachel and Mike did not want her to come.

Mike finally reached the clinic and parked at the side of the one-story building on a large tract of land. He opened the door and helped her out of the car.

When Rachel finally had a break from the painful contractions, she pulled away from Mike. She reached out for Olivia and when the older woman came to her, she put her arm around Olivia and leaned her weight on her. Mike mumbled something, but she ignored him. She wanted as little physical contact with him as possible. And since he couldn't force her to do anything at this time, she didn't have to lean on him.

Her legs felt heavy as she walked into the clinic with Olivia. Just as she sat down on the padded bench in the reception area, another wave of pain hit her and she pressed her lips tightly together so she would not scream. The midwife and a younger nurse called Nancy hurried over to Rachel and carried her away to the birthing room. Olivia followed, but Mike stayed where he was, as men weren't usually in the room during childbirth.

The childbirth was excruciating but thankfully quick. Her child slipped out from her within an hour and after she was cleaned, the midwife handed Rachel her daughter.

Rachel held her baby and wept.

The midwife smiled. "Tears of joy. I know how it feels, especially as this is your first child."

Rachel did not answer. Her emotions roiled as she felt a mixture of joy and deep sadness. Who knew how long she had with her baby before she was taken away?

Olivia lifted her daughter out of Rachel's arms, and Rachel relaxed on the bed. She shut her eyes as despair wrapped itself tightly around her. This baby, as much as Rachel already loved her with all her heart, was one more thing that bound her to this community. To Mike. If only she had given birth to her baby outside Fallow Creek. If only she had succeeded in escaping the first time.

She couldn't stop weeping as she lay on the bed with her back turned to Olivia and the midwife. After a long moment of crying silently, she finally drifted off to a fitful sleep, but not before a consuming sense of hopelessness settled over her. This might as well be the end of her life, because she knew with deep certainty that she would spend the rest of her life in this wretched town, with a callous polygamist whom she loathed.

FOUR

The uncompleted church building and the acres of land surrounding it were totally deserted. Usually during Keith's daily inspections, the place teemed with construction workers, but for the past week, there had been no one around. All work had stopped. He did not blame the workers as there was no more money for their remuneration. Keith had tried to do what he could to continue the work, but as he was not an architect or builder, there was little he could do.

He walked around the unfinished building feeling slightly depressed. If only a part of the church building had been fully completed — even just the main auditorium — there would at least be space for everyone to congregate this Sunday. He had told the builders he wanted the main church, children's church, offices, including his, and other parts of the church completed at the same time. Now he knew that had not been a good idea.

He glanced at his wristwatch. Talking about church service, it was nearly time for the evening

Bible study. If he didn't head to church now, he would not be able to finish preparing his sermon for the evening. He sighed sadly as he walked away from the building. How would he be able to raise the money to complete it now? And was it really God who'd told him to build a bigger church, or had he started it to boost his own ego? As he had done so many times since Mary had called to tell him he had no money left in his account, he asked the Lord to make a way and bring him a miracle.

He got into his old Honda and drove the short distance to the old church. Getting out of his car, he gazed at the tiny building. Mary was right. It was beginning to crumble, but that wasn't why they needed a new church.

He had been the assistant pastor for some years before becoming the senior pastor two years ago. The church had been here for as long as he could remember. There had been another one in Destiny when he was growing up. A larger church, which most of the people here had attended. This small house of worship had had only two dozen members then. As a child, he remembered his parents saying that it was a "church for holy rollers." What would they think now that he was the pastor of that church?

Membership had swelled after he'd taken over from Pastor Raymond and was steadily rising. There was barely enough space to hold all the people who attended the Sunday services. Some people even had to stand at the back during the service. This building had served the town well, but it was time to move on.

Once again, he prayed for provision and then

walked into the church. He immediately made his way to his tiny office behind the pulpit, sat behind his desk, opened his Bible, and began to study for his sermon.

About half an hour later, he raised his head when a knock sounded on his door. The door opened and Jenny Sadler, his dutiful secretary, walked into his office with a huge smile on her face. She was one of the few single women in the church and the only one in her twenties. The other single women who attended were either way older or younger than him.

She stood gazing at him without speaking and he cleared his throat. "Yes, Jenny, can I help you?" He always had the feeling that she had a small crush on him, though she had never said anything about it.

In her high-pitched voice, Jenny said, "Pastor Keith, most people have arrived and are waiting."

Keith looked up at the clock on the wall and raised his brows in surprise. The time had gone by so fast. He said to Jenny, who was still smiling at him, "Where are the worship leaders? Let them start the praise and worship session."

Jenny arched a brow and said, "They're not around today. Susan is out of town and I think Allen is sick or something."

Keith nearly groaned. That meant he would have to lead the worship session today, which he didn't particularly like to do. It wasn't that he didn't like worshiping, because he loved to, but he wasn't a great singer and wasn't comfortable standing in front of the entire congregation and showing just how bad his singing voice sounded. He wanted to tell Jenny to ask one of the other singers to lead the worship session, but he knew that would waste more time. Soon the congregation would become restless and begin to wonder if the service was going to happen this evening. He sighed and, without meaning to, said out loud, "I wish I didn't have to stand in front of the whole church and show just how awful a singer I am."

Jenny looked surprised. "You are a good singer, Pastor Keith. What are you talking about?"

He smiled at her. "Thanks, Jenny. Please give me a minute."

She gave him a sunny smile once again and then left the office.

Keith said a brief prayer, asking the Lord to give him the right words to say when he started his sermon, and then he asked for grace to lead the praise and worship session effectively.

He left his office feeling slightly nervous and stood in the pulpit. He picked up the microphone from the lectern and looked over at the congregation packed tightly together. The church pews, which ordinarily would be occupied by six people, had about nine people sitting on each of them. People stood almost shoulder-to-shoulder at the back of the church, blocking the entrance. Once again, threads of worry ran through him as he thought about what this would mean for the church. He'd been so confident about building a new house of worship, believing that it would be finished in a few months. Now that there was no money left to complete the building, more and more people would probably be turned away as there was no more space for them. He had to find a way to raise money; a way that did not include asking the people to give more than they had already given. He stared self-consciously at the congregation and then raised the first worship song that came to his mind.

Soon, everyone joined in singing with him as he raised one song after another. He soon lost his self-consciousness and focused on God's presence.

Twenty minutes later, he opened his eyes to end the praise and worship session. He noticed that there were people outside the church walking away who had probably tried to enter without succeeding. An overwhelming sadness came over him. When he'd taken over as pastor of this church, his goal had been to see everyone in Destiny saved and attending church regularly. He had taken that goal very seriously, believing it was God's will. Even though he was not an extrovert, he had done the rounds of door-to-door evangelism more than a few times. It had worked, as more people had joined the church. But now, it seemed as though everything would soon come to an end. Who liked to stand in church throughout the service, or sit on a cramped pew, or, worse, be sent away at the door?

He noticed a few eyes on him, people with curious expressions on their faces probably wondering why their pastor was standing in the pulpit without saying a word. He immediately brushed aside his worry, opened his Bible, and began his sermon.

After the Bible service ended an hour later, Keith went to the back of the church to greet his members as they walked out. He shook hands with some and hugged others. He promised to come visit a few of them during the week and said brief prayers for those who asked.

An older couple, Kate and Marvin Carpenter, walked up to greet him. Kate, a plump woman with a constant grin on her face, said to him, "That was a lovely sermon, Pastor. You know I pray every day that the Lord will bring you a lovely girl to serve at your side." She patted him on the shoulder like he was a beloved little boy. "It will happen for you soon," she said.

He pushed down his embarrassment and thanked her. It was not the first time she'd said she was praying for a bride for him. At this moment he was both amused and embarrassed, especially as Jenny was standing behind them, smiling.

The Carpenters finally went on their way and Jenny came up to him. She reached out as usual and gave him a hug. "I will be in the office very early tomorrow," she said, her arms around him.

"That's great," he casually told her, and patted her back in a brotherly hug.

When he pulled away from her, she said, "It's my birthday on Saturday, Pastor Keith. I am having a party. Will you come?"

Keith nodded. "Of course I will come... though I might not be able to stay for too long. The party will be at your house, right?"

"Yes."

"Okay. I will be there."

Her smile stretched from ear to ear. "Thank you, Keith," she said.

He raised his brows slightly, surprised. Not just because she was batting her eyelashes at him, but also because she had called him Keith. She always called him Pastor Keith, never just Keith. Had it been wrong to promise to attend her birthday party?

He brushed aside his concerns. He was pastor of the church. It was his duty to marry people, attend birthday parties, dedicate babies, and officiate funerals. Thankfully, he'd not done the latter except once, for the oldest man in Destiny at the time. Jenny was harmless and he considered her a friend, having known her for years. There was no reason not to attend her party.

Jenny was still looking at him, and he nodded at her to let her know she could leave. When she finally did, he went into his office.

He sat down behind his desk, his mind still on Jenny. It wasn't that he did not like her, because he did. But he liked her as a sister and nothing more. His parents had died early, but what little he remembered about them was that they were inseparable. They loved each other dearly and that was what he wanted with all his heart. He wanted to share his life with someone who made his heart pound; someone who would leave him tongue-tied when he finally met her; in whose presence the whole world would be painted in vivid colors. He wanted to be deeply in love.

"Lord, will I ever meet that person?" he asked, and then sighed loudly. Since he wasn't planning to leave Destiny anytime soon, and there was no one here for him, maybe he was truly destined to be alone.

He put away his musings and packed up his things. Just before he stood up to leave the church, his cellphone rang. He looked at the screen and saw it was Mary.

"Hi, Mary," he said when he clicked the answer button.

Mary sounded worried. "Are you okay, Keith?"

"I am," he answered. "What is wrong? Is it because of the news you gave me about my finances?"

"No," she snorted. "You are still in Destiny?"

"Yes. Where else would I be?"

"Didn't you hear about the hurricane heading that way?"

He sighed wearily. Why wouldn't she just give up trying to get him to leave Destiny? "No, Mary. The hurricane is not headed this way. They've made that clear on all the news channels. You know that. You just want me to leave Destiny."

"Still, I'm worried, Keith. You know the weather report can be wrong once in a while."

"Mary, I will be fine. Nothing will happen here. We have never had a serious hurricane, and I'm pretty sure if we were in the hurricane's path, the authorities would let us know."

"The authorities don't know that a place like Destiny exists."

"Mary, please," he said, exasperated.

"Alright, Keith, I will call you tomorrow to make sure you're fine."

Keith chuckled. "Okay, big sister, I'll talk to you tomorrow."

When he finally walked into his house, he felt lonely. It wasn't a big house. It had two bedrooms, one of which he and Mary had shared when they were growing up, until they were too old to share. Mary had begun to share their grandmother's room with her, while he'd remained in their old bedroom. It was the room he still slept in now. It had never seemed big to him, but today it did.

He shook his head and scolded himself. *That is what you get for obsessing continuously over finding a spouse.* He needed to think less about his marital status and focus more on finding a way to raise money for the new church building.

He spent the rest of the evening reading, making dinner, and eating alone — the latter magnifying how achingly lonely he felt. He ended the evening watching his favorite TV show. After that, he said a brief prayer, and then lay on his bed, looking up at the ceiling, loneliness smothering him.

FIVE

Keith woke up to pitch darkness and a horrifying sound. He sat up on his bed, rubbed his eyes, and listened in bewilderment to the noise that sounded like a dozen freight trains heading toward him. He reached for the light switch above him and turned it on. Nothing. The light did not come on. He remembered his conversation with Mary and fear gripped him. Was he in the middle of a hurricane?

His heart knocked in his chest as he knelt on the bed and drew back the curtains. His eyes widened in astonishment and panic. It was overwhelmingly dark outside and a violent storm was raging. He had never seen or heard anything like it before. It felt like the heavens had been rolled back and the rain was pouring unforgivably on the Earth. Water began to pour in through the window, smashing into his face, and he quickly shut the windows and closed the curtains.

"Oh my Lord, help us all!" he said. The weather report had stated that the hurricane would not make landfall in Destiny. "Only light showers," the man on the news had said. But now Destiny was in the middle of a raging storm. The house began to shake, and Keith's stomach dropped. It felt as though the house was shaking from its foundations and would be uprooted at any moment.

He swung his legs off the bed and grimaced. His feet were nearly ankle-deep in water. Water had started to seep into his house. He stood up immediately. He had to get his flashlight from the kitchen. If only he had taken Mary more seriously… but then, most people in Destiny had believed they would be safe from the hurricane.

He remembered his phone was beside him and picked it up. He pressed a random button and felt intense relief as light, though dim, illuminated his surroundings. Using the light from the phone, he slowly made his way out of his bedroom, wading through the water that was slowly rising in the house. The noise outside grew louder. He heard what sounded like trees smashing down on the ground and what he hoped were not houses being blown up by the force of the wind.

He finally got to the kitchen, opened the cabinet, and brought the flashlight out. Thankfully, he had put batteries in it already. When he turned it on, the whole kitchen flooded with light.

Keith sucked in his breath sharply as he looked around the room. There was water coming in from under the kitchen door and through the window, which had been shattered by a falling tree.

Dread suddenly filled him as he remembered the people in the town, many of whom lived in houses much smaller than his and built with more flimsy materials. He began to pray fervently that no one would be hurt. He looked at his phone to see if he could call anyone, but as he expected, there was no service.

The noise outside grew louder and then the kitchen door suddenly blew open, letting in a gust of wind and sheets of rain that nearly pulled Keith out of his home and into the commotion outside. With great effort, he finally managed to shut the door again and then quickly made his way out of the kitchen.

He heard a horrifying sound outside, like his neighbor's house being torn apart, and started to pray again that no one would be hurt while he waded through water again and went back into his bedroom. The winds kept howling, and then suddenly, as though God had snapped His fingers at the storm, everything ceased. The awful noise, the pounding rain, and the winds falling silent.

Keith opened his bedroom door and stepped out. He began to tour the whole house. The other bedroom, his grandmother's, seemed untouched except for a torn curtain and a hole in the window. He kept going from one part of the house to the other. The kitchen, as he had guessed, was the worst hit. It was almost destroyed. Keith lifted up his voice in thanksgiving to God, because apart from the kitchen, most of the house seemed intact. Except, of course, for the ankle-deep water that had entered the house.

Twenty minutes later, the waters began to recede, and Keith breathed a sigh of relief. Hopefully the other houses in Destiny had been saved as his was. But he couldn't shake the dread he felt as he fervently prayed for the safety of everyone in town.

He opened his front door and saw that it was still completely dark outside. Shining his flashlight into the darkness, he gasped and his heart almost stopped. The destruction outside was indescribable. There were plants and wood floating on the water everywhere, as though a giant had scattered them around, as well as felled trees and cable wires.

He turned to his left and his heart twisted. Just as he had imagined minutes ago, his neighbor's house had been completely destroyed. He stepped out of his house and waded through the waters outside. He saw his car some distance away. Miraculously, apart from debris scattered across it, it looked undamaged.

He headed for his neighbor's house, his fear growing the closer he got. The house was a heap of rubble. *Who could survive this?* he thought. This neighbor, made up of a family of four — Rob, Trina, and their two kids — had lived in this house for a long time.

His heart raced with terror. *Lord, please, no.* And then his fear eased some as he remembered Rob had told him he and his family would be visiting his in-laws this week. Hopefully they had left already.

He reached the destroyed house and began to yell Rob's name and then his wife's. He called out to their two children, a precious eight- and five-year-old who he had grown fond of over the years. He tried to dig through to see if there was anyone in the house, hoping there wasn't. But it was useless. There was too much debris. He would call them immediately once the phone service was restored just to make sure they were okay.

People began to appear with their flashlights,

wading through the water like he was. He smiled when they came near, recognizing most of them. He spoke to Lucy, who owned the small clothing store a short drive from his house, and Andy the baker. He saw others deep in conversation with each other — Bob the carpenter, and Carol, the owner of the bookstore where he bought books and study materials every week. Fear and worry were etched on all their faces.

Some more people gathered with flashlights, brightly illuminating the surrounding area. They talked with dread in their voices about the storm and how much damage had been done to the town.

"The library is gone, pastor," Lucy said. "I saw the ruins on my way here."

Bob said to him, "You're lucky, Pastor Keith. Your house has very little damage. Many people in Destiny were not so lucky. Thankfully, so far I haven't heard of any casualties, though I think some people were hurt. Unfortunately, the phone lines are dead, so we can't call anyone yet to verify."

Matt, one of the builders who had been working on the new church before the work stopped, walked up to him with a devastated look on his face. "Pastor Keith, there's something I need to tell you."

Keith looked quizzically at Matt. "What is it?"

"Unfortunately, the church buildings were destroyed completely."

Keith's heart sank to his feet and he couldn't speak. Finally, he found his voice and said slowly, "Which church building, Matt?" He braced himself to hear what the answer to his question would be. The pain he felt would not lessen no matter which one had been destroyed, but he hoped with all his heart that it would not be the new church building. Even though it wasn't finished yet, that building was the future, the old, the past. The old building held a special place in the hearts of everyone in Destiny, but a lot of money, time, and prayers had been sunk into the new building; a lot of his hopes and dreams for the future. If that building had been destroyed… He didn't even want to consider it.

Matt was looking at the ground, clearly reluctant to answer Keith's question.

"Which building, Matt?" Keith asked again. His heart knocked as he waited for Matt to answer, and yet he did not want to hear what that answer would be.

Matt lifted his eyes to Keith's and slowly said, "I am so sorry, Pastor. Both of them are gone."

Keith shut his eyes as pain shot through his heart. He felt like gathering Matt's words from the air and stuffing them back into the young man. But he could not do that. He had to face the reality of what he'd just been told.

"I'm sorry, Pastor," Matt said again.

Keith opened his eyes, turned around, and went back to his house. He felt weak as he opened his door and walked in. Most of the water had seeped out of the house already, and apart from the carpet that would need to be stripped, the house was okay. But that did not assuage the hurt in his soul. He had believed with all his heart that God wanted a new church to be built so the people of the town would have a sanctuary with enough space to worship in. Now, not only was there no money to complete the building, it was completely gone. Everything he had worked on for months, had sunk money into, all the donations from the people of Destiny from the little they had, all was gone.

"Why, Lord?" he cried out. "I thought you wanted me to build a bigger church for your people. Now we don't even have the old one to worship in." Now that both buildings were gone, what would he do? He was a pastor and that was what he was good at; what he had thought he would do for the rest of his life. But now, it felt like he had no future or purpose.

He swam in doubt and self-pity for a long while and then he heard a still, small voice in his heart. *"The church is not a building, Keith. It's the people that make up my church."*

Keith's eyes widened at the words he heard in his heart. He pressed his lips tightly together and then sighed. He felt awful for wallowing in self-pity when his home was still intact. A lot of the people in Destiny had lost their homes. He prayed with everything in him that it was the only thing they had lost.

"Lord, forgive me," he said, and then stood up. He strode out of his house with renewed determination. Outside, he gathered together the people still on the street and announced that they were all to go out and help as many people as they could with whatever they needed. Surely there would be people who needed help. There weren't enough emergency personnel in Destiny and more hands would be needed. Rescue teams from out of town would probably not get here for hours, if not days. They were the only help some people in the town might have.

He firmly put his worries and fears about the

church and his future behind him. Everyone separated into groups and he went around the town with two men, Theo and Kyle, helping out where they could, going through the rubble to see if there were people who needed rescuing. Buildings could wait, but people couldn't. People were the true church of God and they were who Keith knew he needed to concentrate on now. Hopefully everyone in the town was alive, because if they weren't, he didn't know how he would handle that.

As for his future, he would leave it in God's hands, where it belonged.

SIX

Rachel cradled her baby, Emily, in her arms and sighed sadly. Today was the day the elders were going to come to take her to the Restoration House. Pain shot through her heart and she looked down at her daughter. She kissed her little girl and sighed again, tears running down her cheeks. "I am going to miss you, little one," she said, and then couldn't contain her agony anymore. "Lord, can't you do something about this?" she cried out, not caring if anyone could hear her. She had spent only a month with her precious child, and now they were going to be separated. Who knew when she would see her daughter again?

Mike came and smiled down at her. She looked up at him, despising him. He was actually going to allow her to be separated from her baby. He had promised they would escape somehow, but the weeks had passed and he hadn't done anything. When she asked him why they were still in Fallow Creek, he'd waved her away without a word.

"The elders will be here any minute now to take

you to the Restoration House, Rachel," he said. "Have you packed everything you need?"

Rachel felt like screaming at him. Why was he telling her what she already knew? He had failed in keeping his promise to get her and the baby away from Fallow Creek. More than whatever fate awaited her there, leaving her baby was the one thing that caused her the most heartache.

She stood up and faced off with Mike. "I am not leaving my child, Mike. They will have to cut off my hands in order to separate her from me." She held her baby tight.

The doorbell sounded and she grimaced. She pressed Emily to her breast, panicking, until her baby cried out. Biting her lip, she loosened her grip and kissed her daughter. "I am so sorry, little one," she said. "I won't let anyone take you away from me."

"Rachel, they are here," Mike said. "You have to go willingly or they might call in the security squad to bundle you out."

She bit her lip. *The security squad!* She'd heard others talk about members of the squad literally dragging people who resisted them on the ground and across the street. She also clearly remembered her experience with them that had led to the accident. They were trained to be brutal, and she detested them and the people who had given them so much power. Thankfully, neither she nor her baby had been hurt in that accident. If she held onto Emily now, who knew what kind of hurt would come to her daughter when they tried to forcefully separate both of them? She looked at Mike, who was staring at her impatiently. She didn't trust him to protect Emily from harm if the security squad tried to take her away by force.

Mike looked at her for a few seconds more and then left the room. She rushed to the bedroom window to see if there was any way she could climb out and run without being seen, but it would be too dangerous to climb out with Emily. Plus, as usual, some members of the squad still patrolled the house.

She sat on the floor holding onto Emily and sucked in her breath sharply as she heard footsteps coming up the stairs. Tears poured down her cheeks and she felt as if her heart was shredding into tiny pieces.

The footsteps came closer and closer while she clutched Emily to her chest. The elders finally walked into the room, and Rachel whimpered at their determined and fierce faces. Her heart pounded as Victor Keller, the oldest of the three elders, said to her, "Rachel Cadwell, you are about to be taken to the Restoration House where you will be purged thoroughly of all your sins. You will come willingly with us or be taken by force."

Two squad members came into the room with their fatigues and guns, and Rachel knew she had to relinquish Emily to Mike. She stood up stiffly, feeling completely numb with sorrow, and then looked at Mike. "Please take good care of her," she said, and then kissed Emily's forehead. Mike reached out to take Emily, but Rachel wasn't ready to hand her over yet. She held on and wept.

Emily began to cry and Rachel rocked her while she wept. One of the squad members began to come toward her, and Mike said firmly, "Hand her to me,

Rachel!"

Rachel held onto Emily for a few seconds and then she reluctantly handed her over to Mike. The squad member who had walked up to her started to grab her hand, but she shook her head. "Don't touch me!" she warned.

Victor Keller nodded at the squad guard and he backed away.

"Are you ready to come willingly now?" Another elder asked her.

She said nothing and picked up the small bag she had packed a few of her things in. She began to follow the elders down the stairs, but just before she stepped out of the house, she turned once more to Mike, who was behind her with Emily in his arms. "Please take good care of her, Mike," she said in a voice choked with emotion. She wanted to break down and start crying all over again, but she thought better of it. If she started now, she would not stop.

She followed the elders outside to a waiting car. A squad member opened the door for her and she got into the car. She stuck her head out of the window and stared at Mike, who was standing on the front porch, still carrying Emily. She felt overcome with longing to hold Emily one last time and turned her head away. Wiping the tears from her eyes, she asked the Lord to help her deal with the agony of being separated from her baby.

The drive to the Restoration House was short. When the driver parked in front of the house, Rachel looked out the window and stared at the huge three-story house. She had seen it a few times, but usually when driving past in a car. She had never come this close and she had only known one person who had been brought here, though for what, she didn't know. She didn't know what to expect, but in a way she did not care. There was nothing that could be worse than being separated from one's baby.

Once again, the car door was opened for her, and she stepped out with her bag. She walked to the house with two squad guards behind her. One of them opened the door and she stepped in. She expected to see a furnished living room, but instead the space was empty except for two benches, one on either side of the room, and a small coffee table at the center.

She dropped her bag on the ground and looked up when she heard what sounded like a large group of people chanting from up the stairs. She turned to the squad members for an explanation, but they said nothing to her. Curious, she began to climb the stairs and then stopped when someone called her name. Turning around, she blinked in surprise. Victor Keller, one of the elders who had come to the house to tell her it was time to come here, was looking up at her.

"Wait, Rachel. I need to tell you what to expect in the house," he said. He told the guards who had followed her in to wait outside. When they left, he beckoned for Rachel to come near once more.

She scowled and then came down the stairs. "How long am I going to stay here before I can see my Emily again?" she asked angrily.

He came closer and whispered, "I have a note for you from your husband."

She blinked. "Mike? I just left him. Why didn't he

give me the note himself?" she asked incredulously.

"You will know once you read the note," Victor said and shoved a piece of paper into her hand before turning around and striding out of the house.

She stared after him and then opened her hand. Straightening the crumpled piece of paper, she read the words written in Mike's handwriting. Stunned, she read it again.

Rachel,

My plan is to break you out of the Restoration House this evening so we can leave Fallow Creek. I couldn't tell you at the house because I had to make sure your distress at leaving Emily was as real as possible, or the elders and guards would have suspected that something was amiss.

I will see you soon.

Mike

She could not believe her eyes. She had given up all hope of seeing Emily in the near future, and definitely of ever leaving Fallow Creek. Now Mike was saying they were going to leave that very night. He had not told her how he was going to manage it, but she suddenly felt hope rising in her heart. And then joy coursed through her. She read the note again and whispered, "Lord, please let Mike's plan, whatever it is, be successful."

She would not have to be separated from her daughter again. She couldn't wait to hold Emily in her arms. But that was if Mike's plan succeeded.

She told herself to lower her expectations. Mike's plan might not be successful. But she could not hold down her joy and relief.

If they managed to escape Fallow Creek, she would be free to live the life she'd always dreamt of, and maybe eventually, she would be free from Mike. Because she could not continue to live with him, constantly living with tremendous guilt. It didn't matter what he said or what the people of this town said. Mike was not her husband. He was Olivia's. The earlier she could leave him, the better she would feel.

She jerked her head up when someone slapped her back. Astonished, she turned around and stared into the face of an angry-looking, diminutive woman. *Margaret Foster.* She had seen the woman around the community a couple of times and knew she was in charge of the Restoration House. She had never had any dealings with Margaret or spoken to her. But every time she'd seen the woman, Margaret was wearing a frown. It was clearly her default look.

"What are you doing standing around?" Margaret said, glaring at Rachel. "This is not a hotel and you are not on vacation! You're here to work and attend our renewal classes."

Rachel blurted out, "Renewal classes?"

"Come with me," Margaret ordered. She began to march away, but Rachel stood frozen in her spot. Margaret turned around and barked at her, "Come right now or I will call one of those boys outside to drag you up the stairs!"

Rachel glared at her and for a few seconds refused to obey. Margaret headed toward the door and Rachel moved. She began to climb up the stairs while Margaret followed behind.

Once at the top of the stairs, Margaret led her from one room to the other, rooms with only narrow beds, a desk, and a chair. Some of the rooms were occupied by several women, some by just two. A few were empty.

Margaret led Rachel to a huge space that looked like a large classroom. It had rows and rows of desks and chairs and a huge blackboard at the front with words written in chalk. Before Rachel could read the words on the blackboard, Margaret led her away again. From time to time, women passed by her without looking at her. Most of them stared at the floor as soon as they saw Margaret. Finally, Rachel couldn't hold in her curiosity and asked Margaret what the large room with the blackboard was for.

Margaret glowered at her. "What on earth? You actually thought I have been giving you a house tour? Honey, I'm showing you all the rooms that you will be scrubbing, starting now. That is what we do to every new person who comes into this house. You are shown that hard work is one of the tenants of our faith and one of the things you will need to master in order to be completely purged."

Rachel's mouth fell open, and then, without thinking, she blurted out, "Are you saying that I will be cleaning all the rooms that you showed me, including that large classroom?"

Margaret chuckled. "What? You are way too pretty to clean? You will not just be cleaning, you will be scrubbing every inch of those rooms."

Rachel shut her eyes. Now she knew why this

house had a scary reputation and why Mike was scared for her. Even more baffling was that she knew that what Margaret had told her was not the worst that this place had to offer.

Margaret clapped her hands. "Now get to work," she said. "Go into the room at the end of this hallway. You will find a woman named Patricia. She will give you everything you need to start working."

Rachel didn't move.

Margaret barked, "Why are you still standing here? Go now!"

Rachel hurried away and then looked over her shoulder. Margaret was still staring at her. She reached the end of the hallway and entered the room Margaret had pointed out to her. The room was filled with cleaning supplies, mops, and buckets. The place looked like a store that sold cleaning supplies.

A woman dressed in a long, black, long-sleeved dress appeared from nowhere. Rachel told her Margaret had sent her, and the woman nodded.

"Come with me," the woman said.

Rachel followed her to a shelf filled with a variety of detergents, and the woman told her to pick one. After that, she gave Rachel disinfecting wipes, liquid soaps and floor cleaners, a mop and bucket, and then told her where to get water. Finally, she handed Rachel a scrubbing brush and sent her on her way.

Rachel lugged the cleaning supplies down the hallway, wondering where to start. Mike had told her he would come tonight to rescue her from this place and take her out of Fallow Creek, but she did not know if he was coming in the evening or at night. She could pretend to clean while she waited for him, but if he did not come until past midnight, she would not be able to get away without actually working. She might jeopardize her escape if she called any attention to herself by disobeying Margaret.

She looked into one room after the other and found they were filled with occupants. Many of the women had their heads bowed as if they were praying, and Rachel immediately knew that it was one of the requirements to stay here. They were all probably made to spend hours in reflection in order to "purge themselves of their sins."

She finally found a room that was empty. She knelt on the floor and began to scrub it. She took her time scrubbing the floors, hoping the hours would pass quickly while she cleaned and waited for Mike to arrive. As she scrubbed, she kept wondering what Mike's plan for their escape was. If they were caught, they would never be able to leave Fallow Creek again.

She could not spend any more time cleaning a single room and moved on to the next room. Two women who looked to be in their fifties glanced at her as she entered. She opened her mouth to greet them, but they hurried out of the room as though she had a contagious disease. She frowned and then bent down to begin cleaning. Just like the first room she'd cleaned, she took her time scrubbing the floor and making the bed.

By the time she finished cleaning the fourth room, she felt like lying on the floor. She sighed, exhausted, and then stared out the window, wondering what time it was. It was already dark outside and she could hear voices from down the hallway. The chanting again.

She stepped back from the window and made her way out of the room, leaving the cleaning supplies there. She had to find out what time it was. She remembered that she had seen a small clock on the wall downstairs and headed for the stairs.

She reached the bottom and looked around the empty room. There was no one around. Grateful for that, she looked up at the clock on the wall and her heart began to drum. It was already ten o'clock. Hopefully, Mike would come soon.

The lights suddenly went out, leaving her in total darkness, and she began to panic. What was happening? She could see absolutely nothing. She didn't know the house well and Margaret had not shown her to her room. She sighed. She wouldn't need a room if Mike just came now. *Where are you, Mike?* She did the only thing she could think of. She sat down on the floor and prayed that the lights would come on soon.

She heard footsteps coming down the stairs. Someone was coming down the stairs with a flashlight, which already dimly illuminated the room where she was. She stood up when she heard Margaret's voice. "You!" Margaret glared at her. "What are you still doing here?"

Rachel didn't answer.

Margaret walked up to her and shined the flashlight in her face. Rachel blinked and shut her eyes.

"Answer me!" Margaret bellowed. "What are you still doing here when it's lights out?"

Rachel suddenly grew angry and barked, "How am I supposed to know it was lights out when no one told me? In case you forgot, today is my first day here."

"How dare you speak to me like that!" Margaret snarled.

Rachel threw caution to the wind and said, "I've been working like a slave for hours and nobody has said a word to me. You did not tell me lights out was at this time and you didn't show me to my room. I am not a mind reader, Margaret Foster!"

Margaret's face grew red and she grabbed Rachel's hand. Rachel winced in pain when she squeezed her wrist tightly. "How dare you!" Margaret spat out. "You might be married and related to the richest men in town, but in this house, you are nothing. I am in charge here and you will watch the way you speak to me! I promise I will make your life a living hell, Rachel Cadwell!" She began to pull Rachel up the stairs with her.

At first, Rachel wanted to yank her hand away and tell Margaret off, but she thought better of it. It would be the wrong move to antagonize the woman further. She already regretted her outburst. Margaret would watch her more closely than the others now. Had she destroyed her chance of escaping by provoking her?

She thought about apologizing to the woman but immediately decided against it. That would be too much. Besides, there was no point. Margaret didn't seem like the kind of person who accepted apologies when offended.

She followed Margaret down the hall to an empty room that she had scrubbed and Margaret pointed. "This is your room for now. You will have a new roommate by tomorrow."

Rachel heaved a sigh of relief when Margret marched out and then turned when the older woman called her name. Margaret gave her a wicked smile that chilled her. "Tomorrow, I have a very special surprise waiting for you!" she said in a low voice. "It's a surprise I give to every person who crosses me here. I think you will enjoy it."

She began to walk away as Rachel's heart drummed and then turned back. A member of the security squad appeared beside her. "And oh, I am placing Gavin here by your door to watch you and follow you wherever you go... just in case you try anything funny." She left and shut the door behind her.

Rachel slowly lowered herself to the bed. "What have I done?" she whispered. Her stubbornness had gotten her into trouble here already and probably jeopardized her escape with Mike. How would Mike get her out of here with a guard standing right at her door? She had been stupid, challenging Margaret. Now, she might never have the chance to escape Fallow Creek. Worse, with Margaret angry at her, she might not be released from this house in a long, long time. When would she see her baby again?

She covered her face with her hands and sobbed.

SEVEN

A loud ringing noise continuously sounded in Rachel's ear and she turned on the bed. Where was that sound coming from? She suddenly opened her eyes and jerked up. She frowned at the commotion outside. People were shouting and running. She tossed aside her blanket and jumped out of bed. Quickly, she put on her robe and hurried out of her room to see what the commotion was all about.

The guard that Margaret had posted outside her door wasn't there, but women were running past her, hurrying down the stairs. She frowned in confusion and then realized what was happening: a fire had broken out somewhere in the house. The ringing sound screaming through the house was a fire alarm. She started to head toward the staircase and ran into Patricia, the woman who had given her the cleaning supplies earlier that day.

"Do you know where the fire is?" she asked.

"No, but I need to make sure everyone is out of the house now."

Rachel hurried out of the house with the other women.

Outside, she stood staring at the house, wondering where the fire had started from. She wrapped her arms around herself to try to ward off the cold. She had cried herself to sleep, angry with herself for surely ruining Mike's plan to break her out by challenging Margaret's authority, causing her to post a squad member at her door. Mike had not come again. He had probably tried to break her out already and then found that he couldn't because of the guard assigned to her.

Depression settled over her again. This would be her life now. She had drifted off to sleep depressed. Now, she was awake and still depressed. She wasn't sure she would ever be happy again. Not until she finally left this house and saw her daughter once more. She resisted the urge to cry and instead listened in on the conversations around her.

A group of women beside her were talking about the fire. She knew most of them but didn't know their names. One of them said, "Do you know where it started?"

Another shook her head. "Are you sure it's really a fire? I mean, I cannot see any smoke or any sign of a fire."

"But why would Margaret lie and tell us there's a real fire in the house?"

The other woman said, "I was with Margaret when Patricia came to tell her a fire had broken out somewhere. I think Margaret truly believed there was a fire. Maybe Pat…"

Rachel suddenly gasped as someone grabbed her from behind. She opened her mouth to scream, but the person clamped a hand over her mouth. She tried to struggle, but whoever it was that had grabbed her was too strong for her. The person pulled her away from the house to the back of a white jeep.

The hand left her mouth and just before she screamed, swung her around. Her jaw dropped and then she exclaimed, "Mike! You are here!" Her fear immediately melted away, replaced by overwhelming relief. For the first time in her life, she was truly happy to see Mike.

"Why do you look so surprised to see me?" he said. "Didn't you get my message? I told you that I would get you out tonight." He looked past her and glanced around.

She stared at him in amazement. He had truly broken her out. She knew without a doubt that the supposed fire alarm was planned and caused by him. How he had managed to do it, she did not know. She asked him.

"Get into the car, Rachel," he ordered.

Without wasting time, she got in. Joy flooded her heart at the sight of Emily sleeping in the backseat. Mike came and sat in the driver's seat and she turned to face him. "Thank you so much, Mike. Thank you."

He started the car, drove out into the road, then said to her, "We are not out of the woods yet, Rachel. And to answer your question, I had an ally in Victor Keller. In exchange for his help, I gave him money... lots of money." Mike kept his eyes on the road as he spoke. "Victor paid someone on the squad to start the false fire alarm. He probably had some help from someone in the house. The squad member was also paid to divert the attention of the squad team posted around the house and to make sure that none of them would be looking in your direction when I came this evening to get you."

Rachel sank back on her seat in relief. She already knew the insider in the house was Patricia. She could just imagine the look on Margaret's face when she found out Rachel was gone. She turned around to look at Emily again. Emily looked like a sleeping angel and Rachel smiled widely. She turned and faced Mike. "Who knew that there was greed amongst the elders," she said, slightly amused.

Mike said nothing. His eyes were still planted on the road as he drove.

The drive brought back memories of the night she'd tried to escape, and her heart began to pound with anxiety. The further they drove, the more her anxiety grew. She said to Mike, "You said we're not out of the woods yet. What will we do about the guards at the border?"

She bit down on her lip in nervousness as she waited for Mike to answer. It was all good that he had broken her out of the Restoration House, but if they were apprehended at the border, that would be the end of their plans to escape. They would never be able to leave Fallow Creek again. And she would most definitely be returned to the Restoration House.

Mike finally said to her, "The squad member who Victor paid to divert the other guards' attention at the Restoration House was instructed to immediately drive to the border once he succeeded in his mission. He would tell the squad team at the border that there was an emergency at the Restoration House and that the elders wanted them all there immediately. And they would find an emergency truly once they got to the Restoration House. I just hope he is at the border right now because there's a probability that we left before he did."

Rachel put her hand on her forehead, feeling slightly faint. "Maybe we should slow down to give him time to get to the border and get the other squad members away from there."

"I can't, Rachel. There are other squad members stationed around this road. If I slow down now they will surely get to us. I'm pretty sure one of them is following us now."

Rachel instinctively looked back but couldn't see much in the darkness. She looked briefly at Emily again and then turned back to Mike. "So, what if we get to the border and all the squad team are still there? Once they see me with you, they will know what our plans are."

"Then I'll have to go to plan B."

Rachel's stomach twisted with worry. What on earth was Mike's plan B? She was too anxious to ask what it was. Her strong desire to escape Fallow Creek was not just because of her own wellbeing, but Emily's as well. She didn't want her daughter to grow up in a place where women were treated like property.

Her heart pounded as they approached a large group of squad members in the distance. Their SUVs blocked the road. "Mike, they are all still there," she said in a shaky voice. "What are we going to do?"

"Calm down, Rachel," Mike said. "Stop panicking."

"And why shouldn't I panic, Mike?" she yelled at

him. "Emily is at the back of this car. The squad chased me down when I tried to escape the last time and caused an accident. If anything happens to Emily while we are trying to escape, I will never forgive myself... or you!" she cried out in despair, "We will never be able to leave Fallow Creek!"

Mike did not look at her or react to her tirade. He kept driving and Rachel closed her eyes as the squad team turned their eyes to them. She opened her eyes again just as Mike came to a stop in front of the men. Her heart kept pounding in fear. She saw Daniel, the man who had interrogated her the day she tried to escape Fallow Creek, coming towards them and swallowed. "Mike, we've been caught," she said.

"Hush, Rachel!" Mike ordered.

Daniel reached the car and poked his head into the window on Mike's side. When he saw her, his eyes grew as round as saucers. "You!" he said. Her heart sank as he turned around and waved over two other men.

"Lord, we need a miracle right now," she whispered.

As the men began to approach their car, an SUV drove up from behind Mike's car and stopped right between them and the men with horns blasting. The squad team turned as one to stare at the driver of the SUV that was blasting his horn, including Daniel. He turned back to look at Rachel and Mike, and then put his hand on his rifle. "Don't move," he ordered. "I'll be watching you."

He moved away and Rachel said urgently to Mike, "What are your plans now? What are we going to do?"

"We wait, Rachel."

She turned to look at the squad team and her jaw dropped. They were beginning to enter their cars and drive in the opposite direction. One squad car remained after the rest had driven away. A young man stepped out of the car and came to them. He reached their car and said to Mike, "They are all gone now. They left me in charge of this place."

Mike smiled at the young man and nodded. "Thank you," he said.

The young man stepped back from the car and Mike started the car again and sped off.

Rachel blinked and stared at the road as he drove. Mike had come through for them. She let out a huge sigh of relief and joy flooded her heart. They were going to escape. They were really going to succeed in escaping Fallow Creek. She nearly cried from relief and then turned back in excitement and said in a hushed tone, "Emily, darling, we made it. We are leaving Fallow Creek for good." She thought about something and then turned to Mike. "So where are we going, Mike? And what about Olivia and the children?"

Mike did not say anything for a few minutes and then he answered, "That squad guard back there, the one who helped us, he will drive to the house and get Olivia and the children. Since the border is now free, he'll be able to drive them to the airport where they will meet us. He will be rewarded handsomely for all his help."

Rachel nodded and then asked again, "So where are we going, Mike?"

He turned briefly to her and said, "We are going to the town where my grandfather grew up. A place called Destiny."

EIGHT

In spite of the days spent trying to rebuild the town, Destiny still looked like it had the first day the hurricane swept through it. Since that day, Keith had struggled to make sense of the destruction in the town, asking the Lord a series of questions in order to understand why their beloved town had almost been laid to waste. But there was one thing he was grateful for; a huge miracle the Lord had worked, considering that many houses here had been destroyed. It was the fact that, as far as Keith knew, no lives had been lost. There were people who had sustained serious injuries, who were receiving medical treatment, and many with mild injuries, but everyone was alive.

Still, the fact that many people were now homeless and living with families whose homes were still intact or mostly intact bothered him greatly. What bothered him the most, though, was the destruction of the old and new churches.

As he walked around the town looking at all the damage that had been done, he silently talked to the Lord. "If anyone had asked if it was a good idea to build a new church before the hurricane swept through this town, I would have confidently told them that you wanted me to do so. Now, I don't even know what you're saying anymore. Maybe I have been delusional for a long time, thinking you called me to spread the gospel. Maybe being a pastor is not even what I am supposed to do with my life. If I thought you wanted a church built and now it turns out that wasn't the case, who is to say I haven't heard wrong about my life's calling?"

He walked around the town almost every day, questioning everything — his mission in life, the things that mattered to him or had mattered, and, in some ways, his faith. He still knew that the Lord loved him, but he could not tell what was on God's mind or what God's will for him was.

Mary had called a day after the hurricane, frantic. After she had been assured that he was okay, she had given him a piece of her mind. "I warned you, Keith," she had said to him on the phone. "What if something had happened to you? I would never have forgiven myself... or you."

He had tried to calm her down, but the more he spoke, the more agitated she sounded. She had asked him again to leave Destiny and come and stay with her and her husband and kids in Denver. He had, of course, refused, but she told him she would call again, obviously to try to get him to change his mind.

He had no intention of leaving Destiny, especially at a time when the town needed him. He'd given away most of the snacks and basic necessities he sold in his store to help many of the people who had lost their homes and everything they had. Two families were staying in his house with him. He didn't know how long they would be there. No relief workers had reached Destiny yet and the work of rebuilding the town was still on his shoulders and those of a few people who had volunteered their time and resources.

He raised his hand in greeting when a few people on the other side of the road called out his name with smiles on their faces. He smiled. That was the thing about the people of this town. They were very resilient. Most of all, they were grateful for the things that really mattered — and that was each other.

The flood had almost totally receded from the entire town but the place he was wading through now was still water-logged. He climbed up a steep hill and then continued to make his way through Destiny. From time to time, he stopped to greet someone and then prayed for them. He had already visited a few displaced people, encouraging them with God's word and letting them know he cared. He hated that he couldn't do more. He had been extremely grateful when Mary, in spite of a constant pestering for him to leave the town, had made arrangements with a friend of hers who owned a food company. A large truck had driven into town a few days after the hurricane with hot meals. Once a day, a lot of people went to the truck to get food and water.

But there was still so much that needed to be done in town. The town needed to be rebuilt. Soon, people would begin to leave because two to three families could not keep sharing tiny accommodations for too long. He loved Destiny too much to bear to see the town deserted. Many had taken to doing what they could to help rebuild some of the homes, and Keith had joined them yesterday. But it was apparent to them that they could only do so much, as they were not builders. Most of the builders who had been working on the new church building had been from out of town and had left when the money ran out.

He stopped at a small house that belonged to Gary and Claire Weaver, a couple in their thirties with a young son. Two families were staying with them in the two-bedroom bungalow. He knocked on the door and then entered when it opened. Smiling at Claire, he said to her, "How are you?"

She looked tired, but smiled and told him she was doing okay.

"And where is Gary?"

"He went out to help with the building projects," she said. "The Radfords also went out to see where they could help."

Keith nodded. "And Debra and Shawn?"

"Their three-year-old son developed a fever during the night and they both had to stay up late to take care of him. They are all asleep now in the other bedroom."

Keith said, "I'm sorry to hear that. I will come back later in the day to pray for their son."

Claire said, "You can pray for him right now, pastor. They would really appreciate it."

"But you said they were sleeping."

Claire only smiled and made her way out of the living room, clearly wanting Keith to follow her. She entered a small room with two adults and a child lying on the bed. Before he could tell Claire not to wake them up, she said loudly, "Debra! Shawn! Pastor Keith is here to pray for Luke."

The couple sat up rubbing their eyes and then smiled at Keith. Debra gently woke their son up and then told Keith he could pray for him. Keith went over to the boy and felt his forehead. He felt warm. He prayed that the Lord would heal him completely. After that, he prayed for Debra and Shawn and then for Claire and Gary. He promised to visit them again the next day and left the house.

He continued to walk through town and decided to visit the new family that had just moved to Destiny. He had thought it was a little weird when he'd first heard that a family had moved to town just after the hurricane had ravaged it, but he accepted they had their reasons. His job was to welcome them to the town and try to get to know them.

One of the couples staying in his house had told him where the new family lived. They'd moved into the big house at the edge of town, the couple had said.

Keith had raised his brows in surprise. "The old abandoned house?"

"It's neither old nor abandoned now," Eric had said. "A week before the hurricane hit, some men came and painted the house and mowed the lawn. They also changed the windows, the door, everything that needed changing, really."

Paula, Eric's wife, had said, "And I saw a truck parked in front of the house some days ago. A furniture truck. I haven't been there for some time but I think the house will be furnished by now."

Keith had narrowed his eyes. He hadn't been

in that area for a really long time. Maybe months. He'd had no reason to go to that part of town as the only house that stood there was that old abandoned house. The next house was some distance away. "Did you see the family that moved into the house?" he'd asked Paula.

"No, we did not," Paula answered. "But from the way the finished house looks, I'm guessing it's a wealthy family."

"Like the man who originally owned the house?" Keith asked.

Eric shook his head and Paula shrugged. "I don't know the original owner," she said.

"I don't either, but my grandmother once told me the house was owned by a wealthy man. I cannot remember his name now. When he died, his family moved out and the house went to ruins. The house was not destroyed in any way during the hurricane?"

"I don't think so," Eric answered.

Keith had told them he would visit the new family when he had the time. He had been busy for the past two days, but today he could finally pay the family a visit and welcome them to Destiny. He walked on, passing a couple more houses and then just trees and a wide field. He saw the house from a distance, built on a small hill. He couldn't stop staring at it, amazed by the change. When he reached the house, he stood in front of it for a full minute, gazing in amazement. It looked totally different now, like a real home. A huge, magnificent home. And it had not been touched by the hurricane, which meant it was probably built to withstand them.

He opened the newly painted white fence and

walked up a slope to the front door. He looked around the house. There were four vehicles parked on different parts of the grounds. He turned to the door again. The huge mahogany door was newly polished with a brand-new knocker and doorbell installed. He reached out and pressed the doorbell and then waited.

He frowned when no one came to the door and then smiled in self-mockery as he remembered there was still no electricity in town. He grasped the knocker, knocked on the door, and waited again.

The door opened and a beautiful young woman with dark hair that hung down to her waist and the brightest blue eyes he had ever seen poked her head out and gazed at him. "Yes, can I help you?" she said in the sweetest voice he had ever heard.

For some seconds, he could not speak, and then he shook himself out of his stupor when he noticed the curious way she was looking at him. Embarrassed, he answered, "Umm... I am Keith Thorn, the pastor of the Firm Foundation Church. I just came to say hello and welcome you to Destiny. Is your husband around?"

Before she could answer, a burly man with a bushy beard appeared in the doorway behind her and looked at him with part curiosity and part irritation. "Yes, what do you want?" the man asked in a deep voice.

Keith told him what he had told the woman and then the man's face suddenly brightened. "Oh, you're the pastor that I have been hearing about. Welcome," he said, smiling. He opened the door wide and said, "Please, come in."

Keith was surprised at the sudden change in the man's countenance as he walked into the house. He walked past the foyer lined with flowers and into a massive living room. He looked around him. The only time he had been in a house with such luxurious furnishings was when he visited Mary's boss, an executive of a software company, in Denver. He would never have imagined that such luxury was in Destiny. For a brief moment he admired the house and then he turned to the couple.

"Sit, Pastor," the man said.

Keith sat on the milk-white sofa with huge, fluffy throw pillows. Instinctively, he turned to the beautiful woman and then turned away quickly, scolding himself for looking at her. He said to the man, "You have a lovely home here," and forced his gaze to remain on the man.

The man, who looked about twelve to fifteen years older than his wife, thanked him, and then said, "Please call me Mike." He sat on the couch facing Keith as his young wife sat on the other end. "This is my wife, Rachel," the man added.

Keith smiled and nodded. "You are both welcome in Destiny. It's really unfortunate that you came at this time, when the hurricane has devastated our town. It was such a beautiful town. Have you been here before?"

"No," the man said. "Neither has my wife. But my father was born here. This was actually the house he was born in. But he left as a young boy when his father died."

Keith gasped. "Oh. My grandmother told me about your grandfather. So, your last name is…"

"Cadwell," Mike said.

"Yes. Now I remember. Wow. It is amazing that you have moved to Destiny and into your father's childhood home."

"Yes, it is," Mike nodded and then added, "I had already put together everything that I needed to move here with my family before the hurricane hit. We came here and were really surprised at what we saw. The devastation caused by the hurricane is terrible. I will try to help in any way I can."

Keith said, "We will take any help we can get." He smiled. "I would have invited you to our church service on Sunday, but our church building is gone. We were building a new, bigger church, but that was destroyed by the hurricane as well."

For the first time since the conversation started, the young woman spoke. She said in a soft, velvety voice, "I'm so sorry."

Keith smiled sadly. "It was really hard when I found out. We were building the new church because the old one had gotten too small. It was supposed to contain everyone who wanted to come to church. Everything we had was sunk into building it. The flood swept it all away." Keith blinked, realizing he had been going on and on, and said, "I am sorry for rambling."

Mike smiled. "I like you. And just like I said, I would love to help in any way I can." He lifted a finger and added, "In fact, hold on a minute. I will be right back." He stood up before Keith could say anything more and left the living room.

Keith pressed his lips together and then slowly turned to Mike's wife. He asked, "So, how are you settling in Destiny?"

The lady said in a soft, very feminine voice, "It's

a little difficult because all the stores are closed right now, except for the one near that bookstore. However, I didn't see anything I wanted when I went there. I think whoever owns the store is giving away most of the things in it. I don't know who the owner is, but that person has an exceptionally large heart."

Keith didn't know what to say. If he told her that the store belonged to him and he was the one who had given away the things he had bought for sale, she might think he was being boastful. But if he didn't tell her, she would wonder why when she found out he owned the store. He opened his mouth to tell her as humbly as he could that the store was his, but she said, "How long have you been a pastor?"

He was slightly surprised that she had asked him the question. She had seemed somewhat timid sitting beside her husband and he'd thought that was her personality. Now, without her husband present, she seemed more confident and open. She'd asked her question in her silky, soft voice, but there was a steeliness to it that told him that underneath her quiet exterior was a strong personality.

He said to her, "I actually went to Bible school years ago and was an assistant pastor for a few years. But I became the senior pastor of our church about two years ago." He tilted his head and looked into her blue eyes. "And what do you do, Rachel?" he asked.

He frowned slightly as she looked away. He had seen the embarrassed look on her face and wondered why she was embarrassed. She turned back to him and said, "For now I care for my little baby. But I have always wanted to teach kids. I would love to be an elementary school teacher one day because I love kids and the idea of imparting knowledge to them."

He smiled encouragingly at her. "So why haven't you started to pursue your dream?"

For a few seconds she did not answer and he began to worry that his question had troubled her for some reason. But a moment later she said, "I haven't had the opportunity to pursue my dreams. But now that we are here in Destiny, I think it might happen soon."

He smiled widely and nodded. "We have a beautiful elementary school here in Destiny where the kids go." Suddenly he remembered that the school had been flattened and the kids had not been able to attend classes for days. Sorrow filled his heart. He said to Rachel, "Well at least we did have an elementary school, but it was destroyed by the hurricane."

He sighed loudly and then bent his head slightly, overcome by how much the town of Destiny had lost. He jerked his head up when he felt arms around his shoulders and looked into Rachel's eyes. For a full minute, he gazed at her, surprised that she was sitting beside him now with her arms around him to comfort him. He appreciated her gesture, but it felt inappropriate. What would her husband think if he walked in now? He didn't know whether to shift away from her or to stay.

Footsteps approached the living room and Rachel immediately got up and took her seat again.

He sighed in relief, not just because she had moved away and saved them the embarrassment, but because of the way he'd felt when she had put her arm around him. He wondered at his reaction to her. He had seen beautiful women before, so why was he suddenly so besotted? Why had everything in him come alive at her touch? She was married, for goodness' sake. He had to leave this house right now.

Her husband Mike appeared and Keith stood up. He put on a smile and said, "I have to go now. I still have a few other people to visit."

Mike smiled and nodded. He walked up to Keith and held out a piece of paper.

Keith looked at the paper. It was a check. He looked up at Mike.

"To rebuild the church," Mike said and then thrust the check into Keith's hand.

Keith raised up the check and stared at it. His jaw dropped. He blinked, wondering if he was adding more zeros than what was actually on the check. But he wasn't. He looked up at Mike and asked in bewilderment, "Is this for a hundred thousand dollars?"

Mike chuckled. "That is what is written on the check, isn't it? And there is more where that came from."

Keith's heart nearly stopped and then he began to laugh with joy. "Thank you so much," he said to Mike. He wanted to hug the man, but he wasn't sure he should. "This will go a very long way toward building the church and rebuilding this town."

Mike shrugged and Keith took his hand and shook it. "Thank you," he said again. "I promise to keep you posted every step of the way. You will be able to clearly see how your money is being spent."

Michael nodded. "I love the church of God, so

this is an easy gift for me. I just want to make sure the church is built so people here have a place to worship."

Keith smiled. The man was a Christian then. Which meant his wife probably was also. He said to Mike, "I would love to have you and your wife as guests in my home. I can give you a tour of the whole town when you have the time. You could bring your baby along, too." He turned to look at Rachel and then noticed a strange look in her eyes.

He turned back to Mike when the man said, "I have three children."

Keith nodded. It was slightly strange that the man had said he had three children instead of "we" and then shrugged it off. "So, when can I expect you at the house?" he looked at Rachel and faced Mike again.

"We will send word to let you know when we are free," Mike answered.

Keith nodded. He thanked Mike and his wife once more for their generosity and then left the house. As he walked back to his, he kept looking at the check with wonder and bewilderment. But most of all with joy and gratitude to God. He whispered, "Lord, I asked for a miracle and you provided. And you didn't just provide, you blew my mind. Thank you so much."

He hurried towards his house, almost running. He had to show Eric and Paula the check. And then he would call Mary and tell her about the money and the kind couple who had given it. He would tell Mary that she had been wrong and he had been right. God had truly called him to Destiny, to build a church for His flock. There had been a slight hitch in the plans, but now it had all worked out for good, just as the Bible said it would.

He got to his house and felt every shred of disappointment and despair that had clung to him after the hurricane fall off, replaced with a joyful hope for the future and a certainty that he was at the center of God's will.

NINE

Rachel buttoned her blouse after breastfeeding Emily and laid her gently on the sofa. Emily was already drifting off to sleep and Rachel smiled and kissed her cheek. Taking a deep breath, she picked up the remote control on the coffee table and turned the TV on. She'd hardly ventured out of the house since they'd arrived in Destiny. Everything she needed to know about the devastation the hurricane had brought to the town was on the news. Not that Destiny was on the news. They were mostly showing all the places that had been affected by the hurricane.

She hated to leave the house here because she was ashamed. Destiny was not Fallow Creek. The people here probably lived like other normal people in other places. The men probably had one wife each. The rules that governed this place were different from those that governed Fallow Creek. The people in this town did not know that Mike was a polygamist and that she was the so-called second wife, the one who had imposed her presence on a once happy marriage and snatched the affections of the first wife's husband away from her.

She sighed and turned off the television, unable to concentrate on any of the shows. She had told herself that she would leave Mike once they left Fallow Creek, but it had not been so easy — especially because this town had been devastated by the hurricane. There were no jobs here. Without a job, she had no money except what Mike gave her, which was mostly to purchase things for Emily and for the house. Usually she asked Olivia to help her buy the things she needed so she wouldn't have to go out herself.

She leaned back against the sofa and closed her eyes. She was getting claustrophobic. Soon, she would have to leave the house or she would go mad. But if the people of Destiny found out about her living conditions with Mike and Olivia, she would not be able to bear the wagging tongues that would surely ensue. No doubt, the people would judge her. And they would be right to.

The front door opened and Olivia walked into the living room, carrying bags of groceries and toiletries. She had left the house early in the morning to go to the next town in order to buy all the things they needed in the house.

Rachel rose up immediately to help her with the bags just as Mike walked in from the back-porch. He reached out and pulled Rachel into his arms before she could get to Olivia.

Kissing her firmly, he said, "I haven't seen you all day." He ran his hand slowly down her arm and then looked at Olivia, who had now dropped some of the bags on the floor and was looking at them with hurt in her eyes. "I think I hear the kids arguing upstairs," he said to Olivia. "Go and see to them."

Olivia opened her mouth as though to say something and then shut it again. She averted her eyes, picked up the bags, and then walked past Rachel and Mike. When she left the living room, Rachel glared at Mike. He was playing his foolish games with her and Olivia again.

She said angrily, "I was about to help Olivia with the bags. She should have been the one you went to greet instead of me. I saw you about half an hour ago when you went to sit out on the porch, but Olivia has been out since morning."

Mike shrugged and planted another kiss on her lips. "I know I just saw you thirty minutes ago, but you know I cannot get enough of you. Olivia has had her time with me, but now you have my complete and full attention."

She felt repulsed and pulled away from him. If only she could find a job so she could leave him immediately.

Mike smiled at her and said, "I'm going to take a walk around town."

When he left, Rachel took Emily to her room and laid her gently in her crib. She came downstairs again and sat on the living room couch. Her mind went back to the incident with Olivia and Mike. What had happened was not a surprise to her. It was how Mike regularly behaved. At moments like that, she hated herself for staying with him, for putting up with him. She hated the hurt in Olivia's eyes every time something like that happened. She hated how he fawned over her in Olivia's presence, especially as she was the intruder.

Why are you still with him? she asked herself.

But she had no choice for now. Even though she had said she would leave him as soon as she was free from the awful laws that degraded women in Fallow Creek, as she had no job and therefore no money to take care of Emily or herself, she couldn't leave yet. But she would. The constant guilt she felt about how she was hurting Olivia and sinning against God by staying with Mike was eating more and more into her. Once she found a job, she could then save for a small house for herself and Emily.

But she had to be careful about how she left Mike because he could cause her a lot of trouble, even here in Destiny.

She began to think about her dream of becoming an elementary school teacher and then remembered what the good-looking pastor had said when he visited. He had told her she could pursue her dreams by being a teacher in the elementary school in Destiny. But he had also said that the school was no more. She was sure she needed some kind of training to become an elementary school teacher, which she did not have. She had been too ashamed to tell the pastor that her formal education had stopped at age thirteen.

An idea suddenly popped into her mind. Even if she did not have the qualifications to be a teacher, she loved kids. Surely there were people in Destiny who needed a babysitter to watch their kids. She could babysit for them and get paid for it. The money would not be much, she knew, but it would be a start for her while she planned her escape from Mike.

She pursed her lips. Actually, she did not have to escape anymore. She would just leave him, as they were no longer in Fallow Creek. Once she had saved enough money from her babysitting, she would leave him. But for now, she had to find a way to keep him away from her. She couldn't keep sharing his bed. Even if she couldn't formally leave now, she would stop being intimate with him. That would be hard, considering how forceful Mike could be. Plus, they shared a bedroom. The first thing she would have to do was to find a suitable excuse to move into the guest room.

She sighed wearily. What excuse, she did not know. She stood up as a firm determination entered her heart. If she did not succeed in moving out of Mike's room, then she would have to keep praying for forgiveness until she could save up enough money to leave him. Which meant that she needed to find people who would trust her with their children and pay her to take care of them.

She smiled in self-mockery. She was a stranger in town. Why would anyone trust her with their children?

And then an idea came to her. She immediately headed upstairs and went to Olivia's room. She found Olivia playing on the floor with her two boys. She sighed as Olivia looked up at her with a cautious expression. Haltingly, Rachel said, "Olivia, can you do me a favor?"

For a long moment, Olivia said nothing. Finally, she smiled down at the boys and told them to go outside and play. She looked up at Rachel again and said harshly, "What do you want from me?"

"Can you watch Emily for me? I just want to run

out on an errand. I will be back in no time."

Olivia stared at her while Rachel waited, her heart thudding. When Olivia didn't answer after a full minute, Rachel said again, "Please, Olivia. I promise I'll come back as soon as possible. Emily is asleep right now so she doesn't need that much attention unless for some reason she wakes up and starts to cry."

Olivia sighed audibly and nodded. "Fine," she said. "I will watch Emily for you."

"Thank you so much," Rachel said. "I kept some formula in…"

"I have two kids!" Olivia snapped. "I know how to feed a baby!"

Chastised, Rachel gave her an apologetic smile. "I'm sorry. Thank you so much, Olivia. I will be back before you know it." She left the room quickly and went into the bedroom she shared with Mike.

She stepped out of the floral dress she'd worn constantly in Fallow Creek, which was one of the only four dresses she owned. She put on another dress, a light blue gown. Out of all her dresses, it was the most appropriate to wear in a place like Destiny. Actually, in any other place that wasn't Fallow Creek with its strict dress code for women.

Looking at herself in the full-length mirror, she adjusted the dress. Unlike her other dresses, which were loose and almost to her ankles, this dress was calf-length and slightly more fitted. The sleeves were shorter, just above her elbows, and the neckline wasn't as high as the others.

She gazed at her face. For the first time in her twenty-five years, she wished she could wear some makeup like other women.

She smoothed down her hair and decided to put it up in a bun. Soon, she put it down again and braided it. She looked at herself in the mirror and undid the braid. And then she grunted. *What are you doing, Rachel?*

She smiled in self-mockery as she gazed at herself in the mirror. She knew exactly why she was being finicky about her appearance today when she normally didn't care. It was because she was going to see the handsome pastor with the kind eyes. At least, she hoped she would see him. She didn't even know where he lived or if he would be home.

She forced herself away from the mirror, slipped on a pair of low-heeled sandals, and left the bedroom again. She stopped in front of the nursery and looked in on Emily before continuing on. Downstairs, she picked up the keys to Mike's Range Rover and hurriedly left the house. She hadn't told him she was going out, which would have been an infraction in Fallow Creek. She opened the small fence and got into the car.

As she drove away from the house, she kept looking out the window for someone she could ask for directions to the pastor's house. Destiny was a tiny town and the pastor seemed to be well known. Surely, the first person she asked could easily point her in the right direction. Even if he wasn't at his house, many people here would know where she could find him.

She drove through town, gazing this way and that, appalled. There were destroyed houses, felled trees, and crushed cars everywhere. Having gone out only twice since they'd arrived here, the extent of the damage still shocked her.

Her heart went out to the people in the town, especially those who had lost their homes. This was really bad. She had to find a way to help out instead of secluding herself in her luxurious home, pretending that nothing like this had happened. Yes, she was worried about her reputation, but that didn't mean she could use that as an excuse not to do right.

After gaping at the town for a long time, she finally remembered she wanted to ask someone for directions to the pastor's house. She had just been driving aimlessly through town. A young woman with a blonde bob was walking down the sidewalk, probably heading to the all-purpose store a few feet away. Rachel stopped the car and waved to get her attention.

The young woman turned and smiled. She walked to Rachel's car with her smile intact and a curious look in eyes.

Rachel said to her, "Hi. I just moved here some days ago and I'm looking for Pastor... Keith. I think that's his name. Do you know where he lives?"

The young woman's smile grew wider. "I knew you were a stranger because I've never seen you before. Welcome to Destiny. It's such a shame you moved here just after the awful hurricane, when the whole town is in disarray."

Rachel nodded. "I keep being amazed at how bad everything is."

The young woman said, "Yes, it's really bad. Anyway, my name is Jenny, and Pastor Keith lives on the next street. However, he's not at his house right now."

Rachel felt slightly disappointed until Jenny

added, "He's in his store just over there." Jenny pointed at a small building, the all-purpose store that Rachel had been in before. She was surprised to hear it was his. She had not seen him on the day she'd gone there and he hadn't mention it belonged to him when he'd visited the house.

"It's one of the few places that wasn't touched at all by the hurricane," Jenny said.

"Thank you so much, Jenny."

"No problem," Jenny told her. "I was just heading there to see Pastor Keith myself."

Rachel drove the short distance to the small store and limbed out of the car. She was about to enter the building when Jenny reached her. She smiled, opened the door, and walked in with Jenny behind her. Rachel looked around the store. It was almost empty now. If nothing was being sold here, then why was it still open?

Jenny said to her, "Pastor Keith must be at the back. Let me go get him." She left quickly and Rachel's heart pounded.

Calm down, she scolded herself. *Remember why you are here.* She took a deep breath, forced herself to stay calm, and began to walk around the store, looking at the few remaining things on the shelves.

TEN

The shelves in the pastor's store contained a few knick-knacks, some cookies and candies, a couple of old books, pens, and notebooks. She noticed a pile of hand towels on the bottom shelf.

She smiled at the variety of things sold in the store. It reminded her of the store her mother had owned in Glendale before they'd moved to Fallow Creek. She still remembered those days with nostalgia. She and her brother had been as free as birds and their mom had seemed much happier. She was now dead, having passed away some years ago of a brain tumor and a broken heart. Rachel had blamed her stepfather, Chris, for her death, even though she said nothing to him. Mom had loved him, but he had married two other wives after her and consequently stopped paying any attention to her. Rachel had cut him off completely after her mother died.

She turned around when she heard footsteps approaching. Her heart skipped a beat when the pastor appeared. He looked even more handsome than when he'd visited the other day. Her hands grew slightly damp and her pulse began to race as he smiled at her, and she told herself to calm down. *Remember why you are here, Rachel.* She was here to find out if the good pastor could help her get babysitting jobs so she could finally move away from Mike. Then she could make a decent, guilt-free life for herself and her daughter.

He came to stand in front of her and Jenny stood next to him. For some reason, Jenny had lost her bright smile and was scowling at her and Pastor Keith. For a brief moment, Rachel felt puzzled by that, and then she brushed it off. She concentrated on the handsome pastor and smiled back at him. "Hi! I hope you are not too busy now. I came to talk to you about something really important."

Pastor Keith said, "That's okay. I can talk now." He turned to Jenny and said, "I'll see you later, Jen."

For reasons Rachel didn't even want to acknowledge right now, a thread of jealousy ran through her at the wide smile he gave to Jenny and the way he had called her 'Jen'. Maybe they were an item.

If they were, why would she care about that? He was apparently a single, handsome young man, and Jenny was a pretty, young woman. They looked good together. She should be happy for them; at least happy that there were people like this couple who belonged only to each other, and women like Jenny who did not have to share their men like Rachel did.

Jenny left without saying goodbye to her, and Rachel focused completely on the strapping man before her. She studied his face, his eyes, and then she blinked. *Stop your juvenile crush, Rachel!*

Pastor Keith said, "Let's go into my office and talk." He led the way to a small office at the back of the store. There were study books and two big Bibles scattered on the table. He looked embarrassed as he sat at his desk and started to clear the table. She sat across from him and he said, "Please forgive the mess."

She smiled. "That's okay."

Pastor Keith finally focused on her and said, "What do you want to talk to me about?" Before she could answer, he added, "I have to say, the money you and your husband generously donated is truly making a difference. I re-hired the builders who were working on the new church before the hurricane swept it away. They have started to rebuild it again. Also, we've been able to get more food trucks and basic necessities for people who need it. I cannot say how grateful I am for the money you and your husband gave."

Rachel cringed every time he said, "you and your husband." Guilt had gripped her as he spoke. She wanted to tell him that the donation was not from 'her and Mike' and that Mike wasn't her husband. But she could not bring herself to tell him. What would he think of her if he knew that she had been living with a married man and his wife for years? She was pretty sure he would be shocked and maybe he would want nothing to do with her, which she would deserve.

"What's wrong?" he asked, leaning forward and staring at her with a concerned look.

Rachel forced herself to smile. "Nothing is wrong. I was just thinking about something I have to take care of as soon as possible."

Pastor Keith smiled. "I am glad. I thought it was something I said."

"No." She smiled genuinely this time. "You said nothing wrong."

His eyes caressed her face for a long moment, and then, seeming to catch himself, he blinked and leaned back on his seat. He looked embarrassed again, and to remove the awkwardness of the moment, she quickly said, "You must really love this town. Did you grow up here?"

She groaned inwardly after asking the question. She had asked yet another personal question, just as she'd done when he'd visited the house. Why couldn't she stop herself from asking such personal questions and just focus on asking for a job? She still remembered with embarrassment going over to him and putting her arm around him in the house. She had not thought about what she was doing because he had looked so sad and she'd wanted to comfort him. Later, though, she had chided herself for doing that.

He smiled and a wistful look appeared on his face. "Yes, I grew up in Destiny, and I love this town. I love being the pastor of the only church in town." He looked intently at her and asked, "Where are you from?"

Her heart began to beat rapidly and she quickly said, "I actually came to ask you about a job."

He looked both curious and interested. "I remember you told me you wanted to be an elementary school teacher. Unfortunately, as I told you, we don't have the elementary school anymore. But it is one of the things we plan to focus on soon.

We hope we can rebuild the school before summer vacation is over." He looked like he wanted to say something else but wasn't sure he should.

"I remember you telling me about the elementary school," she said. "Actually, I didn't come to ask for a job as a teacher. I came to ask if you could introduce me to some people who might need a babysitter. The parents could even leave the kids at my home while they go about their business and then get them when they are ready."

Pastor Keith looked up thoughtfully. He faced her again and smiled broadly. "I think that might be a good idea. Unfortunately, many businesses here had to close up and many people don't have that much money. I know there will definitely be people who want a babysitter, but I have to tell you… though I know you don't need the money as much as something to do, the pay will be very small."

If only he knew how much she needed the money. She shrugged. "That's okay. Like you said, I really just need something to keep me busy." She wanted to tell him the truth, that she did need the money, but she couldn't. They lived in a big house and Mike had just donated thousands of dollars. Pastor Keith would either think she was lying or suspect that something was wrong with her living situation. She wasn't ready for him to find out the truth about her.

He stood up and said, "Okay, then. Let's go."

She raised her eyebrows in surprise and asked him where they were going.

He chuckled. "You asked me to find parents who need a babysitter for their kids, didn't you? We are going to find them."

"Right now?" she asked him.

"Yes, now."

"Okay..." she said slowly and stood up.

She followed him out of the office and out of the store. They headed in different directions and then turned around again and faced each other. They both started laughing awkwardly.

He said, "Oh, I'm sorry. Of course you brought your car. I was just heading toward mine."

"I guess we can take your car, Pastor Keith," she said.

He nodded and said, "Please call me Keith."

"And please call me Rachel," she said.

"Okay, Rachel," he pointed at an old blue car a few feet away. "There is my car."

They walked to his car and got in. She sat beside him while he started the engine and pulled into the road. As they drove through town, he intermittently waved to people who heartily greeted him. She surreptitiously studied him. He looked about ten years younger than Mike, which meant he was probably about two or three years older than she was. And he was definitely more handsome. His wavy hair fell down his forehead as the wind tossed it this way and that, causing her heart to flutter. Unlike Mike, who had a heavy beard, Keith was clean-shaven.

Her eyes moved down to his arms holding the steering wheel. He was wearing a grey, short-sleeved T-shirt that showed his strong arms and broad shoulders. Her eyes moved back to his face while her pulse quickened. She couldn't look away. She took in his sparkling green eyes as he smiled and waved to yet another person on the street. She looked at his messy hair again, and then her eyes settled on his full lips.

An image popped into her mind; both of them wrapped up in each other's arms, kissing passionately. Her heart began to pound until it felt like it would burst out of her chest. She knew immediately that she had to look away. But she couldn't.

He turned to her with a huge smile and then raised his brows, looking at her quizzically.

She quickly looked away, embarrassed. Had he noticed her studying him intently?

"Rachel? I asked if you would mind watching older kids as well?"

She shook her head. "No, I don't mind." Her embarrassment grew as she turned away again. *Pull yourself together, Rachel!* What was wrong with her? He had asked her a question and she hadn't even heard because she was so busy gawking at him. She needed to put a stop to her infatuation. She could not afford to be distracted from her goal. The only thing she cared about right now — should care about — was getting a job, saving up money for an apartment, and then leaving Mike. She had to focus all her efforts on her plans for independence so she could make a life for herself and Emily; a life she would not be ashamed of as her daughter grew up.

Keith finally stopped in front of a small house that mirrored some of the houses she had seen as they drove here. She got out of the car when he did and they walked to the front of the house together. Keith knocked on the door, and a short time later, a man, taller than any she had ever seen, opened it and peered at them. A huge smile broke out on his face as he looked at Keith. "Welcome, Pastor," the man said. "Please come in." He turned to gaze curiously at her.

Rachel entered the house and Keith stepped in behind her. He sat down on the couch and she sat next to him. Without thinking, she shifted close so that their knees and arms were touching. She thought about moving away but knew it would look weird. If Keith noticed how close they were sitting, he said and did nothing about it.

She could feel the warmth of his body as he turned to the man who was sitting on the sofa next to theirs. "So, Gary, this is Rachel. She, her husband, and their three children are the family who moved into the big house on the edge of town."

Gary's smile broadened and he nodded. "The house looks amazing," he said, looking at her. "You and your husband did a great job with it."

Once again, as was usually the case when someone referred to Mike as her husband, guilt smothered her. What would happen when all these people in town found out she was a polygamist? Because in spite of how she hated the lifestyle, as long as she still lived with Mike as his "wife" that was what she was — a polygamist. The earlier she could leave Mike, the better for her. She only wished she could leave him immediately. But because of Emily, that would not be possible. She had no means to take care of her daughter apart from Mike.

"I'm sorry," Gary said. "Did I say something wrong?"

"No," Rachel quickly answered. "You didn't." She

felt Keith's eyes on her but did not turn to look at him. He was probably thinking she was strange now. This was not the first time she had zoned out since they'd met today.

Keith said, "Okay, Gary. I brought Rachel here because she needs a job. Just something to keep her busy. She loves kids and she asked me to find out if there were people in this town who needed babysitters. I told her I knew some people. That's why we are here. Are you and Claire interested? She can watch your kids whenever you're busy or just need a break." Keith grinned. "Talking about Claire and your kids, where are they now?"

"They went to visit Claire's mother. They should be back this evening." Gary looked at Rachel and then at Keith. "I will have to talk to Claire first, but we could use a babysitter at this time. I'm busy, as you know, with the hardware store, and Claire seems a little overwhelmed with all the house chores and watching the kids these days. Since they are out of school right now, it's really difficult trying to juggle work and take care of them at the same time." Gary looked at Rachel again. "If Pastor Keith trusts you to take care of our kids, then I trust you too."

Rachel could not help but grin. "Thank you so much."

They left five minutes later, after Gary promised to call Keith once he had spoken with his wife about their request. Outside the house, Keith said to Rachel, "One down, about a dozen more to go."

"Thank you," she said to him. She felt touched by his kindness. She was little more than a stranger to him, yet here he was taking her round town in order to help her get a job. She pursed her lips as guilt once again snatched her joy. When Keith found out about her... She gasped as Keith placed his hand on her arm.

"Are you okay?" he asked.

She nodded. Now he would definitely think she was certifiable.

They got into his car again and Keith began to drive. They drove for a short time and stopped in front of another house. This time, the couple and their kids were at home. As before, Keith introduced Rachel and told the couple that she needed a babysitting job, just something to keep her busy.

Rachel pressed her lips tightly together, feeling guilty. She still hadn't told him the truth — that she needed a job because she needed money. But it was not something she was ready to do yet.

Just like Gary, the couple, who had three boys ranging from four to seven, beamed at her and told her they would trust her with their kids because they trusted Keith.

They went to a third house and had the same reception and then finally Keith drove her to a quaint house with trees all around, some felled. He turned to her with his eyes sparkling and said, "This is my house."

For some reason, her heart began to race. He opened the door and she got out of the car. She followed him to the front of the house, wondering why he had brought her to his house when he hardly knew her. In Fallow Creek, people brought you to their homes only when they felt you were sufficiently trustable or in an emergency. From the smile on his face, there was no emergency, which meant… she blinked. It couldn't be. She'd only met him twice.

He opened the door, allowed her to walk in first, and then went in after her. The first thing she noticed about his house was how cozy it looked. The living room was definitely small. It was the same size as her and Mike's bathroom, but it felt homier than their living room. The furnishings made her smile because it was unexpected and definitely not what she thought his living room would look like. As though he could read her mind, he said, "This house belonged to my grandmother. We grew up here, my sister and I. She took care of us after our parents died."

"I'm so sorry," she said.

"It was a long time ago," he said to her and pointed at the couch. "Please sit," he said.

She sat and once again wondered why he had brought her to his house. She loved the idea of spending time with him, if only to admire his looks, but she was sure that if Mike found out about this, he would go into a jealous rage. Reluctantly, she opened her mouth to thank him and then tell him she had to go, but he said, "I'll be right back."

He left quickly and she sighed. She looked around the living room again and then heard something that sounded like a child's laughter coming from somewhere in the house. She blinked in surprise. Did he have a child? Was he married, maybe to that Jenny, and all this time she was fantasizing about him? And why had she even been obsessing over him when she was living with another man?

A minute later, he came back with a young pretty woman and two little girls who looked about four and six. Rachel gasped in surprise and dread filled her heart. Keith was married? He had kids? She had been ogling a married man?

She pushed aside her surprise and disappointment. Well, it was all for the best. She could finally put aside her crush and concentrate on her goal. She stood up stiffly and forced herself to smile. "Hi," she said to the woman, and then grinned at the children. She looked at the woman again, "You are so beautiful," she forced herself to say.

The woman beamed, thanked her, and said, "You are beautiful, too."

Rachel turned to Keith and said, "You have a lovely wife and your kids are adorable."

The young woman laughed but Keith frowned. He said, "I'm so sorry I gave you the wrong impression, Rachel. Donna here is not my wife. She is married to a friend of mine, Steven. And these are their kids. They are one of the two families living here with me because their homes were destroyed by the hurricane."

An overwhelming relief settled on Rachel, and then she brushed it aside. What did it matter anyway if he was single or not?

Keith said, "Donna told me she's interested in having you babysit her kids, didn't you, Donna?"

"Yep!" Donna said pleasantly. "They are a handful, these two." She looked at her kids, who were now jumping up and down on Keith's couch.

Rachel smiled and told Donna that she would try her best to be a great babysitter. She looked at the kids and beamed, and the younger one gave her a toothy smile.

The three of them stood talking about the calamity that had befallen the town, and then they changed topics and talked about the children's school and the plans to rebuild it. "Rachel wants to be an elementary school teacher," Keith said to Donna.

Donna turned to her and Rachel simply nodded. She quickly changed the topic, not wanting Keith and Donna to know that she was not yet a qualified teacher. She asked where she could buy baby supplies for Emily. They had brought along a huge bag of diapers and other things that Emily needed from Fallow Creek, but eventually they would run out.

"Elizabeth owns a kiddies' store not so far from here," Donna said to Rachel. "Part of her store was destroyed, but I know she is still selling the baby things from the part that wasn't. I'm sure anyone would be happy to direct you to the store."

Rachel nodded. She was sure that was the case, too. The people of Destiny seemed extremely nice and always ready to help out at any minute. It was a shame that they had suffered so much because of a terrible natural disaster.

Ten minutes later, Keith said to Donna, "I think we have to leave now."

They stood up and after Donna hugged her warmly, Rachel left the house with Keith.

In Keith's car, Rachel said, "Everyone was so nice to me today and they all agreed that I could babysit their kids even though they do not know me. It's all thanks to you, Keith."

He shrugged. "No, it's not really me. The people here are just super nice. I hope in due time you will get to know them well and make good friends here."

Without thinking, she said, "I hope you will be the first friend I make." She immediately groaned inwardly and chided herself for her words.

Keith gave her a huge smile. "I would love that very much," he said. "And I hope to make friends with your husband as well."

She nearly groaned aloud. She looked out the window as Keith drove through the town again. Once again, she marveled at how much destruction there was in this town and how resilient the people were. And then she felt Keith's eyes on her. She did not want to turn for fear he would look away, but then she could not resist. She turned to him, but he did not look away. He smiled and said, "Can you and your husband come to Sunday service at a makeshift church?" He chuckled. "Actually, it's just the open ground and it's only a short distance from your house."

Her heart began to race again. Right now, it would be a bad idea for her and Mike to go out together as a couple. And who knew what Mike would do? He was unpredictable and might bring Olivia along, which would be even worse. Then everything she had been trying to hide would be revealed. She said to Keith, "I'm not sure. I will ask Mike and see what he says." But she would not ask Mike and hopefully no one else would.

"That's fine," Keith said, smiling. "I hope you two are able to come and you can bring your children as well. We have three lovely women who take care of the children during our church services. Unfortunately, because we now hold our service outdoors, we need more hands to watch the children and make sure they don't run off somewhere." He narrowed his eyes, a thoughtful expression on his face, and then smiled at her. "Why don't you join our children's department in church and then you can help out with the kids? That will be great for you. More parents will know that if they can trust you with their kids in church, they can trust you with them outside the church."

She bit her lip. How could she pass up on this? And yet she could not afford to have the people here know about her different lifestyle. Not now. She sighed and repeated, "I will let Mike know."

Keith nodded and focused on the road again.

They finally got to his store and Keith got out of the car. She did too, and he walked her to her car. He shook her hand and said, "I'm glad you came out today."

"I had a great time with you, Keith," she said, and then pressed her lips tightly together, mortified. Why was she always putting her foot in her mouth? Why had she said she'd had a great time with him? It sounded as though they had gone out on a date, which would be weird since she was married, or at least he thought she was.

He didn't say anything for a long while and then spoke. "I hope I'll see you and Mike at the service tomorrow."

She said nothing and got into her car. Starting the car, she drove off without looking at him, knowing he was still standing on the sidewalk and gazing after her. Her mind stayed on him all the way to the house and even as she entered the living room.

Her eyes widened with dread as she came face

to face with Mike. He had a look in his eyes that she had only seen once. She remembered that day clearly. The day he'd looked at her like he was looking at her now. It was a year after they'd had their so-called 'spiritual marriage'. She had gone to visit her brother, Taylor, and met one of their childhood friends in his house, a young man named Carl.

Usually, in Fallow Creek, married women did not spend more than a few minutes talking to other men, but because she was with her brother, she'd thought nothing of it. And neither had Taylor or Carl. They'd sat on the front porch of Taylor's house talking and reminiscing about old times. At one point, Taylor got up and went indoors to get something. Rachel continued to talk with Carl. And then she frowned when Carl suddenly looked fearful as he looked away from her.

She glanced in the direction he was staring at and then shuddered. Mike was coming toward them with a look of rage on his face. He stood in front of them and, with his eyes blazing, glared at Rachel. "So this is where you have been." He turned to glower at Carl. "Talking and whiling away your time."

She could clearly see the jealousy in his eyes, and she wondered what he possibly thought she had been doing with Carl in Taylor's house. She had not been prepared for the punch Mike threw at Carl and the fight that ensued after. It had been totally humiliating. He had literally dragged her home and then had not let her out of the house for weeks after. Unfortunately for her, the law of Fallow Creek was on his side and there was nothing she could do about it.

Now, he had the same look in his eyes. She knew she had to explain herself quickly before he did whatever he was thinking about doing. Before she could speak, he said, "I saw you. I saw you with that pastor who came here the other day." He was staring at her with a scornful look. "You were driving past and you did not see me."

She shook her head. "Michael, it's not what you think. Keith was just showing me around because I asked him to."

"Keith, is it? You are a liar. I saw the way you were looking at him and the way he was looking at you, too."

Rachel bowed her head. What could she say about that? What Mike said about the way she was looking at the pastor was true. But what she had not noticed was that the pastor was looking at her the same way. But she was sure it wasn't so. Mike was probably exaggerating because of his jealousy.

"Look at me!" he commanded.

Rachel lifted her eyes and staggered back at the look in his. She was sure that at any moment he would hit her. She stepped back even further from him and said, "Nothing happened, Mike. I have better things to think about than being involved with some pastor."

"Yes, like your daughter, who you left all alone."

"I did not leave her all alone, Mike. I told Olivia to watch her." She suddenly gasped and fear gripped her. Had something happened to Emily? Was that why Mike was mad? She began to hurry past Mike in order to check on Emily, but Mike grabbed her arm. She winced in pain as he applied pressure. She tried to snatch it away from his grasp but he held on even tighter and snarled, "Where are you going?"

"Please let go of me! You are hurting me, and I need to go check on Emily."

He let go of her and she hurried past him. He said, "You are not going to leave this house for a long, long time."

She did not look back or answer him. She had to get to her daughter and make sure she was alright. As for what Mike had said, this was not Fallow Creek. He had no right to imprison her in this house.

She hurried upstairs and went into Emily's room. Emily was not in her crib. She went out of the room again, worried. Hurrying to Olivia's room, she heaved a huge sigh of relief when she saw Emily in Olivia's arms.

Olivia shot her an angry look. "You said you were going to come back in no time. It's been hours since you left the house."

"I'm so sorry, Olivia," she said. "I had something really urgent to take care of." She walked up to Olivia and took Emily out of her arms. Kissing her baby's cheeks, she thanked Olivia for taking care of Emily. She left the room again, but instead of going to the bedroom she shared with Mike, she went downstairs and entered the guest bedroom. Without a doubt, Mike would soon come in and try to intimidate her and force her to go back to their bedroom. She had to find a good reason for why she wanted to stay in a separate bedroom.

She was a little surprised when Mike walked into the room with Olivia. She had expected him to come, but not with Olivia. She knew exactly what Mike was going to say. He was going to tell her that he was disappointed with her for spending time with another man when she was married. He would let her know that he was serious about her not leaving the house until he said so. But he could not control her movements in this town as he had in Fallow Creek.

She bounced Emily on her knees while her baby gurgled. Looking at Mike and Olivia, she said, "Please, Mike, I am tired. Can we talk about it tomorrow?"

"Rachel, hand Emily over to Olivia. We need to talk."

"I told you we'll talk about it tomorrow," Rachel said, frustrated.

"No, we will talk about it now." Mike turned to Olivia and said, "Take Emily back to her room."

"No!" Rachel held onto Emily. "She's staying here with me."

Mike grabbed her hand and squeezed it tight until she cried out in pain. He held her hand away and Olivia took her baby. He did not let go of her until Olivia left the room with Emily.

"Now, listen to me," Mike said. "I don't know what has come over you since we came to this town but let me tell you that things have not changed. Just because we are not in Fallow Creek anymore doesn't mean you can do whatever you want."

Anger rose up in her and she screamed, "Yes, Mike, it does! Things have changed. Really, I'm not even married, no matter what you tell yourself."

He stared at her with derision. "You are the one lying to yourself. We are married before God."

"No, we are not! And especially not before God!"

Mike stared suspiciously at her, and she regretted what she had just said. If he knew that she was planning to leave him again, he would not only keep her from going out of the house for a short while, he would not let her out ever. And not only that, he would hover over her continuously and would give her no breathing space. He definitely would not listen to any explanation she gave as to why she could not stay in their bedroom with him. In fact, he would force her to be intimate with him... every day. She felt like throwing up at the thought and the urgency she felt to get away from him increased.

He gave her a cold smile and said, "I know what you are thinking. It's not going to happen."

She glared at him, wondering what he was going to do.

He walked out of the room and then she heard the door click and lock. Her heart sank as she stood. He had locked her in. She went to the door and began to pound on it, screaming for him to let her out. When she was tired, she sank to the floor and wept. His plans were even worse than she had thought. He not only planned to lock her in the house, but in this room. And she knew without a doubt that he would come at night and force himself on her, telling her that he was only taking what was his.

"Lord, I have to get out of this house today," she whispered. "Please, help me get out." There was no way she could continue staying in this house. She had to find a way to escape now and take Emily with her.

But how would she be able to get out of this bedroom, and how would she be able to get Emily without Mike or Olivia seeing her? And even if she succeeded in leaving with Emily, where would they live?

These thoughts ran through her mind as she stood up and paced the room. However, in spite of the impossibility of the situation, she knew one thing: she was going to try to get out of this house this very night, no matter what. Even if it meant that she and Emily would sleep on someone's front porch.

ELEVEN

Glancing at her wristwatch, Rachel saw it was ten minutes past midnight. She had been waiting until midnight when she was certain everyone in the household would be asleep. She had continuously run through her mind different scenarios of how she could escape the house. First of all, she had to escape this room. She had fallen asleep at around eleven o'clock, and now she had to put the final plan she had settled on into motion.

There was no way out of this guest room except through the window. She would climb out of it. It would be relatively safe since the guest room was on the ground floor. Once she was outside the house, she would head to the staircase at the back of the house that ran from the top of the house to the bottom. She would climb the staircase, crawl into the nursery through the window, carry Emily out as quietly as she could, go down the stairs and unlock the door. She would flee into the night with Emily and take refuge in Pastor Keith's house.

She'd decided on Pastor Keith as she knew no

one else in Destiny and he had been kind to her. Hopefully she would be able to find his house quickly. It might not be easy, especially as she was going on foot. She had decided that taking one of Mike's cars was not an option, as the cars were parked very close to the house. Once she started the ignition, Mike would probably hear her and her plans to escape would be thwarted. Besides, she didn't want anything that belonged to him.

Climbing out of bed, she opened the window, and then blinked in surprise and dread. It was raining outside. It wasn't very heavy, but she couldn't carry Emily out in this rain. She stepped back into the room and looked around for something to use to cover her baby from the rain. Finding nothing, she grabbed the duvet from the bed and then threw her legs out the window. She landed on the ground and quietly made her way to the back of the house.

The house was lit brightly outside, powered by the generator Mike had bought the day after they came to Destiny. She climbed up the stairs as slowly and as soundlessly as she could. When she got to the top, she took a deep breath as her heart began to pound. The ledge which ran around the house was narrower than she had previously imagined. It would be extremely difficult to carry Emily on this ledge. But she had to get her daughter out.

She made her way carefully down the ledge to get to Emily's room. She had to pass by Mike's bedroom in order to get to Emily's. For some reason, as she passed by his room, she could not resist looking in. And then her heart seized with fear. The curtain was slightly open and the bedside lamp was on. Mike was on the bed, reading, and beside the bed was Emily's crib.

Rachel bit her lip in frustration and anger as she stared at Mike. When Emily began to cry, Mike stood up from the bed and went to bend over the crib. He looked into it and lifted Emily up into his arms.

Panic flooded Rachel. She should have known that something like this would happen. Mike always had everything planned out carefully. She wasn't sure if he had guessed that she might try to escape, but knowing him, he had decided not to take any chances. He probably knew that she would never leave without Emily.

He put Emily back into her crib and walked toward the bed. Rachel jerked back so he wouldn't see her and shut her eyes as she leaned against the wall, praying for wisdom. She wanted to enter Mike's room now and grab Emily, but that would be foolish.

Mike was clearly confident that she would not leave without Emily. Having Emily with him was the way he'd decided to make sure that the few times he wasn't watching her, she would not think of leaving. And she would have stayed if they were still in Fallow Creek. But he had underestimated her desire to leave and had pushed her past what she could bear. Living in Destiny had opened her eyes to how different her life would be without him; how much better. She would not remain a prisoner forever in Mike's house to do with as he pleased. Most of all, she could not continue to violate her conscience and the growing certainty in her heart that God wanted her to leave.

"Lord, how can I leave without Emily?" she

silently prayed.

She looked out into the distance. The rain was heavier. She had to leave now. But she would be back as soon as she figured out a way to get Emily out of this house. She headed to the stairs once more and then made her way down. She looked up at the house one last time and felt a mix of emotions. On one hand, she couldn't wait to leave, but on the other, she wanted to stay because of Emily.

The rain began to fall even harder and she knew she had to make a decision right now. She took a deep breath and then gave in to the urge in her heart, an urge she believed was from God. She had to leave now and get Emily out later. In order to do that, she would have to tell Keith her secret. The thought sent shivers down her spine. He would be disgusted by her once he found out everything, she was sure, but there was nothing she could do about that. She turned around, covered herself with the duvet, and ran far away from the house.

The rain beat down on her mercilessly as she jogged on. The farther away she went from the house, the darker everything became. Soon, she could not see her way in the darkness and the rain made it much worse. In her plans to leave Mike, she had not put the weather into consideration, or the fact that there was still no electricity in Destiny.

She kept walking, but she knew she was hopelessly lost now. She was cold, miserable, and afraid. The farther she walked, the more certain she was that she was going the wrong way. She looked around her but could see nothing. She was ankle-deep in water, as the ground was waterlogged because of the rain, and she was drenched through.

The rain had soaked the duvet and her clothes.

She began to shiver from the cold and knew that if she did not get out of the rain soon, she might get pneumonia. How awful it would be if she died out here and Emily had to stay and grow up with Mike. She began to sob, but she kept walking. If there had been some source of light, somewhere, she could have searched for a house where she could plead with the owners to stay for the night.

The problem was that she could not see anything at all. It was a starless night and everywhere was pitch black. Also, Mike's house was on the edge of town and after it, empty tracts of land. She was almost certain there were no houses where she was. For all she knew, she could be heading out of Destiny.

Finally, exhausted, she sat down on the ground. Her teeth were chattering now, her tears mingled with the rain. She started sobbing loudly, not just for herself, but for her daughter. She felt physically and emotionally broken. At least there was one good thing that had come out of not being able to take Emily out today. In this rain, Emily would have been soaked through. If something bad had happened to Emily because of that, Rachel would never have forgiven herself.

She had been completely stupid deciding to leave the house today even after seeing how heavy the rain was. And she had overestimated her knowledge of the roads in this town and her ability to find a house she'd only been to once. But she had been desperate to leave Mike. She had done what she thought was right and was being punished for it.

She kept sobbing as she sat there, not knowing

what would happen to her. She prayed, asking the Lord to cause the rain to stop. If it did, at least she could sleep out here without the fear that she would drown if there was another flood. However, even if the rain stopped, dying from cold would still be a huge probability.

She wrapped her arms around herself to try to ward off the cold, but it did no good. She was shivering uncontrollably now. Finally, she stopped sobbing, and lifted up her eyes to the sky. She shouted, "Lord, if I am going to die, please take care of Emily for me!"

She did not want Emily to grow up in a polygamous home. If Rachel died, that might solve it. But on the other hand, knowing Mike, he would not waste any time bringing another woman into the house. He was the kind of man who gathered possessions, including women, and was never satisfied with what he had.

After praying, she bit her lip and closed her eyes. An overwhelming sense of hopelessness settled over her and she embraced it. She lay down on the wet, cold ground, weary, and closed her eyes.

***

Keith sat up on his bed and rubbed his eyes. He threw his curtains open and fear gripped him. It was raining heavily. He immediately knew it was what had woken him up. Since the hurricane, he had developed a fear of storms and this one raging outside reminded him of the day the hurricane had devastated Destiny. The rain was not as heavy as that day, but even then, the rain had not come down heavily until some hours into the storm.

He jumped out of bed, picked up the flashlight from the floor beside him, and turned it on. He began to pace his room, praying, "Lord, please let it never happen again."

A deafening crack of thunder sounded, shaking the house. Keith began to pray for the town again and for the weather. He frowned as he felt a gentle tug in his heart. He felt a strong desire to pray for something. He shut his eyes. No, someone. Someone he knew was in danger. He could sense it somehow. He began to pray, not knowing for whom he was praying. He prayed for his sister, the members of his church, Rachel, all the people in Destiny who came to his mind. He asked the Lord to protect them and keep them safe.

After a while, he stopped praying as he felt a deep sense of peace settle over him. He climbed into his bed again.

***

Rachel opened her eyes and sat up. Her ears perked up. Footsteps sounded in the darkness and then she could see someone coming toward her.

She blinked, wondering if she were seeing things, and then knew she wasn't. Two men were headed in her direction with bright flashlights. They were under umbrellas and their eyes were fixed on her.

She stood up unsteadily, her heart beating wildly, and waved at them. She couldn't speak for a few seconds and then found her voice. She called out weakly, "Please help me."

The men hurried to her and, without speaking,

linked her arms with theirs. She stood between them, leaning against them as they walked. They held on to her, shielding her from the rain with their umbrellas. One of them gently asked, "Where were you going this late and in this rain?"

She began to cry again, but this time with relief. "I was going to Pastor Keith's house, but I lost my way. Do you know where he lives? Can you take me there?"

"Everyone in this town knows where Pastor Keith lives," the other said. "We will take you there. Don't you worry about it."

She thanked them weakly and then looked around the area where they were. Illuminated by the men's flashlights, she could see they were in an open field and there were no houses around, just as she had guessed.

They were almost carrying her as they walked. She was grateful for them and for the umbrella over her. But she was still extremely cold and still shivering. Soon, she grew weaker and weaker. One of the men carried her while the other held an umbrella over her. She began to feel herself dozing off. She jerked awake when she heard a loud knock.

"We are here," one of the men said to her. He knocked again on Keith's door and smiled at her. "You are safe."

***

Keith groaned and threw the covers aside, unable to sleep. He couldn't stop thinking about how much work still needed to be done for the town. He thought about the generous donation given by the Cadwells to rebuild the church and help the people of Destiny. Once again, for the hundredth time since the donation was given, he prayed for Mike and Rachel, asking the Lord to bless them. Mike Cadwell had said in not so many words that he was willing to give more to see the church and town rebuilt. He had told Keith not to hesitate to tell him if there was any way he could help.

As much as Keith hated the idea of asking again for help after the man had given so much, he knew he had to eventually. He would do anything, humble himself and beg if he had to, in order to see the town of Destiny and its people back to where they were before — fully happy again. His mind had settled on the elementary and middle schools, especially because of Eric and Paula's kids who lived in the house with him. The couple worried continuously about their children; about when they would be able to start school again. The school had to be rebuilt, and since Mike had promised to help wherever there was a need, Keith would have to go and see him soon and ask for his help.

His mind traveled to Rachel and their day together. He had enjoyed being with her, more than he would ever admit. He had been surprised when she said she'd enjoyed the time spent with him, but he had been happy about it. He began to wonder what she was doing now and then smiled in self-derision. *What else would she be doing?* Of course she was asleep. He scolded himself once again for thinking constantly about her. She was a married woman, for goodness' sake.

He shook his head and forced Rachel from his mind. He stretched out on his bed again and tried to go to sleep, and then sat up immediately when he heard a loud knock over the sound of the rain.

He frowned. Who on earth could be at his door at this time of the night? He got out of bed again, turned on his flashlight, and stepped out of the room. In the living room, he glanced briefly at the clock on the wall and his frown deepened. It was a few minutes past three o'clock. Who was paying him a visit at this ungodly hour?

The knock sounded again and he walked to his door. He opened it and loudly sucked in his breath.

"Rachel!"

She was huddled over on the floor, drenched with water from the rain. She looked exhausted and her eyes were shut. "Oh, Rachel, what happened to you?" He quickly lifted her up in his arms and carried her into his living room. Gently, he placed her on the couch, knelt beside her, and swept her dripping wet hair from her face.

She opened her eyes and looked up at him. She smiled weakly and he said to her, "Wait here, Rachel."

He chided himself as he hurriedly left the living room. *Wait here. As if she is in any state to get up and walk out of the house.*

He got to his bedroom, feeling confused, and tore the blanket from his bed. And then he sighed. She needed more than a blanket. She had to change out of her wet clothes into something dry before he wrapped her up.

He hurried to the living room, lifted her up again in his arms, and carried her to his bedroom. He lay her on his bed and then went through his closet, trying to find something she could change into. He found nothing appropriate he could put her in except a pair of navy-blue pajamas, which would be too big for her. Still, they would have to do. He got his towel from the bathroom and then stood looking at her on his bed. She was too weak to dry herself and change into the pajamas, and he couldn't do it. He did not want to wake any of his house guests, but he needed help right now.

He went to knock on the door of the other bedroom. He entered and apologized for barging in when Eric and Paula sat up on the bed. Eric's flashlight was on, dimly illuminating the room. Their two children were sleeping on a mattress beside the bed. Keith's other guests, Jude and Michelle, had left his house yesterday with their children.

"I'm so sorry to wake you up," Keith said, his flashlight by his side, "but I need your help, Paula." He told them briefly about how he found Rachel at his door and that he needed Paula's help to get her out of her wet clothes and into dry ones. "I found a pair of pajamas of mine that I haven't worn for her to change into, but they will be too big. Do you have something better for her to wear? If you do, can you please bring it along with you?"

Paula had stood up before he'd finished speaking and opened the wardrobe. She grabbed some clothes from it and hurried out of the room with Keith.

They entered Keith's bedroom and found Rachel curled up on the bed, the duvet covering her whole body and half of her face. Paula immediately went to work. She pushed aside the duvet, gently sat Rachel up, and then began to unbutton her dress.

Keith turned away quickly and left the room.

In the living room, he sat down to wait and then stood again, unable to sit still. He paced the living room, worried about Rachel. What had happened to her? Why did she leave her house in the middle of the night in this weather?

More and more questions kept running through his mind about her and then he began to panic slightly when Paula didn't come out. He thought about going back to his room, but he was not sure he should. Paula might still be dressing Rachel, and it would definitely be worse than awkward if he walked in on them.

He kept waiting, tapping his foot impatiently and continuously, praying that Rachel would be okay. Maybe he needed to call Dr. Kingston. From the way Rachel looked when he had found her at his door, she had been in the rain for a long time and she'd been shivering. She might catch a cold or worse if she did not get medical attention soon.

Paula came out to the living room and smiled at him. "Sit down, Pastor Keith," she said. "I think Rachel will be okay. I made her a hot drink with our portable gas heater and then put her in your bed. She's warm now and asleep."

"I want to call the doctor," he said.

Paula nodded.

He reached for his phone on the coffee table. Phone lines had finally been restored a day ago. He prayed electricity would follow. Dialing the doctor's number, he waited as it rang and rang. When it stopped ringing, he sighed loudly and dialed the number again, praying the doctor would answer this time. He gave a sigh of relief when Dr.

Kingston did. After he told the doctor about Rachel and the condition he had found her in, Dr. Kingston asked if she had a fever. He looked at Paula and said, "Rachel doesn't have a fever, does she?"

"No, she actually looks quite well."

Keith told the doctor what Paula had said.

"Okay, I will come by first thing tomorrow morning... just to check and make sure she is truly fine."

After the call ended, Keith went into his room with his flashlight. He walked slowly and soundlessly to the bed and gazed at Rachel as she slept. He felt a tug in his heart as he watched her pretty face. It took everything in him to not reach out and caress her cheek. He backed away and left the room.

Sitting on the sofa, he faced Paula and said, "I hope she's really okay."

"You saw her," Paula said. "She looks fine."

He nodded but still he continued to worry.

Paula stood up, came over to put a hand on Keith's shoulder, and smiled. "Stop worrying. She will be as good as new by tomorrow. Now you need to try to get some sleep."

When Paula left, Keith stretched out on the couch. He tried to sleep, but he could not. His mind and emotions kept churning as he thought about Rachel and why she had come to his door, soaking wet, in the middle of the night. He wondered where her husband was now, and if he would come looking for her tomorrow.

Keith kept looking at the clock on the wall, willing it to be morning so that the doctor could come and check on Rachel. An hour later, he finally fell asleep.

TWELVE

Rachel slowly opened her eyes and stared into the face of a middle-aged man with kind eyes and a warm smile. She blinked as she stared at him. She wanted to ask who he was and where she was, but she shut her eyes as a wave of nausea swept over her. She licked her lips and opened her eyes again. She was parched. "Can I have some water?" she asked the man and then struggled to sit up.

Someone hurried up to her and placed their hands on her shoulders. "Don't try to sit up, Rachel. Just rest."

She coughed and looked into Keith's handsome face. He looked terribly worried as he gazed at her. Immediately the events of yesterday came rushing back to her, and she groaned. "Emily," she said weakly.

Keith put his hand on her forehead and turned to the other man. "She's not warm anymore," he said.

The man who Rachel guessed was a doctor nodded. "Apart from a slight runny nose and a cough, which I will give her medications for, she's perfectly fine. She just needs to rest for a day or so and she will be completely okay. She's actually lucky to have come to you in time because that rain last night was too heavy for anyone to be outside."

Rachel cried out again, "Emily... my daughter."

Keith gave her a small smile. "Your daughter? I'm sure she's safe at home. But I will get word back to your husband that you are here as soon as the doctor leaves so that he can come and pick you up."

Her eyes grew wide and she shook her head vehemently. "No, no, don't do that. Don't tell Mike where I am."

Keith gazed at her with worry and surprise on his face.

The doctor said, "Don't let her get too agitated." He wrote down something on a piece of paper and then handed a package to Keith. "This is for her cough." He smiled at Rachel and then faced Keith again. "Let me know if there are any new developments with her health. But I think she will be alright."

The doctor started to leave the room and Keith thanked him. After he left, Keith came and sat down on the bed next to her. He reached out as though he was about to smooth down her hair and then drew back his hand again.

She said to him, "I have to get my daughter, Emily."

Keith stared silently at her for a few minutes and then asked, "Why don't you want me to contact your husband? Surely, you want him to know where you are so he can come and pick you up, and then you can see your daughter."

She sat up and slowly leaned her back on the

pillow. She gave Keith a tired smile. It was time she told him everything. She looked into his eyes. If only things had been different, were different, maybe she would express her interest in him. She remembered how he had carried her into the house last night and gently laid her on his bed. He had vacated his bed for her and she did not know where he'd slept. She said in a tired voice, "Thank you for what you did for me yesterday."

She suddenly remembered the two strangers who had saved her life and said to Keith, "The two men who brought me to your house, do you know who they are? I'll have to visit them soon and thank them for what they did for me."

Keith frowned. "What two men, Rachel?"

Rachel stared quizzically at him. "The two men who brought me to your house," she said. "I was hopelessly lost yesterday and who knows what would have happened to me if those men had not come along and helped. I thought you saw them?"

"I didn't see any men," Keith said.

"Are you sure?"

"Yes, Rachel. I am pretty sure." Keith looked up and then turned to her again. "That is really weird."

Rachel frowned and then shrugged. "I guess they left before you opened the door." Remembering the strangers who had helped her reminded her again of her daughter. She had to get Emily out of Mike's house and bring her here. And in order to do that, she had to tell Keith everything. If not, she would have nowhere to go, nowhere to stay, and nowhere to bring Emily. She was going to ask the pastor for a huge favor and the least she could do was tell him about her whole life; everything she feared, no matter what he would think of her afterwards.

"Keith, I have something to tell you. It's something really hard for me to say, but you have to know."

Keith gazed at her and said, "What do you have to tell me?"

She took a deep breath and pushed through her reluctance. "Keith, Mike is not my husband."

Keith's eyes grew wide, and then he shook his head. He didn't say anything for some seconds and then he spoke. "I am so sorry. I just assumed that you were married, especially since I saw you in the house together. But you have children together, don't you?"

She said slowly, "We have a child together, but Mike has two other children from his wife; his real wife. I am Mike's second wife," she said, and then added quickly, "but not his real wife."

Keith arched his brows. "I don't understand."

"Where I come from, the men marry more than one wife. Since it's not legal, they marry additional wives in a ceremony they call a spiritual union. That's why I said I am not really married to Mike. However, I am considered his second wife."

Keith's mouth fell open and he stared at her. She shut her eyes, unable to look at his face anymore. He looked so confused, so put off by what she had told him. She was sure he had never have imagined such a thing. She knew she had to press on, to make him understand. And then maybe he would not think so badly of her as she was sure he did right now.

She began to tell him about her childhood, how she and her brother grew up free until their mother 'got converted' by the man she later married. She told him about their move to Fallow Creek and the indoctrination into the new religion. She talked about the life at Fallow Creek, how women were treated as property with very few rights. She told him about the lack of freedom she had faced, how she had met and then married Mike, and how she had always wanted to escape. She talked about the day she'd finally tried to, before being caught by the security squad. She spoke about how she had given birth to Emily, about pitying and continuously feeling guilty about Olivia because she was living with the woman's husband even though she had first lied to herself that she was truly married to Mike.

Finally, she told him about the Restoration House, how Mike had arranged for them to run away and how they had come to Destiny. She said to him, "I couldn't bear it anymore, Keith. I couldn't bear the guilt and the shame, the loathing I felt for Mike every time he touched me, and the loathing I felt with myself for continually living in that situation."

She told him how she had left the house and tried to escape with Emily, but had not been able to because Mike had taken her to his room. She talked about how she had wandered aimlessly and hopelessly in the darkness until the two mysterious men had come to rescue her. She finally said, "You were the first person I thought about when I decided to escape because of how kind you had been to me." She smiled. "Actually, you are the only person I know here."

He was looking at her with wonder and confusion

and something else she could not place. She took his hand instinctively and watched him stare down at their joined hands. "Please, Keith," she said. "You understand now why I don't want Mike to know where I am and why I have to get Emily out of that house as soon as possible."

Keith said nothing for a long while and then he finally nodded his head. "Wow! I would never have imagined that you have been living in such a difficult situation, Rachel." He reached out and this time he tucked a strand of her hair behind her ear. He smiled at her and said, "I promise I will do everything I can to help you bring your daughter here."

An overwhelming sense of relief ran through her as she looked at Keith's face. He wasn't judging her and he didn't appear to think any less of her. He was such a good man.

He frowned again and said, "But Mike is Emily's biological father, isn't he?"

Rachel sighed and said, "Yes, he is."

"And has he ever done anything bad to her?"

"No."

Keith said, "It might be tough to get Emily from him."

She nodded. "I know. Still, I want to fight for her to live with me. I don't want her to grow up in a polygamous home with Mike. Even though I have left, I am pretty sure Mike will find someone else soon because it's the way of the men in Fallow Creek. But I am sure he's going to make my life a living hell before he finally lets me go. And I know that one of the ways he will do that is to try to keep me away from my daughter. But that cannot happen." She looked into Keith's eyes again, pleading with him to please help her.

"I will do everything I can to help you, Rachel," he said. He touched her cheek gently and she felt a shock of electricity run through her. "I'll try to get your daughter to you, but it won't be easy."

Rachel placed her hand over the hand he'd laid on her cheek before he could withdraw it. "I know it won't be easy," she said, gazing into his eyes, loving how his hand felt on her cheek and how he was looking at her as if she were a rare treasure. "But I believe it can be done. Especially since this is not Fallow Creek."

"The first thing I have to do is return the money Mike gave me," Keith said, "or, at least, what remains of it. Unfortunately, a large chunk of the money has already been spent. But I need to return the rest to him. I would never have taken the money if I had known the sort of person he was."

Rachel looked at Keith as he stared at the wall in front of him. He looked worried and she knew he was thinking about Destiny, about how he would rebuild the town, the church, and the other projects he'd told her and Mike about when he'd visited the other day. Mike had told him he would help rebuild the town and give whenever he was called upon to do so. But now that she'd told him all her problems, she knew he would not take any more money from Mike. Consequently, all the rebuilding would stop...all because of her. She immediately regretted coming here and telling him about her problems. How could she stand in the way of the town being rebuilt? She wanted with all her heart to leave Mike and have absolutely nothing to do with him, but she did not want to take away the chance the town had to come alive again.

"You look worried," Keith said, gazing at her.

She said to him, "Now I wish I hadn't told you all this about Mike and me. Maybe you should hold off on confronting and giving Mike back that money. I will find another way to get Emily out of the house."

"No," Keith said. "It would be wrong for me to keep the money after all I know about him now. I will return the rest of the money as soon as I can."

"But what about the town and the church?" Rachel said to him. "It has to be rebuilt for the sake of the people here. I will not be able to live with myself if because of me, Mike withdraws his offer to provide the funds needed to rebuild the town."

"I know it will be hard," Keith said, "but the Lord will provide another way for the church and the town to be rebuilt."

"But..."

"No, Rachel," Keith shook his head. "Don't try to convince me otherwise. You know it would be wrong to keep the money and then continue taking money from Mike. Besides, I think this might be a lesson from the Lord, His way of teaching me not to depend on any man as my provider. As the town's provider. God is our provider, not Mike. He will provide all the funds needed for the church and the town to be rebuilt again."

Rachel stared at him and desire began to grow in her heart. And it was not just desire for him, though it was there, but it was for the kind of relationship he had with God. She had always considered herself a Christian, but now she knew that she wasn't much of one. In spite of her many excuses, she'd been living with a married man. She'd always wanted to be closer to God but somehow, it had never happened. But Keith sounded like someone who was close to God and trusted Him with everything. She wanted that.

"We will go to Mike's house tomorrow and tell him you want your daughter."

She shook her head. "I can't go back there," she said. Fear built in her heart as she thought about going back to Mike's house and getting trapped there. "I don't ever want to be with Mike again."

"You're not going to be with him," Keith said. "This is not Fallow Creek, Rachel. This is Destiny. He has no right anymore to try to entrap you or force you to stay with him. You don't belong to him and, actually, you never did." He looked deeply into her eyes and smiled. "The Lord will make a way, somehow, so we can get your daughter to you. We will have to go to court."

She wanted to believe that she could actually win a custody case over Mike, but she had so many doubts. She said, "I don't have a job right now and I have no home of my own. Mike is wealthy. I doubt that any court would give me custody of her now."

"Then we will wait, Rachel. We will get you a job and then a home, and then you can fight to get custody of your daughter. For now, you need to confront Mike. We will go to your house together and do that. And then you will tell him firmly that you want to see Emily. She's your daughter. He cannot keep her away from you."

Rachel wished it would be that easy. But Keith did not know Mike. He hated when something he believed belonged to him was taken away and now that she had left him, he would be enraged. Especially if she showed up with Keith. He would definitely go into a jealous fit and her chances of seeing Emily anytime soon would be nil. "I will go alone," she said to Keith.

"No, I don't think that is a good idea."

She smiled weakly and said to him, "You just said I am no longer in Fallow Creek. I am in Destiny and here, I am a free woman. I don't belong to Mike and he has no right to me anymore. I think it would be a good idea to go alone, but I will let him know that I have told others about him and what he is capable of. I will warn him that if he tries to hold me against my will in the house, he will have the whole town to answer to."

Keith shook his head as he gazed tenderly at her. He said softly, "I still think I should go with you."

"No, Keith," she said. "If you go with me it will make Mike mad with jealousy. He hates seeing me with any man and it might make things worse. It would be better for me to go alone and try to reason with him and then get him to let me see my daughter."

Keith did not say anything for almost a full minute and then he nodded. "Okay, Rachel. Let's do this as a compromise. I will go with you, but I will not enter the house. I will stay some distance away while you go into the house so that I make sure you come out safely."

She couldn't resist and took his hand again in hers. "Thank you so much. I'm so glad that we are friends."

He suddenly looked downcast and she wondered why. He opened his mouth to say something and then closed it again. He gave her a curious smile and squeezed her hand. "Yes, I am glad we are friends, too."

He stood up with their hands still joined together and she pursed her lips. She did not want him to go and held onto his hand. He looked down at her and smiled again and then gently pulled his hand away from hers. He said softly, "You need to get some rest now, Rachel. Tomorrow, we will go to Mike's house."

She began to tell him that she was strong enough to go today, but he firmly told her that she had to rest. "We will go tomorrow."

She watched him leave, feeling slightly uncertain. She had said something that hurt him, but she wasn't sure what exactly it was. He turned around at the door and beamed at her, and her concerns melted away. She smiled back at him and then thanked him again for everything.

"You need to stop thanking me for taking you in, Rachel. It's what any decent person would have done." He turned around and then left the room, shutting the door slowly.

She shut her eyes and lay down on the bed again. She inhaled deeply as she covered herself with his duvet. The bed and the duvet smelled of him — spicy cologne, soap, and a scent that was distinctively him. She inhaled deeply again and smiled. She felt so at peace anytime she was with him and even lying on his bed right now, taking in his scent. He made her feel like everything would be alright, no matter what was going on in her life.

She whispered, "Lord, thank you for bringing him into my life." And then she added, "Please,

Lord, Keith has a beautiful relationship with you, and I want it too. With all my heart."

She suddenly felt a deep peace come over her as she felt God's overwhelming love surround her, covering her like a warm blanket on a cold day. And then waves and waves of love went through her, melting away all her shame and guilt. For the first time since she was a child, she felt no iota of guilt or shame. She smiled as joy filled her and then she began to feel sleepy. Before she drifted off, she whispered a prayer of thanksgiving to God, and then closed her eyes and fell into a peaceful sleep.

THIRTEEN

Mike Cadwell ran his fingers over his hair again and again as he paced his living room floor. He looked down at his first wife, Olivia, who was sitting on the sofa with Emily in her arms and asked for the hundredth time, "You're telling me you don't know where Rachel went? Did she just disappear into thin air?"

Olivia looked up at him, her eyes pleading. "Please sit down, Mike. Rachel is an adult. I am sure she is fine."

Mike glared at her. "She's been gone for almost two days now. I wouldn't be so worried if she hadn't left Emily. How could she have just upped and left?" He snapped his fingers. "Just like that?" He would have gone to the police if he didn't loathe them so. His brief experience with them in Fallow Creek had showed they only brought trouble.

"Have you asked around town to see if anyone has seen her?" Olivia asked.

Mike narrowed his eyes in anger and glowered at her. "Really, Olivia? I have been gone the whole morning asking people in this town if they have seen her, and yet you are asking me if I have been asking for her around town?"

Olivia didn't say anything for a short while as she burped Emily. After that, she said, "I think the fact that Rachel did not take Emily with her means that she's okay and will definitely come back. There's no way she would leave permanently without her daughter. She loves Emily way too much."

Mike stepped away from Olivia and went to look out the window, as if the action would cause Rachel to appear outside. If Olivia was right, Rachel had run away again. But at least he knew she would have to come back because of Emily. Still, he couldn't bear the thought of her being somewhere other than here at his house where she belonged.

He turned around and went to the mantel near the TV set. Grabbing the keys to his BMW, he turned around and said to Olivia, "I am going to look for her again."

Olivia sighed but said nothing. Mike strode out the front door, got into his car, and drove out into the road.

As he slowly drove through Destiny, he looked this way and that, hoping to see Rachel. It was a small town and it would surely not be impossible to find her on the street. Unfortunately, because they were new to town, many people did not know him or Rachel yet. He described her in detail to some of the people he stopped to talk to, but none of them had seen her.

He drove past a row of houses, some of them partially destroyed and some still standing proudly, having defied the hurricane's wrath. He narrowed his eyes as he saw someone familiar and his heart began to pound. Rachel had just come out of one of the houses, followed closely by that Pastor Keith. He had seen them together in some old Honda a few days ago and now here they were exiting a house together.

Mike watched them looking at each other with longing and he shook with rage. They were about to enter that same old car he'd seen them in days ago. He drove his car closer and then stopped some distance away from the Honda. He regarded Rachel from the top of her head to the soles of her feet with anger and despair. He should have known that she would come to this wretched pastor's house when he had seen them together the other day, gallivanting around town.

They entered the car and drove away, and for a short while he thought about following them. However, he changed his mind and decided to go back home. He knew if he confronted them in the open it might not go in his favor. Whatever was going on between Rachel and that pastor, he was going to squash it. Rachel would come to the house today or, at the most, the next day, because of Emily. He would deal with her and that wife-stealing pastor. To think he had said that he liked the young pastor and had given him a check to build his church! He'd told him that there was more money where that came from, but that would not happen again. He deeply regretted ever giving money to that so-called pastor.

He took a deep breath to calm his anger, started his car, and drove back home.

**

Staring at the clock on the wall from the couch where he lay, Keith sighed. It was already seven in the morning, but he had hardly slept. He'd spent the night tossing and turning, thinking about Rachel and all she had told him the day before. He had not stopped thinking about all of it since she'd told him her story. The fact that she had been living in a polygamous relationship had shocked and surprised him. But it had not dampened his attraction to her. What bothered him the most was how she had described the way Mike treated her. He'd been disgusted by it all.

Her revelation that she was truly single and not married had left him with a mixture of confusing emotions. On the one hand, he felt exhilarated and excited that there was a possibility of a relationship with her, but on the other hand, he didn't think he was supposed to do anything about his attraction. In a way, she was still attached to Mike. But the most important reason why he didn't want to tell her how he felt was that she'd just left a crazy lifestyle behind. He wasn't sure it was God's will to pursue her, nor that she needed to be pursued by a man right now after all she'd been through.

Being at the center of God's will had always been important to him. But he couldn't help the way he felt about her. He was not going to do anything about it except help out until she could find her feet and get her baby from her ex.

He sighed again. She was in his bedroom right now, sleeping in his bed. He pictured her in his mind, her long dark hair splayed on his pillow, her slim body tucked under his duvet. She was so achingly beautiful. He felt an overwhelming desire to go into his room just so he could look at her, and then stifled it the way he had done when the same desire had come over him yesterday and the day before.

He turned on the couch and groaned. How long would she stay in his house? How long in his bed? His longing for her was increasing daily, and it was getting harder and harder to control it. Thankfully, Paula and Eric were still living in the house with their children or he didn't know what would have happened. They acted as chaperones, though unknowingly.

He continued to picture Rachel, her beautiful face, the way dimples appeared on her cheeks when she smiled and how soft her cheek had felt when he had laid his hand on it. He chided himself for thinking constantly about her, but he couldn't stop. He stood up to go to the bathroom to take a shower and clear his head, but Paula and Eric walked into the living room.

"Good morning," they greeted cheerily.

"Good morning." He smiled at them. When they told him they wanted to speak with him, he sat down on the couch again.

They sat on the sofa and faced him. "So, we want to thank you for everything you have done for us and our children," Eric said. "We will never be able to thank you enough for taking us in when our house was destroyed."

Paula said, "We have really enjoyed staying in your house and we will miss this place." She looked around the living room and then faced Keith again. "But it's time to go."

Eric said, "It's time we got out of your hair, Keith,

so you can take your house back."

Keith's eyes widened and he began to shake his head. "You guys don't have to leave now," he said, starting to panic. He had just thanked God for their presence here, which acted as a barrier between him and Rachel. If they left, it would just be him and Rachel in the house. Who knew what would happen then?

"It's okay, Keith," Eric said. "Just as we said, we've had a really good time staying here." He chuckled. "As you know, all good things must come to an end."

Paula shook her head at Eric and said to Keith, "You know we have been building that log house near the lake. It is finished now, and so it's time to move."

Keith ran his fingers through his hair and sighed. "I guess it's the right thing to do, especially because of your kids, but I will miss you guys so much." He thought about his selfish reason for wanting them to remain in his house and pressed down the desire to ask them to stay longer.

They chatted for a few minutes more and then Paula and Eric got up to leave the living room so they could start packing. Just before they left, Keith remembered he hadn't asked them when exactly they were leaving.

"When are you leaving?" he asked.

"Tomorrow morning," Paula said.

Keith shut his eyes as dread washed over him. In a day's time, he would be alone with Rachel. When Paula and Eric had left the living room, he leaned back on the couch and prayed silently for help, especially for his longing for Rachel.

It wasn't just his longing for her that made

him dread being alone in the house with her. He whispered to the Lord, "What will people say when they find out that Rachel lives here with me?" It would be really inappropriate. It was a tiny town. People would soon find out and then word would spread that their single pastor was living with a woman he wasn't married to. It was not the kind of testimony he wanted. It would definitely affect his goal of seeing everyone in town have a personal relationship with God and attend church regularly.

He sighed heavily, confused about what he was going to do. *There's nothing you can do,* he thought. It wasn't like he was going to kick Rachel out of his house. He wouldn't be able to do that even if he wanted to. Which he didn't.

He groaned at the confusion he felt. On the one hand, the thought of being alone in the house with her caused his pulse to race with excitement, but on the other, he was fearful of the fact.

He thought again about what he and Rachel had discussed two days ago. He couldn't believe that she had actually lived with Mike as a second wife. They had decided to go to Mike's house together, but he would wait in the car some distance away from the house while she went in alone. With all his heart, he wanted her to get her daughter because that was what she wanted; that was what would make her happy. And there was nothing he wanted more than for her to be happy. He wondered how Rachel's discussion with Mike about taking Emily away would work out.

Probably not so well, from all that Rachel had told him about Mike. But he knew she had to try. It was unlikely that Mike would agree, but it would be a chance for Rachel to see Emily. After that, he would help her in her quest to find a full-time job, become financially independent, and then be in a position where she could fight for full custody of her daughter. Babysitting would give her something to do but would not pay enough for her to gain the kind of financial independence she needed.

His mind soon traveled to the new church building project that had begun again because of Mike's donation. His heart sank. He had to return the rest of Mike's money. Once again, because of lack of finances, the building would soon stop. They had been having church services in an open field, but it was not always feasible, as people were exposed to the elements. Last Sunday, after the heavy rain the night before, they had not been able to hold the service on the open ground.

He lifted his eyes to the ceiling. "Lord, please, I ask for provision," he prayed.

Apart from his goal to see that Destiny got a new church, the town still needed money to rebuild many of the houses that had been destroyed in the hurricane and provide basic amenities for some of the people who had lost every single thing they had. He had been so excited when Mike had given him the check and told him there was more where that came from. Now he had to return the money, or at least half of it as half had already gone into the building projects.

He chuckled in spite of himself. "Lord, I guess I have to depend on you completely for everything we need now." He had tried to get a loan from the bank yesterday but had been refused because he had no collateral.

He leaned forward on his seat just as Rachel walked into the living room and his heart did a flip. Her hair was messy, her eyes still looked heavy from sleep, and she was wearing a drab black robe. Still, none of these took away from her exquisite beauty. He sucked in his breath sharply as she faced him and smiled at him.

She yawned and said, "Hi, Keith." She came and sat on the sofa across from his.

"Hi," he breathed. His heart pounded as Rachel stood up and came to sit on the couch beside him. She searched his eyes and said, "You look worried. What is it?"

He sighed and gazed at her, wondering if he should tell her what was on his mind. He did not want to bother her with his problems. She looked genuinely concerned about him, and he decided to unburden his heart. "I'm just worried about the ongoing church building project and the various houses that we were already beginning to rebuild. Everything has to stop now. I just don't know what to do."

He began to tell her in detail about building projects, his fear and worry now that it had all stopped since he had decided not to use the money Mike gave him. He also told her about trying to get a loan from the bank and being refused. "What I worry about the most are people who lost everything in the hurricane and those who have no homes now. The need in Destiny is great. I know some other towns the hurricane also affected have help from the government, but Destiny is so tiny that I think we are not on the map at all. Every day, I feel this great burden to help my town, but I just don't know how anymore."

She smiled sadly and placed her hand on his shoulder. "I don't have much," Rachel said, "but there are some expensive wristwatches that Mike bought for me that I haven't ever used. When we get to Mike's today, I can get them all. I can sell them in order to raise money for the town."

He looked at her and smiled in appreciation. "Thank you, Rachel. I'm sure that will go a long way in helping out. But we still need a lot more."

"I know," Rachel said, sounding worried.

He stared at her for a long moment, wanting to take her in his arms and kiss her but knowing with a deep certainty that he shouldn't. He finally pushed down the desire and said slowly, "There has to be a way that we can raise funds for Destiny."

Rachel's eyes lit up. "What about organizing a concert of some sort using the people in the town who can sing?"

Keith wanted to tell her that people in this town did not have much money to donate, but she immediately said it herself with her eyes downcast.

He smiled at her to let her know he appreciated her idea and then said, "What about creating a donation page on social media platforms where people can go and donate to Destiny?"

Rachel's eyes lit up again and she said, "Yes! And you can create a website specifically talking about the great need in Destiny and everything that has been destroyed by the hurricane. We can have a link where people will be led to a page where they can donate whatever amount of money they want."

Keith felt a little glimmer of hope light up in his heart. He wasn't sure it would work out but there was no harm in trying. "I know a few guys in Destiny who are great with social media and someone who builds websites. I can call them now and bring them on board."

Rachel's smile widened and Keith picked up his cell phone from the coffee table. He called the Stryker brothers, Frank and Nick, who were barely out of their teens, and told them of his idea. They were excited about it and promised to visit him in the evening so they could discuss the idea further. Keith also called a young lady named Zuri who built websites and told her about his plans.

After she promised to see him the next day, he ended the call and faced Rachel. "So, you heard everything. We will see how it goes."

She gave him a heart-melting smile, and again he thought about Paula and Eric's decision to move out the next day with the kids. He became nervous, especially as she was so close to him that he could reach out and touch her if he wanted. He suddenly blinked in surprise as the standing lamps and ceiling fan lights suddenly lit up. For a second, he stared at them and then he shot up from the couch with joy as he realized that electricity had returned. Rachel was also on her feet beaming and, without thinking, he reached out and gathered her in a tight hug.

His body immediately felt like it had been set ablaze, and he gasped as desire coursed through him. He drew back from her and then sharply sucked in his breath as he noticed the look in her eyes. Her eyes were glazed with desire, probably just as his were, and for a long moment they stood gazing at each other, the atmosphere around them crackling with the longing they felt for one another.

Keith could not resist any longer and pulled her into his arms. He brushed his thumb across her lips, his heart beating wildly. Finally, unable to bear the tension in him anymore, he leaned in to claim her lips with his, but jerked back when someone banged on the door.

He groaned and reluctantly stepped away from her, still shaking with desire. He went to open the door and then staggered back, doubled over in pain, as a punch landed in his stomach. He looked up at the face of the man who had punched him even as he held his stomach, groaning. He narrowed his eyes at Mike.

Mike walked into the center of the living room while Rachel went to put her arms around Keith. "Why did you do that?" she shrieked, glaring at Mike.

"You whore!" he bellowed at her. "I didn't believe it at first when I saw you together yesterday," he looked at Rachel with an accusing expression, "but I thought there had to be some kind of explanation. I thought you would come straight to the house to see your daughter at least. I waited for a long time, but you didn't come. I knew then that I had to come here myself. Now I know why you didn't come to see your own daughter, who you left just like that. You've been very busy being the whore you are."

Anger shot through Keith, and he straightened in spite of the pain in his stomach. He put himself between Rachel and Mike and faced off with Mike. "How dare you speak to her like that?"

"You better step back right now if you don't want me to hit you again!" Mike lunged at Rachel, but Keith pushed him back.

Mike glared at Keith and then looked past him, glowering at Rachel. He yelled, "You are my wife! You shouldn't be living with another man. You have to come back with me now!"

Keith said coldly, "She's not your wife and never will be."

Mike's face turned red, and he swung at Keith again. This time, Keith dodged his blow and shook his head.

Rachel screamed again and marched up to Mike. "Listen, Mike, I don't belong to you. I'm not going back with you, but I will come to get Emily. She belongs with me."

"No, Rachel, you belong with me," Mike said. He grabbed her hand and tried to pull her out of the house, but Keith pulled her out of his grasp.

Mike screamed with rage and reached for Rachel again, and Keith knew he had to make a quick decision. He abhorred violence and he had never hit anyone, even as a child. But this time, as Mike grabbed Rachel again, Keith punched him hard in his midsection. Mike stumbled back and then crashed to the ground.

Keith looked down at Mike's unmoving body and groaned. "What have I done?"

Rachel knelt down beside Mike and felt his neck for a pulse. She looked up at Keith and said, "He's fine. He'll live." She stood up again, and Keith blinked in surprise when she hugged him tightly. She drew back and said, "Thank you."

She left the living room, and Keith placed his hand on his forehead and took a deep breath. Rachel returned with a bowl of water and a towel, and Keith knelt down beside her as she put a damp towel on Mike's forehead. Keith kept asking the Lord to forgive him for punching Mike, but he'd had no other option at the time. He knew he would probably do it again if Mike ever tried to hurt Rachel or drag her out of the house against her will.

They both sat on the floor beside Mike, Rachel dabbing the damp towel on his face continuously while they waited for him to wake up.

Rachel said, "Should we call the doctor, Keith?"

They both looked down at Mike as he stirred. He opened his eyes, shut them again, and then opened them once more. Moaning, he slowly sat up and then looked at Keith and Rachel. He uttered a string of obscene curses, causing Keith to draw back in revulsion.

He slowly stood up with his hand on his stomach and then cursed at Keith and Rachel again. He groaned, no doubt from pain, and then focused his gaze on Rachel. "You will never see Emily again! I promise you that!"

Rachel narrowed her eyes and said, "You cannot stop me from seeing my daughter, Mike. Just because we are not together anymore doesn't mean I don't have a right to see Emily. In fact, I want her with me. She is still really young and she needs me now."

Mike laughed out loud and then fixed her with an angry stare. "You really think I'm going to let her stay here with you while you're living in this abomination?"

"The real abomination was living with you and your wife," she said.

Mike shrugged. "If you don't come back home, I

will make sure you never see Emily again."

"I'm never going back to live with you. Never ever again!"

Mike stared at her for a long moment, and then he nodded. "Then you will have to learn to live without your daughter, Rachel." He opened the door and left the house before Rachel or Keith could say anything more.

After he left, Rachel sank onto the sofa and covered her face with her hands. Keith immediately went to her and put his arm around her. "Don't worry, Rachel," he said. "We will find a way to get you to see Emily again and bring her to stay with you. This is not that strange town you lived in before you came to Destiny. We have laws here that are on your side."

"But what can we do?" Rachel asked, looking at Keith with tears in her eyes.

"We will go to the police," he said. "They will pay Mike a visit and get him to let you see your daughter. After that, we will try to get a job for you and then you will go to court and fight for custody."

"But it will all take such a long time, Keith."

"I know," he said. "But I think it will be worth it in the long run. For now, though, we will go and get the police involved so you will at least be able to visit your daughter."

Rachel nodded and then stood up. "Just give me a minute," she said. "Let me go and change and then we will go to the station together."

After she left, he kept thinking about how her presence in the house had already made his life even more complicated. Not only did he have to worry about getting the finances for rebuilding the church and the town, he had to go on this journey with Rachel to get custody of her daughter from that wicked Mike. He sat down on the sofa and sighed. It was going to be a long journey and a difficult one, but he would do anything for Rachel. She was worth it all, even if right now he did not know if they were meant to be together.

FOURTEEN

The Destiny police station was much smaller than the one Rachel had planned to take refuge in when she was fleeing Fallow Creek. She walked into the police station with Keith, feeling slightly afraid. The only explanation she had for the way she felt was the constant indoctrination they'd been put through in Fallow Creek about law enforcement agents not being friends to their way of life.

As though Keith sensed her fear, he put his arm lightly around her shoulders and smiled at her. "It's okay," he said.

She gave him a small smile and then took a deep breath to calm her nerves. She noticed only two officers in the building and remembered Keith had told her there were only three police officers in the town, including the sheriff.

Keith greeted them warmly and smiled when they thanked him for all that he was doing for the town. After he had made them promise to attend the open ground service on Sunday, he led Rachel down a narrow corridor and to a slightly open door that had the name "Ezra Reed" etched into the wood.

Keith turned to Rachel and said, "The sheriff," and then knocked lightly on the door. Without waiting for an answer, he entered the office and Rachel followed him in.

A bald, fifty-something-year-old man looked up at them through his glasses. He closed the file he had been perusing when they came in and smiled widely at Keith. He turned to look at Rachel with a curious expression on his face and turned back to Keith. "Hey, Pastor!" he said. "You came to see me today."

"Hi, Ezra," Keith said. "We are actually here for something very important."

The sheriff pointed at the seats in front of his desk and Keith and Rachel sat down. He kept looking at Rachel curiously and Keith said, "This is Rachel Cad…" he turned to her with an embarrassed look on his face.

She smiled to let him know it was okay and then said, "Dalton, that is my maiden name."

"Rachel Dalton," Keith said to the sheriff. "She moved to Destiny a few weeks ago."

The sheriff nodded. "So, what can I do for both of you?"

Keith turned to her and said, "Can you tell him everything?"

Rachel pressed her lips tightly together. The last thing she wanted was to tell yet another person in Destiny about her past crazy life, but she had to if she hoped to ever see Emily again. She took a deep breath to try to let go of her nervousness and then began to tell the chief about her so-called "marriage" to Mike in Fallow Creek. Shame washed over her as he raised his brows and gave her a strange, puzzled look. She pressed on and told him about running away from Mike and coming to Keith's house because she couldn't bear to continue to live the polygamous lifestyle any longer.

She paused for a few seconds to catch her breath and then continued. She told him about her desire to take her daughter to live with her once she could get on her feet and then finally told him about Mike's unexpected visit and his threat.

"I know Mike," she said. "He meant what he said about not allowing me to ever see Emily again unless I come back to him. If I ever go back to that house to try to see my daughter, I know he will not let me leave again." She cried. "I don't want to go back, but I want my daughter."

Keith put his arm around her shoulders again and Ezra Reed held out his hand. "Don't you worry about it, ma'am," he said. "I will send Officer Gamble with you when you are ready to visit your daughter and make sure your husband…" — he cleared his throat — "the man you've been living with doesn't touch you and lets you leave without any hassle."

Rachel smiled tentatively and nodded. Five minutes later, she and Keith left the police station together. She felt more hopeful after the promise that the sheriff had made to her. When she went to Mike's house to see Emily and get her things, a police officer would go with her. Mike would have to behave himself. Most of all, she would be able to see Emily with no problems.

***

Rachel sat in Keith's car staring out the window at the town of Destiny. The sun was setting in the sky and, as usual, she marveled at the people she saw, leisurely strolling to wherever they were going, easy smiles on many faces despite the state of the town now. They were probably glad to just be alive. Hopefully, they would find a way to rebuild their homes and lives soon. Keith was confident that the Lord would provide everything needed to do that, and she was beginning to be as confident in God's provision and help as he was. It was impossible not to have some of Keith's resilient faith rub off on her when she was living with him. She turned when Keith placed a hand on her shoulder. "How do you feel?" he asked.

"A little nervous," she answered. They were going to Mike's house now, and as the sheriff had promised yesterday, a police officer followed behind in a police car. A conflicting mix of emotions warred in her — anticipation and fear. She took a deep breath to try to calm her nerves. She was not looking forward to going back to Mike's house or seeing him again, but she could not wait to see and hold Emily in her arms. It was all she had dreamt about since she'd left the house; or, at least, one of the two things she had dreamt about. The other was about the kind and handsome man sitting beside her now. She turned and smiled at him, grateful that he was here with her.

He took her hand, and her heart began to race wildly when he wove his fingers through hers. She did not know what to make of it, his threading their fingers together while he drove and focused on the road.

Don't read too much into it, she told herself. He was a kind pastor and he was probably holding her hand now to encourage her because she was nervous. Reading way too much into his actions would only lead her to disappointment and heartbreak.

But her heart revolted. Surely, the look in his eyes when they had almost kissed yesterday, before Mike interrupted, was not one of random kindness. He had looked at her with such intense desire that her knees had weakened and her breath had stopped.

She sighed. Still, a relationship was the last thing she needed now after the relief of leaving Mike. She had to learn to stand on her own feet without a man.

She looked at Keith again, studying his handsome profile. If there was anyone, though, who could make her forget her decision to find herself without a man, it was Keith. And already, being with him these past few days had made her believe that she could have true love; the love of a good man. It was just that she wasn't sure she should be involved with Keith. That girl, Jenny, at the store the other day, had clearly been jealous of her. Rachel wasn't sure what their relationship was. Having already intruded on Olivia's relationship for years, diverting her husband's affection away from her, though unknowingly, it was the last thing she wanted to do to another woman. Until she knew he was a completely free man and that Jenny wasn't interested in him, she would not encourage nor express any kind of feelings toward him.

She slowly removed her hand from his and then

shut her eyes ruefully when he looked at her. The thought that he would believe she did not like him weighed heavily on her heart, but she had no choice. She'd already lived with guilt over what she'd done to Olivia for years and she was done with it. She turned to look out the window again and then, for some reason, she blurted out, "What about Jenny?"

As soon as the words left her lips, she groaned inwardly and then chided herself. *Why did you ask that, Rachel?*

She felt too ashamed to turn and look at Keith, but she could feel his eyes on her.

"She's good," Keith said slowly. "At least, I think so. I haven't seen her since the day you both came to my store."

Rachel's heart began to pound with hope, but she told herself to calm down. That visit to his store had been just over a week ago. Since there were other means of communication like phones, it was not a big deal for people who were in a relationship not to see each other for a week. Besides, maybe Jenny was out of town. She asked him if Jenny had left Destiny.

He chuckled and she resisted the urge to turn and look at him. "I don't think she's out of town," he said. "She usually tells me whenever she plans to leave, which is mostly to visit her brother in Denver."

Rachel pursed her lips. He certainly knew a lot about Jenny, which meant they might really be in a relationship. Even if there was a chance that they were not, what he'd said just now about Jenny, and the way Jenny had looked at him that day at his store was enough for her to believe that she liked him a lot, or was probably in love with him. There was no way she was going to get in the middle of that after what she'd done to Olivia. She could still see Olivia's eyes, the way they always looked whenever she and Mike retired to their bedroom together. Even though she hated the idea of sharing a bedroom with Mike when his first wife stayed in a separate bedroom, she had thought she had no choice. Thank God for Destiny and for finally being able to leave him. Now, if the Lord would only help her get her daughter out of that house the way He had helped her escape it, she would be tremendously grateful.

They began to approach Mike's house, and she inhaled as anxiety and dread washed over her.

Keith parked in front of the house, and she turned to smile gratefully at him. If he had been hurt by how she'd removed her hand from his earlier, he did not show it. He smiled broadly and then told her in a soft voice that he would be praying for her while she went in. They had decided that his presence in Mike's house would only enrage her ex and make matters worse. Since she was going into the house with the police officer, she had nothing to fear, she'd told him. She would ask to see Emily and, after spending time with her daughter, she would get her things.

She got out of the car and waved at him. Somehow, his smile and promise to pray for her instilled more confidence in her than the police officer already walking behind her as she made her way to the front door.

She reached the door and turned to look briefly at the young policeman behind her in uniform. He gave her a small, encouraging smile, and then she turned and knocked on the door.

A moment later, the door opened, and Olivia peered at her. Olivia's eyes widened in obvious surprise and she exclaimed, "Rachel, you are here!" She looked at the police officer behind Rachel and her eyes grew even bigger. "What's happening?"

The policeman told her they were here to make sure Rachel was allowed into the house to see her daughter, gather her things, and then leave without any problems. He had a smile on his face, but the tone of his voice was firm.

Olivia opened the door wide, and Rachel and the police officer stepped into the house. Rachel took a deep breath and looked around the living room. She didn't know what she was expecting it to look like. It still looked mostly the same with its expensive furnishings, but the spiral staircase seemed to go on and on as though reaching towards the sky. The ceilings were very high. Now that she had been staying at Keith's tiny house for a while, it seemed way too high, and the living space too large.

Olivia looked at Rachel and then at the police officer and said in an uncertain voice, "So, Rachel, you're not planning to stay?"

"No," Rachel answered.

Olivia looked quietly relieved and once again a thread of guilt ran through Rachel. She felt even more confident of her decision to leave Mike, even though she might not get full custody of Emily immediately. It was simply the right thing to do even if she did not loathe Mike, which she did for making her live this sinful life for so long. Not that she did not blame herself, but a large part of the blame fell on him as well.

"Emily is in her room?" Rachel asked Olivia.

Olivia nodded. "She is."

Rachel began to climb the stairs and then she paused. "What about Mike?" she asked over her shoulder. "Is he home?"

"He's upstairs, in his bedroom. I want to warn you, though, Rachel. You know you have to pass his bedroom in order to get to Emily's room. Mike will probably know when you pass by. He checks on Emily at least a hundred times a day now. I think he has gone mad with paranoia."

Olivia's kids ran down the stairs, yelling and chasing each other. They stopped in the living room as they saw the officer and stared up at him with uncertainty in their eyes. The police officer smiled at them and the boys gradually smiled back. They turned to Rachel and then came to hug her briefly before running out of the house, chasing each other once more.

Rachel looked at the police officer and then her eyes settled on Olivia. "He will be coming upstairs with me so that Mike will not try to stop me from seeing Emily or leaving the house."

Olivia still looked uncertain and followed Rachel and the officer as they climbed the stairs.

At the top of the stairs, Rachel paused again for a few seconds while she tried to gather herself together. She squared her shoulders and began to march to Emily's room, hoping that somehow Mike would not see or hear them walk past. But she knew that was unlikely. Even if he were asleep, Mike was a light sleeper and had always been extremely wary of his environment, even at home.

Now that Olivia said he checked on Emily way too many times a day, the probability of them not being seen or heard was very small.

She prepared herself to confront him as she marched past his room to Emily's. She entered Emily's room and immediately rushed up to her baby's crib. A sob of relief escaped her lips as she looked down at Emily, and she lifted her out of her crib. She held her baby close to her, feeling her soft body, and then pressing Emily's cheek on hers.

Emily chortled and Rachel held her slightly away to inspect her. "You look well." She smiled at her.

Emily grinned as though she understood what her mother had just said. She reached out and grabbed a handful of Rachel's hair, and then chuckled again, her blue eyes sparkling with mirth.

"I can see that you're happy to see me," Rachel said, tears in her eyes. She never wanted to be separated from Emily again, but she knew she couldn't stay with her daughter right now. She swung around when Mike's voice thundered from behind her, "What on earth is happening here?"

Mike was standing at the door staring angrily at the police officer and then at her. He pointed at the officer and then looked at Rachel with fury in his eyes. "What is he doing in my house and why are you here with him, Rachel?"

The police officer calmly told Mike what he had said to Olivia at the front door. Mike interjected between his words. "I don't care about what you're saying! You are intruding. I need you to leave right now!" He turned to Rachel when the police officer didn't move. "Tell him to leave now!"

Rachel hugged Emily close and said, "I won't. I

have to gather all my things first and then I will leave your house forever."

Mike glared at her. She knew from the look on his face that he'd thought he had won. He had thought she was here for good, unable to stay away from Emily any longer. Well, he was wrong.

She started to carry Emily out of the room to go to Mike's bedroom so she could get her things, but Mike blocked her.

"You're not taking my daughter out of this room."

The police officer started to intervene, but Rachel shook her head. She turned around and went to place Emily gently in her crib. She would cause no problems today. All she wanted to do was see her daughter and then get all her things out of this house. She lingered for a while at the crib looking down at Emily and cooing at her. Finally, she sighed and began to head toward the door.

Mike was still standing there, blocking her way. She looked at him and he gazed at the officer, who was standing behind her. She smiled slightly, knowing the police officer was looking at Mike, daring him to try to stop her from leaving the room, the house.

Mike huffed and then stepped away from the door. Rachel went out of Emily's room and walked to Mike's bedroom. For almost a minute, she glanced around the room, and then the bed, shuddering. The room and the bed brought back memories that she wanted to forget completely. She turned around and flung the closet open. Bringing out the large suitcase that Mike had used to pack her things and his when they'd left Fallow Creek, she opened it and began to yank her clothes out of the closet and throw them into the suitcase.

She could feel Mike's eyes and the police officer's on her as she packed, but she did not turn to look at them. She finally finished packing her clothes and shoes and then went to the ornate armoire near the door and opened it. She brought out the boxes of wristwatches and jewelry that Mike had bought for her, which she had barely worn, and looked at them. She had promised Keith that she would sell them and donate the proceeds to the building projects in Destiny and, looking at them now, she knew she would get a good sum of money for them. She picked up two of the boxes to take them to the suitcase and then blinked in surprise when Mike said, "She cannot take those things with her! They belong to me!"

She stared at him, but he was looking at the police officer. "I bought those expensive things for her, but they belong to me."

The officer said calmly, "I think since you bought them for her, they are hers."

Mike shook his head. "They are mine. I bought them with my own money. She cannot take them with her. I will allow her to take the other things that I bought her, but she cannot take the jewelry. I insist."

The officer looked up thoughtfully while Rachel's heart pounded.

Mike said again, "She cannot take them. I gave her all the jewelry as a token of our marriage. Some of them I gave her on our wedding week, and the others through the years as a symbol of our love and union. Now that she has decided she doesn't want to be with me any longer, they should automatically go back to me. She should not have them."

"We are not married and never were!" Rachel exclaimed. She already knew that Mike was going to win this one. If it were not for the fact that she wanted to use the jewelry to help rebuild Destiny, she would never even have thought of taking them with her in the first place.

The police officer looked at Rachel with a resigned expression on his face. "I think he might be right."

Rachel shut her eyes as her heart sank. She'd promised Keith that she would sell the jewelry and donate the money to help with the building projects in Destiny. He'd been so worried about the lack of funds and she'd been happy she had a way to help. What would she tell him now? He would be so disappointed. The money from the sale of the jewelry would have gone a long way in helping this town and its people. She sighed heavily and then placed the boxes back into the armoire.

She looked down at the suitcase that she'd packed all her things into and locked it. She began to wheel it out of the room and again Mike followed her and the policeman out. She went to Emily's room again, walked to the crib, and then smiled sadly when she saw that Emily was fast asleep. She backed away quietly.

Mike said in a mocking voice, "So you are now going to live in sin with the fake pastor?"

She glared at him, angry at his insinuation, but also feeling slightly guilty. She and Keith had no intention of 'living in sin', but she could see how her staying with him would look to other people and how it could affect his reputation. Mike knew her well enough to know how to push her buttons. He knew that her reaction to his suggestive statement would be guilt. She pressed her lips together and walked past him, determined not to let him see how his statement had affected her.

The police officer thankfully took the suitcase from her as they made their way down the stairs. They got to the bottom and Rachel looked around the living room again and then up the stairs longingly. If only she could take Emily with her.

She sighed and turned her eyes away. The police officer was already at the door with her suitcase and Rachel turned to smile at Olivia, who was standing in the middle of the living room, gazing at her and Mike.

Mike said scornfully, "You belong to me, Rachel. I won't let you disgrace me by living with another man. You will return or you will never see Emily again. This little fiasco you pulled today with the policeman will not happen again. I promise you."

She looked at him, her heart racing at his threat. She began to walk away from him and he followed her. He said to her, "I mean it, Rachel. Come back to me or..." He did not finish his statement, but she understood exactly what he meant.

She followed the police officer out of Mike's house, still troubled. Mike had sounded confident when he was spewing out his threats. She knew that the fact that she was staying with Keith was hard for him to swallow because of his pride and jealousy. She was his property, at least that was what he thought. That was how most men in Fallow Creek saw their women.

She got to Keith's car and found him leaning

against the car, waiting. He reached for her and this time, she did not resist or pull away when he took her hands. He looked deeply into her eyes and said tenderly, "Everything will be alright, Rachel."

Tears began to fall down her cheeks as she thought about Emily and about Mike's threat. Even though she had the law on her side here, at least to an extent, Mike was a wealthy and determined man. If she planned to fight him for full custody in court, he would get the best lawyers. He could provide everything Emily needed now, while Rachel had nothing to give to Emily at this time. Mike had the upper hand.

Keith looked like he was about to say something, but he pressed his lips together again. They both watched the police officer put her suitcase into the trunk of Keith's car. After that, they thanked the officer for his help, and then he got into his patrol car. They waved at him as he backed into the street and drove away.

She looked at Keith again and knew he wanted to hug her but was hesitant to do so, probably because of how she had pulled her hand away when they were coming here. But at this time, she simply needed comforting. She needed to feel Keith's arms around her.

She wrapped her arms around him and sighed deeply when his arms went around her. For a long moment, they stood beside the car holding onto each other. He ran his hand up and down her back as she buried her head in his shoulder. All she wanted was to stay in his arms forever, but unfortunately, she couldn't.

Keith stepped away from her and beamed.

He told her once more that everything would be alright and then got into the car. She got in as well and then stared at Mike's house as Keith reversed the car and finally drove away.

FIFTEEN

They got to the front of Keith's house and he turned off the ignition. She opened the door to get out of the car, but he put his hand on her shoulder and she turned to him. He said, "I have to go to my store now, but I just want to make sure you are okay."

She smiled at him and nodded. "I'm fine," she said softly.

He searched her eyes, and she felt like he could read her mind. For some reason, she did not feel intimidated or bothered by that. She had told him all her secrets and he still hadn't pushed her away. She knew she could trust him completely.

Keith kept his eyes on hers while her heart continued to race until she felt like it would burst out of her chest at any moment. What was it about him that sometimes left her speechless and weak-kneed in his presence? Was it his good looks or his unusual kindness? It was both of these, but more.

She suddenly gasped as a deep longing for him rose up in her. She blinked as she realized that she was in love with him. How had she fallen in love with him so quickly?

His eyes moved to her lips and her longing increased until she trembled. When he cupped her face in his hands, she knew he was going to kiss her. She shook with anticipation and then guilt as she remembered her decision not to get involved with him knowing that some other girl who had been here before her was in love with him as well.

She wasn't sure how he felt about Jenny, but she would not do this to another woman.

And yet, as his lips touched her cheek and as he trailed kisses down from her temples to her chin, she felt too weak with longing to pull back. All she wanted was to feel his lips on hers and to feel his arms around her again.

She groaned as he kissed the corner of her lips, her heart threatening to explode. And then Olivia's face appeared in her mind, and she remembered the day the woman had begged for just a little time with Mike. Rachel immediately pulled away and wrapped her arms around herself. "I'm sorry," she said in a haunted voice.

Keith looked like he had been punched in the stomach. He blinked rapidly and then leaned back against his seat and shut his eyes. "I'm sorry, too," he said. "I shouldn't have..."

She cut in. "No, you did nothing wrong, Keith. It's just me." He still looked really hurt, and she felt tears well up in her eyes. She had hurt him and it was the last thing she wanted to do. She quickly opened the door and stepped out of the car. She looked at him through the window. "I'll see you later," she said.

Once again, he searched her eyes. and from the

look on his face, she knew there was something on his mind; something he wanted to say to her. And yet, he said nothing. A small smile touched his lips and he looked away from her. Without saying a word, he started his car again and drove off.

She pressed her lips together tightly and pushed down the sob rising in her throat. Entering Keith's house, she sat down on the sofa, her emotions roiling with a multitude of worries and fears. She had seen Emily and, as happy as she was about that, the fact that she would not see her again for a while tore at her heart. And then there were Mike's threats. Thinking about them made her tremble with fear.

And yet her body shook now, not from the fear of Mike's threat, but from Keith's touch. She could still feel his lips on her cheek, her chin. The excitement and anticipation that had run through her at that moment lingered still. She clearly recalled the love and longing she had felt as he looked at her, as though she were everything he had ever hoped and prayed for.

She muttered, "I cannot be in love with him." And yet, she was. But she could not, would not do anything about it. When they had been together in the car and everything in her wanted to kiss him like she'd dreamt of doing for days, the memory of the pain and hurt in Olivia's eyes caused by Mike's annoying obsession with her had been enough for Rachel to pull away. Keith and Jenny had known each other for years according to what Keith had told her yesterday. Surely, there had been some kind of interaction between them which had been enough to give Jenny hope that Keith would one day come to love her the way she clearly loved him.

Rachel's heart kept beating as confusion flooded her soul. She wanted Keith for herself, but it would be wrong and selfish to act on her desire. She stood up and began to pace the living room. Keith would return later on and she was certain that their expressions of affection for each other that had started in the car would continue in the house. And then where would that lead?

She was sure of how she would feel about herself if anything untoward happened between her and Keith. She clearly remembered Mike's insinuation. He probably wasn't the only one in Destiny thinking that way. And if his accusation actually proved true, what would happen to Keith if people found out? She could not afford to ruin his reputation, neither would she stay here and let him fall in love with her and draw his heart further away from Jenny. The girl deserved to be with the man she loved before Rachel fell in love with him.

Rachel bit her lip. She had to leave this house.

But where would she go? And Keith had promised to help her get a job so she could ultimately get custody of Emily. How would that happen if she left?

Calm down, Rachel, she said to herself. She was panicking, unsure of what to do, knowing that whatever she did would have undesirable consequences.

She tried to figure out what to do as she paced the living room, but everything she came up with was undesirable to her. She knew the right thing was to leave the house, and yet she didn't want to.

You have to, Rachel. You have no choice.

She sighed wearily and began to head to Keith's room to pack up the few things he'd bought her. And then she groaned as she remembered that her suitcase filled with her clothes, the one she had taken from Mike's house, was still in Keith's car. In her hurry to get away from Keith before they kissed, she had left it in the trunk of his car. She marched into his room with determination. That would not stop her from leaving.

She looked around the room she'd been sleeping in for the past few days and then went to bring out the dress she had worn to his house on the day she'd escaped Mike's. She went into the bathroom, got her toothbrush and toiletries, and stuffed everything into a plastic bag she found in the kitchen.

Smoothing down her hair, she quickly braided it. She straightened her dress and then went to the living room with the plastic bag containing her things. Before she left the house, she glanced around sadly. Compared to Mike's lavish house, Keith's was like a cubicle, but while she had been eager to leave Mike's mansion, she felt overwhelming sadness at the thought of leaving this house. She would miss being here and seeing Keith every day. Sorrow filled her heart and she mourned for what she and Keith would have shared had the situation been right.

She reluctantly opened the front door and sighed sadly. "Lord, please give me strength," she said. Since the day she'd told the Lord that she wanted the kind of relationship Keith had with Him, she had felt God's presence constantly with her. She prayed more often and leaned on the Lord more than she had ever done. But now it was hard to trust that everything would work out for the best. She wasn't even sure where she was going to go, but she knew she could not leave Destiny without Emily. How Keith would react to her leaving, she didn't know, but she knew he was different from Mike and that it would not affect his willingness to help her gain custody of her daughter.

She left Keith's house and began to make her way down the street. Somewhere between his front door and where she was now, she had decided to go to Paula and Eric's new house. The couple had been kind to her when they lived with Keith, especially Paula. Rachel knew she would be imposing by asking them to accommodate her for a while, but she had no choice. She had to do it to protect Keith's reputation and free herself from perpetual guilt. Her leaving would give Keith and Jenny a chance to be together and maybe she could even try to help Jenny get closer to Keith. It might not make up for the years she had spent with someone else's husband, but it would go a long way in helping another woman get the desire of her heart.

The walk to Paula and Eric's was a long one. She had heard Keith say that the couple now lived in a tiny house near the only lake in Destiny. Eric had built the house with some help from his friends. She was sure she would easily find the house once she reached the lake. Even if she could not stay with the couple, they might be able to help her find somewhere she could stay until she could have her own home. How she would manage that, having a house of her own in this small town without a job, she did not know. It felt like her future was up in the air and she did not even know exactly what she was doing. But what she was doing now, leaving Keith's house, was the right decision.

She got to the couple's house and stood in front of the door. It was a small log house built with felled trees taken from all over the town. For a long moment, she could not bring herself to knock at the door. This was really presumptuous of her. She'd come to this couple's house, a couple she hardly knew, just because they had been nice to her at Keith's. The house looked really small and the couple had kids. There was a big chance that there would be no space for her here. If so, she hoped Paula or Eric would point her somewhere else where she could stay.

She sighed with worry as she remembered that many people in the town who had lost their homes were staying with friends and acquaintances. There might actually be nowhere for her to stay in this town, and that would be a disaster.

She breathed a quick prayer again, asking for the Lord's help, and then knocked on the door. When there was no answer, her worry grew. She knocked again and sighed with relief when the door opened.

Paula stared at her in surprise and then the surprise quickly melted off her face. She beamed. "Hi, Rachel! What a pleasant surprise!"

Rachel smiled uncertainly.

Paula opened the door wider and Rachel stepped into the house. The living room was as small as she had expected, but cozy. Most of the furniture was made from logs. There were only three chairs and a table in the middle of the room. Rachel sat on one of the chairs.

Paula sat on another and faced Rachel. She

smiled. "I haven't seen you since the day we left," she said.

"Yes," was all Rachel could say. She swallowed and then decided to tell Paula why she'd come. "It might be presumptuous of me to come to you for help, but I am desperate," Rachel said in a small voice.

Paula stared curiously at her but said nothing.

Rachel continued. "As you know, I was staying at Keith's house, but I had to leave because I didn't think it was right to go on staying with a single man, especially in this very small town. I don't want Keith's reputation ruined because of me."

Paula's eyebrows shot up. She leaned forward as Rachel talked, and when she finished, Paula said, "Is that the only reason you left?"

Rachel stared at her and Paula smiled. "You've fallen in love with him, haven't you?"

Rachel was taken aback and lost for words. She did not know whether to deny it or tell Paula the truth.

Paula said, "It's okay, Rachel. It's Keith Thorn we are talking about. I can imagine it would be easy to fall in love with him. You are, aren't you?" Paula asked again.

Rachel did not say anything for a long while and then she nodded. "Yes." There was no point hiding it.

Paula smiled. "I knew both of you were going to fall in love the day you arrived at Keith's. I could see the way he looked at you and how worried he was about you. And now, I can see it in your eyes, Rachel. How much you care about him." Her smile turned mischievous. "I know why you don't want to stay with Keith any longer. Apart from your fear of 'ruining his reputation', you are scared of what will happen between you two if you continue to live with him?"

Rachel nodded slowly. She looked down at the floor for a few seconds and then looked up at Paula again. She said haltingly, "Do you know anywhere I can stay until I am able to get a house? I don't know anyone in this town to ask except for you and your husband."

Paula chuckled and then stood up. She came and put her hands on Rachel's shoulders. "Yes, Rachel. You can stay here."

Rachel looked up at her. Paula was an exceptionally perceptive woman. Relief flooded Rachel and she stood up. She looked into Paula's eyes and apologized. "Thank you so much," she said. She looked around the house, slightly worried. "But what about your husband? Will he mind me staying here?"

"I'm sure he won't mind," Paula said. "He's not at home right now. He took the kids to visit their grandparents, but they will be back in the evening. I'll speak to Eric then, but you don't have to worry about it. I am pretty sure he'll have no problem with you staying with us."

Rachel thanked her again, and Paula said, "Come, let me show you to the room you will be staying in. Unfortunately, we have only two bedrooms because this house was built in a hurry, but there is a small space in the house that we haven't yet decided what to do with. We were thinking about making it my husband's study, but I think the Lord let us keep that space for you."

Rachel was incredibly touched. She thought about something and grew worried again. She said, "Please don't tell Keith I am at your house if you see him. Please." She looked at Paula with her palms together, pleading.

Paula didn't say anything for a short moment, and then she nodded. "I won't tell him. I promise." She led Rachel through a tiny kitchen and then to the small empty space. She said to Rachel, "As you can see, it's very small and empty, but I have a cot somewhere in the house. Please wait here and let me go get it."

She left quickly and Rachel glanced around the space. She walked to the window and opened the curtains. Looking out the window, she smiled at the expanse of land before her. "Thank you, Lord," she whispered gratefully.

Paula came back again with the cot, bedsheets, a blanket and a pillow. She quickly made the bed for Rachel and then stepped back. She smiled and said, "I'll go and start preparing dinner. You can lie down and rest and I will bring your food to you when it's ready."

"No, Paula, let me come and help you."

"Don't worry about it, Rachel. I insist. Stay and rest. The food will be ready in no time."

After Paula left, Rachel sat on the cot that would be her bed from now until she moved out of the house. Her mind went back to Keith and she wondered how he would feel when he came back and found her gone. She felt terrible at the fact that for the second time today, he would be very hurt because of her. Her heart ached for him and for Emily. She sighed again. She had to get used to the ache in her heart because this would be her life for months to come, until she could find her feet and get her daughter.

But what if that never happens? There were no jobs waiting for her to apply for in Destiny, and Mike would probably win whatever case she brought against him. She worried for a long time about it and then forced herself to put her worries away. She had to think positively. God was on her side. She had to depend on Him for favor. He would help so she could get a job somehow and a house, and then get custody of her daughter, even if it ended up being shared custody.

She shut her eyes, her heart still aching. She might be able to get rid of some of the pain she felt when she finally got custody of Emily, but without a doubt, the pain would never completely leave because there was one thing she could not ask the Lord for. One thing she wanted with all her heart but would never ever get. And that was a chance to be with the man she had fallen in love with. She would have to live with that pain for the rest of her life, or until the day the Lord took it away from her.

SIXTEEN

Keith frantically checked every part of his small house, looking to see if there was a spot he hadn't yet checked where Rachel would be hiding. He had come home half an hour after he'd left her with his emotions in tatters and unable to concentrate on the meeting he'd had with the brothers who were running the social media campaign for donations for Destiny. He had asked for the meeting to be postponed. They had looked at him strangely, especially as he was the one who had called the important meeting and told them how quickly they needed to start the campaign.

There was something as equally important to him that he needed to take care of at home, and that was Rachel. He had left her after she'd pulled away when they were about to kiss — after her rejection had shaken him to the core. When she'd pulled her hand away from his on the way to her ex's house, he had been hurt but had recovered quickly, believing she wanted her space because of what she was about to do. But in the car in front of his house, she had seemed to welcome his expressions of love. He had seen it in her eyes; she had feelings for him. And he loved her. He'd admitted that to himself a day ago. It had broken his heart when she'd pulled away, especially when she left the car and he knew she couldn't wait to get away from him.

Normally, he would let it go, but Rachel drew out emotions in him that he had never felt before. He would go on his knees and beg her to have him if that would make a difference. Which he'd planned to do once he got to the house. With her, he had lost all sense of shame, and he didn't even care anymore what the people of the town would think about him when they found out she was staying in his house. But when he got home, he'd found her gone. Her things were gone. He had searched everywhere for her but had not found her. He didn't know where she would have gone and told himself to calm down. Maybe she'd just stepped out for a walk or something. But still, he couldn't stop worrying. What if he had pushed her away by kissing her? What if that had been too much for her?

He had waited impatiently in the living room, praying she would return to the house, but after waiting for hours without any sign of her, he had called the station to find out if she was there. He knew the chances of her being there were small, but still he'd called. As expected, they told him she wasn't. He had gone out searching for her. He had chided himself for worrying so much. She was safe in Destiny, he was sure. And she wouldn't return to Mike because she hated the life she'd lived with him.

But he couldn't stop worrying. What if she

had? What if the thought of being away from her daughter for much longer had overridden her desire to stay away from Mike and she'd given in to his threats?

Keith had shuddered. If she had gone back to Mike, he didn't know what he would do. But he knew his heart would never recover. He went to the places he thought she might be, which were only two places — Gerald's bookstore because she liked books, and the small grocery store on the next street. Part of the store had been destroyed by the flood and all the groceries there carried away, but the owner, Fred Baker, had begun to restock little by little, and Keith had taken Rachel there once to buy some food.

He found Rachel at none of these places. He'd walked back home, hoping against hope that she had returned while he was away. He thought about going to look for her at her ex's, but he gave that idea up quickly. The only reason she would be back there now was if she'd changed her mind and decided she couldn't afford to stay away from Emily, even if it meant getting back together with Mike. If that were the case, it would be utterly selfish of him to ask her to leave, no matter how painful it would be for him.

He got to his house and opened the door, hoping she was home, but when he didn't see her, he had started to frantically search the whole house for her again, calling out her name as he did. Finally, he told himself to stop. She was not in the house.

He stood in the middle of his living room, wondering what to do, and then he remembered he still had her suitcase in the trunk of his car. He quickly went to get it and brought it into the house. A flicker of hope lit up in him. Her suitcase was here, filled with her things. That meant that she would soon return for it. Maybe he could convince her then not to leave, or at least show her that he loved her and then rip through whatever reservations she had about a relationship with him.

He went into the kitchen to prepare dinner for himself and also to keep his mind busy instead of worrying about Rachel. But as he cooked, he continued to worry. He prayed again and again that she would come back soon if for nothing else but to get her luggage. It would give him the opportunity to speak with her.

He finished cooking and dished out his food. Carrying his plate of lasagna to the living room, he sat on the sofa and began to eat. Then he dropped his plate on the coffee table, his appetite gone.

He glanced at the clock on the wall. It was almost seven p.m. He took a deep breath and turned to look out the window, hoping against hope that he would see Rachel walking toward his house. But he did not. He turned around again, leaned back against the sofa, and placed his leg on top of the coffee table. He pictured her sitting across from him, smiling. He knew exactly what he wanted to tell her, but if he did not know where she was, how would he pour out his heart to her?

He couldn't stay still any longer and stood up from the couch. He went around his house once more, asking the Lord for wisdom. He went into the room where Paula and Eric had stayed with their kids and looked around the room. It was empty, as he'd expected. He began to back away and then blinked when his eyes fell on an empty shampoo container on the floor. Without a doubt, it had been Paula's.

Suddenly, his pulse began to race. He put his hand on his forehead and sighed. Paula. Of course. Why had he not thought of that? Rachel and Paula had gotten along well when Paula and Eric were here. Paula had been very nice to Rachel and had helped her get totally well after Rachel arrived with a cold. Rachel had told him that she liked Paula and that they would have been good friends if Paula had remained here.

Quickly, with no patience to look for his car keys, he left his house in a hurry. He jogged to Paula and Eric's, praying with all his heart that Rachel was there. If she wasn't, he was not sure where else to look.

He got to Paula and Eric's log house and rang their doorbell. He waited, tapping his foot impatiently. As he lifted his hand to ring the bell again, the door opened and Paula looked out at him. She smiled, and then suddenly looked sheepish.

"Hey, Paula! How are you?"

"Good," she said in a small voice.

He stared intently at her and asked, "Paula... please. Is Rachel here?"

Paula looked down slightly and then looked at him again. "Rachel? Who... is Rachel?"

He immediately knew that Rachel was here and shook his head. He said urgently, "Paula, I need to speak to her. Please!"

Paula looked down again and didn't say anything for a moment. Then she lifted her eyes to Keith and gave a loud sigh. "How did you know Rachel was here?"

"Your shampoo bottle."

She frowned. "What?"

He shrugged. "Please, Paula, I need to see her."

Paula said, "I'm sorry, Pastor Keith. She made me promise not to tell you where she is. She doesn't want to speak with you."

Keith placed his hands gently on Paula's arm and looked into her eyes. "Paula, if you don't let me in, I will sit out here on your porch... every single day, until you do. And if I catch a cold or get pneumonia, it will be your fault. You don't want to be responsible for that, do you?"

Paula huffed and shook her head. "Okay, I will let you in!" She opened the door and he walked in. He hugged her briefly and then followed her out of the living room, through a short hallway, and to a door. Paula called out to Rachel and opened the door.

He did not wait for Paula to ask him into the room. He walked past her and entered.

Rachel was sitting up on a cot on the floor. Her mouth fell open when she saw him. She looked past him to Paula with an accusing look on her face.

"I'm sorry, Rachel," Paula said. "I had to let him in. He really loves you, you know. This sort of love is hard to come by these days."

She left the room and Rachel turned her gaze to Keith and gave him the same accusing look she had given Paula. "I did not want you to know where I was," she said.

Without invitation, he sat beside her on the cot. He stretched out his legs and then turned fully to her. "Rachel, why did you move out of my house?

And why did you pull away when we were kissing in the car?"

Rachel looked away and then shifted slightly away from him.

He turned her face back to his and said softly, "Tell me what's wrong, Rachel. Why did you just up and leave?"

She gave him a hard look, stood up, and folded her arms. She said in an equally hard voice, "I did not want to put your reputation at stake!" When he stood, she turned away again.

Once more, he turned her around to face him and sighed loudly, frustrated at her. "I don't care about my reputation!"

"You should," she said. "You are the pastor of this town and everyone looks up to you. How would it look to the people here if you're living with a single woman you're not married to?"

He smiled at her and said tenderly, "A single, beautiful woman who I am desperately in love with?"

Her face turned red as she blushed, and then she pressed her lips tightly together. Tears formed in her eyes and she said, "You cannot fall in love with me, Keith. Jenny is in love with you. That is the other reason why I left. I promised myself after I left Mike that I would never again do to any woman what I did to Olivia."

Keith stared quizzically at her. "What did you do to Olivia?"

"I stole the affections of her husband. Olivia loves Mike, but she had to share him with me for years, and Mike stopped paying any attention to her once we got together. I have lived with that guilt for a long time." She stared into Keith's eyes to try to make him understand. "From the way Jenny looked at you that day at the store, I knew without a doubt that she loves you. I cannot be with you, Keith, when I know she will suffer because of it. No matter how much I..." she bit her lip and said nothing more.

He took her hands and stared intently into her eyes. He said fiercely, "No matter how much you what?"

She shook her head and he said, "Please, Rachel, I have just told you that I love you."

She said quietly, "I love you too, but it doesn't matter. We cannot be together. You've known Jenny for much longer than you've known me and she loves you. I am sure you will come to love her too if you just try."

He ran his fingers through his hair and nearly bellowed in frustration, but he took a deep breath to try to calm down. "Okay, Rachel," he said, "I understand what you are saying. But I won't come to love Jenny one day, because I love you. I'll never stop loving you no matter how much you try to push me away. I don't want anyone else. I want only you, Rachel."

She lowered her eyes and cried, "Didn't you hear all that I just said? We cannot be together, Keith. It isn't fair to..."

"Stop it!" he cut in. He stared her down. "What isn't fair is you ignoring how I feel and what will happen to me if you reject me. I cannot help the way I feel. I don't love Jenny. I love you."

"But what about Jenny's feelings?" she asked, her eyes downcast.

He cupped her cheeks and said, "Jenny deserves someone who will reciprocate her love. That person is not me." She still looked unsure and he said again, "You just told me about Olivia and Mike, so you understand the way a person can feel to be with someone who they love but who doesn't love them back. You wouldn't want that for Jenny, would you?"

She looked conflicted for a few seconds, and then she nodded slowly. "I guess you're right," she said.

"So," he smiled, "you said you loved me a moment ago. I want to hear it again."

She pursed her lips and didn't say anything for a few seconds. Finally, she whispered, "I love you."

He chuckled and said to her, "Rachel, you can do better than that." He drew her into his arms and kissed her with everything in him. When she melted in his arms and kissed him back, he reluctantly pulled away from her.

She looked dazed as she gazed at him.

He took deep breaths and said slowly, "Now say it again."

She whispered, "What?"

"That you love me."

"I love you, Keith. With all my heart."

His heart soared and he beamed. He pulled her into his arms again and kissed her once more. She clung to him, but he pulled back. She tried to reach for him, but he said, "Tell me again."

She told him again that she was in love with him and he let her draw him close and surrendered to her passionate kisses.

Completely lost in her embrace, he opened his eyes when he heard a cough behind him and became fully aware of his surroundings again. Rachel pulled away from him, and Keith turned to the door. Paula was standing there, looking at both of them with a huge grin. She said, "Food is ready! Keith, you must join us."

Keith asked, "Are Eric and the kids back?"

"Eric called to say the kids wanted to remain at their grandparents' today. but he will be back soon." Paula smiled once more and then left the room.

Keith faced Rachel. She smiled shyly at him, and he took her hand. He threaded his fingers through hers.

Keith's stomach rumbled and Rachel laughed. "Someone is starving."

Keith chuckled. "It's your fault, Rachel. I couldn't eat at home because I was so busy worrying about you. But I am actually glad I haven't eaten. We will eat Paula's dinner together like we are on our first date."

"But Eric will come back anytime soon and he and Paula will join us," Rachel said.

Keith shrugged. "Then it will be a double date."

Rachel giggled. "I have never been on a date."

"Well then, we will have to make it the best date ever," Keith said.

They left the room hand-in-hand. Keith's heart raced with joy and exhilaration, and he felt happier than he had ever been. Rachel had told him she loved him, and after years of waiting for the one God had chosen for him, he had finally found her. He could not wait to show her off to everyone in Destiny.

SEVENTEEN

It was already eleven o'clock at night before Keith got up from Paula and Eric's living room sofa and announced that he had to leave. Eric and Paula hugged him and retired to their room, while Rachel saw him to the door.

He gave her a lopsided grin as he stepped out of the house and said, "Are you sure you won't come back to the house with me?"

She shook her head. "You know the best thing for us right now is for me to remain here."

His smile turned mischievous, and he said, "You are right, Rachel. It's best you stay here. With the way you feel about me, I am pretty sure you will not be able to keep your hands off me at the house."

She stared at him and then broke out laughing. He laughed along with her, and she said, "You are right. I wouldn't be able to keep my hands off you, so for your safety, it's best we live in separate homes."

He chuckled and said, "I guess I have to go now." But he did not move an inch. "I will bring your stuff for you tomorrow."

She smiled; her eyes fixed on him. For a long moment, neither of them could take their eyes off each other, or speak. She studied him as she loved to do whenever they were together. His good looks, sparkling green eyes, and smile always melted her heart. She loved everything about him, and with all her heart she wished she could go back to his house with him so she did not have to wait until tomorrow to see him again. But it would be a really bad idea, especially right now. If only he did not have to leave. She could stay here with him forever, just gazing at him and basking in his love.

"I don't want to go," he said, his eyes searching hers.

She smiled sadly. "Me neither."

He took her hand. "Let's go for a walk."

She raised her eyebrows. "Now?"

"Yes," he said. He looked up at the sky and she looked up with him. The stars were generously sprinkled in the sky. "It's so beautiful," she said and looked at him. He was looking at her.

"Yes… it is," he said, his eyes fixed on her.

Once again, desire ran through her body as their eyes remained fixed on each other. "Walk with me, Rachel."

She nodded and stepped out of the living room, shutting the door behind her. They strolled on the path by the lake, sometimes looking up at the stars, but mostly just talking. They passed by houses that were still standing and well-lit, and many that were destroyed. They walked by rubble and debris and felled trees and heaps of now broken furniture swept out of homes by the flood. There were few people about and Rachel relished the moment as they walked alone through the streets. She could not remember the last time she'd felt this happy. No, ecstatic.

They talked about the town and about the brief meeting Keith had had with the Stryker brothers concerning the social media campaign to raise donations for the town. After that, Rachel told him with tears in her eyes how much she missed Emily every day. Keith stopped for a minute to wipe away her tears with his thumb and then they continued to walk again.

Their discussion soon moved to less serious things. They talked about their childhoods. Rachel told him about growing up in Glendale before her mother packed her and her brother off to Fallow Creek. "We lived near a lake, and Taylor and I liked to swim in it. Sometimes we caught small fish and then threw them back into the lake."

She sighed sadly, remembering how much freedom she'd had at the time; how she'd laughed and played with her brother before her childhood was snatched away from her.

"Where is your mother now?" Keith asked.

Rachel felt the familiar sadness that settled in her heart whenever she thought about her mother. She said softly, "My mom died some years ago from a brain tumor."

"I'm so sorry," Keith said. "Mary and I lost our parents when we were very young. I hardly knew them."

"I'm sorry," Rachel said. "I know you told me you grew up with your grandmother. The house you live in now, she left it to you when she died?"

"Yes," he said. "I love that house. It brings back so many happy memories with my grandmother and my sister." He turned to look at Rachel. "Where is Taylor now?"

Rachel pursed her lips. "Taylor is still in Fallow Creek."

Keith searched her eyes and said, "I'm really sorry, Rachel. I guess if you could, you would have gotten him out of Fallow Creek when you left."

Rachel shrugged. "Actually, many men there seem to have comfortable lives, and Taylor especially. He's one of the wealthiest men in Fallow Creek. He's done very well for himself. He owns a construction company and builds all the houses in the town." She could not hide the disgust from her voice as she said, "The last I heard, he was shopping around for a second wife. I am pretty sure he's not planning to leave Fallow Creek anytime soon."

"But Mike left."

She nodded and then told him in more detail than she had before about all the circumstances that had led to their leaving the town. "I tried to run away just a week or two before we left. I was not successful."

He grinned. "I am glad you finally succeeded in leaving or I would never have met you."

"I am glad, too," she said. Their conversation soon returned to Destiny and the church building project. As they talked, she began to feel chilly and wrapped her arms around herself. She paused and then looked up at the stars again.

Keith said, "You are cold, Rachel." He drew her close and wrapped his arms tightly around her, sending a different kind of chill, a pleasant one, through her body. She trembled when he claimed her lips, kissing her again and again.

She returned his kiss and they stood there, kissing and clinging to one another. After a long while, they pulled apart and grinned at each other.

They continued to walk through the town, talking about their aspirations and plans for the future. When the conversation moved to Emily again and how Rachel could get full custody of her, she told Keith that she was worried about how long it would take. She had to first find a job, get a house, and be fully financially independent before she could even talk about getting custody of Emily. She pressed her lips tightly together as worry and fear began to snuff away the joy she had felt just a few seconds ago. She said, "What if I have to leave Destiny since there are no jobs here?"

He blinked a few times and stared at her with a look of horror. "Well, if you were to leave Destiny, I would miss you very much."

"You know it will be almost impossible for me to find the kind of job I need in order to have any chance to get full custody of Emily in Destiny. I will probably have to leave soon. Without a proper job, my own home, and enough money to take good care of my daughter, the chances of any court granting me custody of her will be nil."

"No, Rachel, stop saying that. The Lord brought you here to Destiny for a purpose and he will find you a job and a house. You won't have to leave."

She opened her mouth to tell him that she wasn't sure that would happen, but he said again, "Stop worrying about it, Rachel. God will work it out somehow."

She wasn't sure things worked that way. The fact still remained that there were no jobs in Destiny. The longer she stayed without work or a house of her own, the longer Emily stayed without her mother. Her baby needed her. She wanted to tell Keith all these things, but she did not want to put a damper on this special moment with him. She brushed away her concerns and focused solely on him.

"We haven't raised much money yet from the social media campaign for Destiny, but we're hoping that as time goes on, more and more people will find out about it and then donate."

"I'm so sorry I wasn't able to get the jewelry when we went to Mike's." Rachel said. She recalled how angry Mike had been, how he had gone into a rage while insisting that the jewelry now belonged to him and that she could not take it. She shuddered. What would have happened if the police officer had not been there?

Keith took her hands again. "You've apologized before, Rachel. It wasn't your fault. Mike was fully to blame for that. Anyway, even though the money from the jewelry would have helped some, it's probably for the best that Mike took it back. I don't want any money from that man. As hard as it was, I was glad when I transferred the remaining money he gave me back to his account. As soon as we get enough money from donations, I will pay him back what we've already spent."

She shut her eyes. She did not want to think about Mike now or talk about him with Keith. Memories of her time with Mike seemed to soil this time with Keith. She changed the subject and asked him once more about the social media campaign for Destiny.

"I have another meeting with the brothers tomorrow. I want you to come to the meeting with me."

She frowned.

"Don't worry, Rachel. It's not going to be held at my house. It will be at theirs."

"It's not that, Keith. I don't know anything about social media and campaigns since we hardly used social media in Fallow Creek."

He arched his brows and said, "You don't need to know anything about social media. I just want you with me at the meeting. I believe you have a lot to offer Destiny."

She doubted it but said nothing.

Keith pulled her arm around his waist and tucked her hand into his denim pocket. Her hands immediately warmed up and she smiled gratefully at him. He took her other hand and kissed the backs of her fingers.

They had taken the longer way to Keith's house, but they finally arrived. They stood in front of his door, facing each other. Rachel felt slightly sad that their glorious time together had come to an end but comforted herself with the fact that she would see him again tomorrow.

She said sadly, "I really enjoyed our walk. I wish it didn't have to end, but I'm glad I will see you again tomorrow." She hugged him tightly and then drew back. Grinning at him, she said goodnight, and then started to turn around. When he held her hand and pulled her back, she smiled and looked inquisitively at him.

"Are you kidding me, Rachel? I'm not going

to leave you to walk back to Eric and Paula's by yourself."

She gazed curiously at him. "But I can't go in. Remember what we talked about?"

"Yes, I remember," he said dryly. "I'm going to walk you back."

She laughed, but he didn't join in. "I just walked you to your house, Keith," she said incredulously. "Now you want to walk me back and then walk back alone to your house again?"

"Yes. That's the plan."

She gazed at him with a smile and said, "But you don't have to. Destiny is safe. You know that."

"Yes, I know. Still, I'd feel much better if I walked you back and made sure you got home safely."

She giggled when he took her hand again, excitement rushing through her. He was going to walk her back again. Their night together didn't have to end yet.

They walked back slowly, talking about everything, completely absorbed in each other, forgetting all their troubles and everything around them. They finally reached Eric and Paula's and Keith sighed. "Well, this is where I say a final goodbye, at least until tomorrow."

He hugged her and they held onto each other, not wanting to let go. Finally, Keith pulled back and opened the front door. He leaned in and gave her a tender kiss and then turned around and walked away.

She kept staring at him until he disappeared from sight and then she entered the house. She made her way to the tiny room that would be hers for however long she stayed in this house. She still felt giddy from her time with Keith, but after she settled down on the cot ready to sleep, all the excitement and giddiness evaporated, and fear took over.

She felt like crying as she thought about the brief troubling conversation she'd had with Keith, before his perpetual positivity had drained away her worry. Despite what he had said to try to calm her fears, she had to leave Destiny soon. She had no choice if she wanted a chance of gaining custody of Emily. She and Keith would still be together, but it would be a long-distance relationship. She had heard how difficult long-distance relationships were and everything in her dreaded the thought of being in one. Still, that would be the only option she and Keith had. Their love for each other would have to sustain them no matter where she moved. But the thought of not seeing him every day was almost unbearable.

She shut her eyes and his face immediately appeared in her mind. She had taken mental pictures of him at every moment they were together and she could see his face very clearly. She had to leave Destiny, the town she was growing to love, soon. But, hopefully, the mental pictures of him would be enough when she couldn't see him in person. She would hold his image close to her heart and live for the moments where they would be able to see each other face to face and be in each other's arms.

She shut her eyes and, for a long while, she could not sleep. Finally, about an hour later, she fell asleep with Keith's face in her mind, his eyes glowing, a huge smile on his face.

EIGHTEEN

For the hundredth time since he'd met Rachel, Keith couldn't get her out of his mind. He lay on his bed tossing and turning, not just because of the intensity of his feelings for her, but because of his worry. He could not forget the discussion they'd had just hours ago. She'd poured her heart out to him and told him she might leave Destiny. She had to get a job and a house in order to have any chance of gaining custody of her daughter. He couldn't imagine her leaving when they had just found each other and had declared their love for one another.

"Lord, please don't let her leave."

He sat up in his bed and turned on the light, finally giving up on falling asleep. Rachel was right. There were no jobs in Destiny, especially now with the destruction caused by the hurricane. Rachel had no choice but to find a job outside of town.

An overwhelming ache settled deep in his heart as he thought about that. There had to be something he could do.

And then it came to him. He shut his eyes. The

idea had been at the back of his mind when he was talking with Rachel, but he had dismissed it, thinking it was too soon. But it wasn't. He loved her with all his heart and she loved him, too. Even though they had not known each other for very long, he knew he couldn't live without her. He had no doubts whatsoever that she was the one for him and that he wanted to spend the rest of his life with her.

Excitement began to run through him, and he felt like running out of the house to Eric and Paula's now and telling Rachel what was in his heart. He could hardly contain himself.

He stood up from the bed and hurried to the room that had been his grandmother's. The room still smelled slightly of her — powder and lavender. Opening the large mahogany wardrobe, he searched through the folded clothes until he found a small wooden box. Opening it, he brought out a smaller blue box and then opened that as well. He smiled as he gazed at the emerald ring with the gold band. The ring had belonged to his grandmother, but she had given it to him before she passed. "To propose to that special girl, when you find her," she'd said. Now he had found that special girl, he couldn't wait to give her the ring and ask her to marry him.

He closed the blue box and took it with him out of the room. When he got to his room, he sat on the bed again. Tomorrow, he would ask Rachel to marry him as soon as possible, and then when she did, she would come and live with him and everything he had would be hers. He didn't earn much from his pastor's salary, but sales from his store, which had stalled for some time, were beginning to pick up again. He still didn't have much, but all he had would be at Rachel's disposal so she could quickly file for custody of her daughter.

He lay down on his bed again and tried to sleep now that he'd stopped worrying about Rachel. But he still couldn't. His mind kept buzzing with anticipation. He looked at the clock beside his bed. It was only four a.m.

He kept imagining the moment when he would kneel before Rachel and ask her to marry him. The only thing he worried about was the time. He wanted them to get married as soon as possible so he could legally take care of her and then her daughter. But what if Rachel didn't want to get married so quickly?

Stop worrying, Keith. Rachel wanted to get her daughter out of Mike's house as soon as possible. Surely, she would see that marrying him was the best thing to do.

He felt almost giddy. After being single for years and not knowing if he would ever find the right girl for him, the Lord had literally brought Rachel to his doorstep.

Gradually, sleep took over him.

He woke up at eight o'clock in the morning and immediately went to shower. He had to get to Eric and Paula's quickly in case Rachel planned to go out early today. He would take her to Stephanie's for breakfast and then hopefully they would spend some time, maybe at the park or the lake, just talking and getting to know each other better. After that, he would walk her back to Eric and Paula's and then hopefully propose to her there, because that was where they had both fully expressed their love for each other.

He dressed quickly in a pair of jeans and a short-sleeved striped shirt and ran a comb through his hair. Finally, he picked up the blue box with the engagement ring in it and opened it again. He smiled as he gazed at his grandmother's ring that would soon, hopefully, become Rachel's. He closed the box once more. His heart started to pound as he imagined himself asking Rachel to marry him and her saying "yes," and happily rushing into his arms. He could imagine how sweet their kiss would be as a newly engaged couple.

He left his room quickly and strode to the living room, hastening to get out of the house so he could get to Eric and Paula's house as soon as possible. Just before he got to the living room, he remembered that he had promised Rachel he would bring her suitcase to her today. He went back to his room, walked to the corner where he had placed it, and wheeled it out of the bedroom, into the living room. He grabbed the keys to his car from the coffee table and carried the suitcase out of the house.

As he drove to Eric and Paula's, the suitcase in the trunk and the engagement ring tucked safely in his pocket, he rehearsed again and again the words he planned to say to Rachel. They had eagerly and earnestly declared their love for each other the day before, but today, he planned to pour out his heart to her, too, and show her just how much he loved her.

He waved to a few people who called out greetings to him as he drove. He saw the florist was open and he stopped to buy Rachel some flowers. When he got into his car again and began to drive, he looked into his rear-view mirror and frowned. There was a black SUV following close behind. He did not recognize it and now that he thought about it, it had been following him for some time. He slowed down so the SUV would overtake him, but the driver slowed as well. He increased his speed and the driver did the same.

His frown deepened. "What is this?" he muttered. Why was this car following him so closely? He drove even faster and the SUV behind increased its speed once more to match his. He began to approach a long stretch of road with no houses on either side and his body suddenly jerked as the SUV hit him from behind. His eyes widened in shock as he realized that the driver behind him was out for him.

He kept speeding, trying to outrace the driver, but his old car was apparently no match for the SUV. He almost hit his head on the steering wheel when the driver smashed into him again. He held on tighter to the wheel. And then the SUV hit him a third time.

"Lord, please help me," he prayed, and once again tried to outrace the vehicle. His car began to screech, complaining about the unusual speed. The SUV hit him again and, once more, he tried to stay on course, but he lost control and began to career off the road. He pressed his brakes hard as he speedily approached a huge tree, but he was going too fast and it was too late. He felt himself flying out of his seat as he smashed into the tree. He flew through the window and landed somewhere on a grassy field. Excruciating pain shot through him and his vision blurred.

He tried to stay awake but felt himself fading away fast. His body was wracked with pain and he cried out again, asking the Lord for help. He fought the darkness creeping in on him and then remembered his grandmother's engagement ring in his pocket. He wondered if it was still there, as he could not feel his legs, and his mind went to Rachel and panic set in. With all his heart, he wanted to see her again, but he felt himself fading fast. Before he slipped away, a terrible sadness filled his heart. He would never see Rachel again or get the chance to marry her.

***

Rachel stood up from the sofa, unable to sit still. She dialed Keith's number as she had done a hundred times in the last hour. She listened as his phone rang and rang, but there was no answer. Frustrated, she glared at her phone and resisted the urge to smash it against the wall.

She looked at Paula, who had just walked into the living room, a worried expression on her face. Paula was holding a basket, and in it was her husband's lunch. She said to Rachel, "You still haven't gotten through to Pastor Keith?"

Rachel sighed. "I haven't." She began to pace the living room, and then glanced at Paula and said, "Why won't he answer my calls, Paula? Why?"

Paula went and put her arm around Rachel. "Shhh... Rachel, stop worrying. Pastor Keith is a big boy. I am sure he's fine."

She shook her head. "But Eric called to say he didn't see Keith in his house when he went to check on him."

"That doesn't mean he's not okay."

"He is supposed to be here by now. He told me he was going to come by early this morning, Paula," Rachel said frantically. "I haven't known him for long, but from the short time I have, I know Keith never fails to keep his word. It's already two o'clock and he's still not here, and he is not picking up his calls. I really think I should go to his house."

Paula gave her a small smile. "Remember why you both made a decision not to go to his house for now. Besides, Eric said he is not home. He would have answered his landline if he were."

Rachel sighed loudly. "I can't just stay here waiting. I'm getting sick with worry."

Paula gave her a sympathetic smile. "I am sure he's okay. It's only been a couple of hours since he promised to come. I think he's busy somewhere in town. That's probably why he has not been able to pick up his calls. I'm sure he will call you back as soon as he can," she said.

"It's not like him to ignore my calls," Rachel said.

"I do not think he is ignoring your calls, Rachel." Paula placed her hand on her shoulder. "Alright, Rachel. Since you are so worried, I will check in on Keith again at his house after I have dropped off Eric's lunch for him at the site."

Rachel nodded, feeling slightly better. Paula had promised to check in on Keith. She made Paula promise that if she didn't find Keith at his house, she would check his store.

Paula hugged her and told her she would be back soon and hopefully with news about Keith. After Paula left, Rachel dialed his home line again and listened as it rang and rang. She huffed when he still didn't answer the phone and called his cell phone number again, expecting it to ring again without him answering. Instead, an electronic voice said, "The person you are trying to reach is unavailable. Please try again later."

She bit her lip and then marched into her room to get her purse. Despite Paula's optimism, she knew something was wrong. She had to go find him. She would first check his store and then his house. If she didn't see him, she would walk through the whole town searching for him if she had to.

After she had gotten her purse from her room, she headed towards the front door. On her way to his store, she would ask around for him. Destiny was a small place. Someone had surely seen him today.

Just before she opened the door, a loud knock sounded, causing her to jump back in surprise. And then her heart soared with relief and joy. She rushed to the door, ready to fall into Keith's arms and let him know he had scared the living daylights out of her by not answering any of her calls.

She flung the door wide open and gasped. Fear ran through her as she recognized the man standing at the door, who definitely was not Keith. She immediately tried to shut the door, but the man, a squad guard from Fallow Creek, held it firmly open and walked in. She opened her mouth to scream, but the man grabbed her around the waist and covered her nose and mouth with a napkin. She kicked and tried to free herself from him without success.

She tried to scream again, but the napkin

muffled the sound. She began to get weaker and weaker, and then felt herself losing consciousness and being lifted from the ground. The man hoisted her over his shoulder as she faded away.

***

A strong antiseptic smell assaulted Keith's nose, and he grunted. He slowly opened his eyes and looked up at an IV pole and a small bag filled with liquid hanging on the pole. He frowned at the tube running from the bag to the back of his hand. He was clearly at the hospital.

He tried to sit up and groaned when excruciating pain shot up his arm. He winced as the memory of the accident instantly flooded his mind. He began to panic as he recalled that he had been on his way to Eric and Paula's to propose to Rachel when he had been hit hard by that madman in the SUV.

He tried to sit up again as he remembered his grandmother's ring. Where was it now? Was it still in his pocket? Dread ran through him as he looked down at his body. His clothes were gone. He was wearing a hospital gown. The ring had been in his pocket. He shut his eyes tightly, praying that he had not lost his family heirloom.

More details of his accident kept rushing back to him and he groaned. The accident had not been an accident at all. That driver who had crashed into him had followed him almost all the way from his house and had kept hitting him again and again until he crashed into that tree. That troubled him deeply. Who on earth would want to harm him in Destiny? He loved the people of this town and he was sure they loved him back. And yet it was clear that someone was trying to get rid of him. But who could that be? He remembered that he'd not recognized the car that hit him and sighed.

Once more, he struggled to sit up and then succeeded in doing so, but not without painful consequences. Pain shot up from his arms to his shoulder and from his waist to his neck, and he moaned. He had to get out of this hospital gown right now, find his clothes, and make sure his grandmother's ring was still in the pocket of his jeans. And then he had to leave this hospital so he could go and propose to the love of his life. He tried to swing his legs to the ground, but he just could not manage it.

He blinked in frustration and gritted his teeth as he tried again. If not for that awful accident, he would be engaged to Rachel now and they would probably be in each other's arms, celebrating their love for one another and their future wedding plans.

His determination to leave the hospital grew. He slowly put his legs on the floor and began to lift himself up. His eyes widened in terror as he crashed to the floor, his legs unable to hold him.

Why can't I stand up? What is wrong with my leg?

But instead of the answer to his question coming to him, another answer did. Mike. That was the only person he could think of who had something against him. Mike had made threats when he'd appeared at the house unexpectedly. From all that Rachel had told him about Mike, he had not expected the man to be capable of murder, but he should have. A man who kept someone against her will and forced himself on her on several occasions would be capable of anything, especially if something he thought he owned was taken away from him.

Suddenly, terror raced through his veins. As certain as he was that Mike had been behind his accident, he also knew that Rachel was in danger. "I have to get out of this hospital," he whispered. He tried to lift himself off the floor by holding onto the hospital bed, but his legs did not want to obey, and he fell down again.

He groaned in pain and turned to the door as someone came in and screamed. Jenny was standing at the door, staring at him with a look of horror on her face. She ran out of the room shouting, probably for the doctor.

Dr. Kingston and a nurse rushed into the room with Jenny at their heels. Dr. Kingston and the nurse lifted him off the ground and forced him to lie down on the bed again, ignoring him as he complained bitterly.

"I have to leave this hospital right now," he said to them, panicking. "I have to go to Rachel." He looked past the doctor, who was sticking a needle into his arm, to Jenny. Her eyes were filled with fear as she gazed at him. "Jenny, please I need to..." He blinked as he suddenly felt himself fading away again. He tried to speak once more. "Jenny, please tell me..." but his tongue felt heavy and he couldn't find the right words. His eyes began to close and his world went black again.

NINETEEN

From deep within her sleep, Rachel heard a baby chuckling. She tried to open her eyes, but she couldn't. She felt something crawling all over her face and shook her head to try to shake whatever it was off. Once again, she tried to force her eyes open, asking the Lord for help. Finally, she opened her eyes and then shut them again, wondering if she was still asleep and dreaming.

She opened her eyes once more and stared into Emily's smiling face. She blinked in astonishment and sat up. Someone had laid Emily beside her on the bed while she slept. She gasped, and overwhelming joy flooded her soul. Lifting Emily into her arms, she kissed her baby's chubby cheeks. "How come you are here?" she whispered and kissed Emily again.

She wrapped her arms around Emily, happily sniffing her, her heart bursting with happiness and amazement. Emily laughed and Rachel said, "What are you doing here, little one?" And then her heart jumped into her throat as she looked around the room and realized where she was. "No, Lord. It can't be. No!" She was back in Fallow Creek.

She held Emily away from her so she could inspect her. Her daughter didn't seem to have any injuries or bruises, and with relief she hugged her once more. Emily gurgled and then, as she usually did whenever Rachel carried her, she grabbed a fistful of Rachel's hair and put it in her mouth.

Rachel held her baby close while she shook with anger and despair. She began to clearly recall the squad guard who had walked into Eric and Paula's when she'd opened the front door. He had placed a handkerchief over her nose and mouth, and she had passed out shortly after. She was in Mike's house, in his bedroom, which meant that Mike had sent him to bring her back here against her will. She suddenly remembered what she had been doing before Mike's goon had kidnapped her, and fear gripped her once again.

Keith, where on earth are you? She looked around her. Her phone was nowhere in sight, nor was her purse. She kissed Emily's cheek again and swallowed a sob when Keith's face appeared in her mind. Now that she had been brought back here, would she ever see him again?

She stood up from the bed, still holding onto Emily. She could not bear the thought of never seeing Keith again. She had to find a way to escape. And yet, even as the thought crossed her mind, she knew there would be no way this time. If Mike had been desperate enough to come back to Fallow Creek knowing he might lose everything he had — the punishment for men who just upped and left the community — it meant he was serious about making sure she never found a way to leave him again. She was stuck in this place.

Rage and misery warred in her. What right did Mike have to force her back to this place — back to him? She had finally been free for the first time since she was a child. Free to be her true self and to be with the man she loved. Now she had come back to this wicked place where she would become enslaved and entrapped once again. Her only solace was the tiny person in her arms now and the God she had drawn closer to in Destiny, thanks to Keith.

Keith! Sorrow filled her soul, and she cried out once more. How would she live without ever seeing him again? She instinctively grabbed the curtain behind her and pulled it back. She looked out the window and sighed. As she'd suspected, members of the security squad were all around the house.

Emily began to cry and Rachel bounced her up and down on the bed, singing softly to her, trying to soothe her. She prayed for deliverance in her heart and thought about Destiny, about the nice people she had met who had treated her as an equal, both men and women. She thought about Eric and Paula, how worried they would be once they found out she had disappeared. She thought about the dreams that she had shared with Keith. She had never shared her dream with anyone except for Taylor, but that was years ago when they were kids. Even then, at that age, she had dreamt of being a teacher. Her role model had been Mrs. Madison, the nice teacher who'd taught English at the public school she and Taylor had attended before their mother moved them to Fallow Creek and turned their lives upside down.

She bit her lip as her mind settled on Keith again. She had been trying to call him for hours before she was kidnapped. She prayed with all her heart that Paula had found him.

She jerked up her head as the door suddenly opened. Mike walked into the room, followed by two squad guards. Rachel smothered the urge to lunge at him and tear his eyes out. She glared at him and said, "You wicked man! You kidnapped me and brought me here by force. What do you hope to gain by being with a woman who hates your guts?"

For a short moment, anger and hurt burned in Mike's eyes and then disappeared again. He sneered at her and put his hand in his pocket and brought out a phone. "This is your phone, Rachel. You have several missed calls from someone named Paula."

She gasped. Paula would probably have news of Keith. She reached desperately for her phone, but Mike held his hand away and chuckled. "It feels good to have Emily in your arms again, Rachel, doesn't it?" He turned around and nodded at one of the men. The man approached her and she shrank back and held Emily tightly. She screamed when the man forcefully took Emily away from her.

"Take my daughter to Olivia," Mike said to the squad member and pushed Rachel back as she tried to reach for Emily.

"Give me my baby!" she shrieked and stood up from the bed. "Give her to me right now!"

The second guard came and forced her hands behind her back, and she struggled to free herself. Mike said to her, "Welcome home, Rachel. This is where we belong. This is our home."

She wanted to spit at him, but she restrained

herself. She would not let him see how badly his words had affected her. She said scornfully, "You came back to Fallow Creek because you could not live like normal people. You had to come back to this weird place because you are weird."

He laughed. "You are also weird, Rachel. I came back because I finally had to admit that there is no place like Fallow Creek." He shook his head. "You thought you could leave me to be with that pastor. It's why I also returned. Here, women know their place. This time you will never be able to escape again."

Bile rose up in her throat and she wanted to curse him for taking her away from the town that she had grown to love and the man she was desperately in love with. She glared at him instead and said nothing.

He shook his head and said to her, "Like I said, don't even bother to try to escape this time. I have hired a bodyguard for you. After you are released from the Restoration House, he will follow you everywhere."

The Restoration House. She remembered that awful place and shut her eyes, nauseated. She would be separated from Emily again.

"And also, there's nothing for you anymore in Destiny. That pastor you were fooling around with has been taken care of."

She sucked in her breath sharply and her head buzzed. She said in a shaky voice, "What do you mean, taken care of?"

Mike tilted his head as he stared at her. "I mean that the pastor is dead, Rachel."

Her knees buckled, and she would have fallen to

the ground if she weren't being held up by the squad guard. She shook her head and screamed, "You are a liar, Mike! Keith is not dead! You just want me to think he is!"

Mike chuckled and nodded. He turned around and told the other security guard who had taken Emily away from her to give him his phone. Mike began to punch some buttons on the phone. "He is dead, Rachel. I knew you were not going to believe me so I made sure my man took pictures." He held out the phone to her and said, "Look."

She stared at the picture on the screen and then let out a scream as horror and revulsion filled her. On the screen was Keith lying on the ground, unmoving. A short distance away was his red Honda mangled beyond repair.

Mike withdrew the phone again and said to her, "So you see, I am not lying. That Keith is truly dead."

This time she strained to tear out his eyes. "You did this!" she spat. "I knew you were evil, but I did not know you were the devil himself." She couldn't stop screaming and trying to get out of the guard's grip so she could get to Mike and wipe that evil smirk off his face. She wanted to draw his blood the way he'd drawn Keith's.

Mike said, "That pastor tried to take what belongs to me. He messed around with the wrong person."

"I don't belong to you!" she screamed. She glared at him. He had wanted her to stay with him at all costs and because of that, he had killed Keith. She would rather die than be with Mike now... but he had Emily. She began to sob and angrily sobbed.

Mike seemed to be enjoying her agony, and she had to gather herself together. But she could not get the image of Keith lying on the ground beside his mangled car out of her mind. She began to weep again.

Mike turned around and left the room. The guard holding her let go and walked out of the room as well, closing the door behind him. She rushed to the door to try to open it, but it was locked. She banged on the door and screamed for her daughter. When it was clear they were not going to open it for her, she walked to the bed and collapsed onto it. She curled up into a ball and thought about Keith, about the last time she'd seen him; the way his eyes had looked when he'd gazed at her and told her he loved her.

Sadness and weakness consumed her body. She shut her eyes and forced herself to go to sleep to escape the crushing sorrow she felt.

She jerked awake at the sound of loud voices approaching the room. She sat up on the bed and shifted back, leaning against the wall as the door opened. She narrowed her eyes as three of the town elders walked into the room with Mike. When Taylor walked in behind them, she leaned forward, surprised. Outside the room were about five guards.

She sprang out of the bed and went to hug Taylor, happier to see him than she had ever been. Taylor put his arm around her as she struggled through her anger and tears to tell him everything that had happened. Finally, after she finished, she said to him, "Can you please help me?"

Mike and the other elders stood around, looking

at her and Taylor with interest and derision. She focused on Taylor and asked him again to please take her and Emily away from Mike's house.

Mike said, "You're definitely leaving the house soon, but without Emily. Like I said before, you will be going to the Restoration House."

She ignored him and said to Taylor, "Emily is my daughter. She has to come with me." She turned to give Mike a cold stare. "I do not want her staying with him. He is a monster."

One of the elders said, "You will be going to the Restoration House, but you cannot take your daughter there. Babies don't go there, as they do not need to be restored."

She glared at the man who had spoken. Mike had also fled Fallow Creek and yet she was the only one being punished.

As though he could read her mind, another elder said, "Your husband has been pardoned by us on one condition; that he swears he will never try to leave Fallow Creek again. He has sworn that he never will. You, on the other hand, are clearly unrepentant. You will go to the Restoration House, but since you have tried to run away before, twice, you will not stay there to work and attend just the regular classes. You will have continuous teachings to help you renew your mind faster. This time, there will be no one to help you. And don't even bother trying to escape. The elder that helped your husband with your escape has been removed from our ranks. From what your husband has told us, he regrets leaving Fallow Creek, and from your defiant attitude, we see why."

The oldest elder amongst them, Rayford Young,

shook his head and said, "That's the way women are. Just like Eve deceived Adam, they end up leading men astray." He looked at Mike and added, "Your wife led you astray, Brother Mike, but we are glad you have come back to your senses and returned to Fallow Creek where you belong."

Rachel listened to them with growing anger and despair. They were going to force her to leave her daughter. For how long, she did not know. She tried to remain calm as she asked the elders, "When will I be able to see my baby again?"

One of them answered, "When your mind has been sufficiently renewed and we know that you have completely changed. You will return then to your husband's house and submit to him completely, and then you will be reunited with your daughter."

Another elder said, "You will not be released until we are completely satisfied that the wicked rebellious nature in you has been crushed."

Mike's eyes searched her face, and he said in a cold voice, "I did everything for you, Rachel. But you chose to repay me by leaving me for another man."

The elder who told her Mike had been pardoned said, "You will never get the chance to escape Fallow Creek again to spread lies about us."

Mike took a step toward her and stopped in front of her. He said, "If the thought to escape even crosses your mind, you will never see Emily again. Your future happiness relies on your ability to submit and be fully obedient."

She looked at Taylor, pleading with her eyes for help. As children, they had been very close and somehow could read each other's feelings. She hoped there was something of that closeness still left between them. She prayed he would remember and speak up for her. But instead, he said, "I'm sorry, Rachel. The elders are right. You should submit to your husband. The Restoration House will do you good. You'll see. It's just to renew your mind and..."

"It's not just to renew my mind!" she shrieked. "Have you ever been there, Taylor?" She stared at him. Of course he had never been there. Why would he? He was a man, and a wealthy one at that. There was no reason for him to ever visit the Restoration House. He was on his way to take a second wife. Men like him enjoyed everything about Fallow Creek. It was how the elders ensured that everybody in the community remained obedient to all the strange rules. It greatly favored the strong and powerful — usually the men, who in turn silenced the weak and made sure they lived in complete compliance.

Taylor said nothing and Rachel closed her eyes, feeling totally hopeless.

Rayford Young said to her, "You can pack a few things now and you will be taken directly to the House."

She stared at him, fear racing through her. "Now?"

"Yes," he said.

She began to pace the room and then stood in front of the men again. "I thought I would have some time with Emily before being taken away to the Restoration House."

Rayford Young immediately glanced at his wristwatch and said, "We have other matters to take care of, so you have to hurry and pack your things now."

She turned and stared at Mike. "At least bring Emily to me so I can say goodbye to her."

"There is no time, Rachel," Mike said. He turned to the squad member he had referred to as her bodyguard, the man who was to watch her constantly when she returned to the house. "Help her pack her things, Ben."

The guard approached her, but she barked at him, "Don't touch my things!"

She flung the closet door open and then stepped back and groaned when she remembered that all her things had been with Keith. The night they'd strolled through Destiny, he had told her he would bring her things the next day, but now he was no more. A sob rose up in her throat again, but she swallowed it. She would not break down in front of these men.

She turned to them and said, "I have no things to pack."

"Then we will take you to the house now," Rayford said.

As they walked down the corridor and past Olivia's room, Rachel heard Emily crying. Everything in her wanted to push past the men and guards and rush into the room to get her child, but she knew there was no use. She would not get far, not from the elders or Mike, and especially not from the guards.

She walked down the stairs, in front of her the elders, Mike and Taylor, and behind her, the squad guards.

Inside the black jeep that would take her to the Restoration House, she looked up at Mike's huge home and at Olivia's bedroom window upstairs. If only she could have a glimpse of Emily now. She turned to look at Mike, who was standing in front of the house. His countenance was like stone. She turned away, distressed. The elders walked away. Taylor stared at her through the car window for a few seconds with sympathy in his eyes and then he, too, walked away to his car.

She sat in the back seat with a squad guard while the driver got into the vehicle. She stared straight ahead as they drove to the House, numb. When they arrived, she sighed. She did not want to get out of the car. All she wanted to do was run away to Mike's house to get her daughter, and then flee Fallow Creek. But her thoughts were just useless imaginations. She could do none of the things she was thinking about.

She finally got out of the car when the squad guard opened the door for her. He walked behind her while she made her way to the front door. He opened the front door of the House and she walked in. She glanced around. It looked exactly the same as the last time she was here.

Margaret, the sour-faced woman who had promised to make her life a living hell the last time she was here, came down from the stairs and walked up to her with a triumphant look on her face. She nodded at Rachel. "You're back," she said gleefully. "Well, then. The elders tell me you are unrepentant and therefore are to attend the special classes for people like you."

Rachel said nothing. There was nothing to say. No punishment that Margaret could mete out and no brainwashing in one of those classes she talked about would be a greater punishment than leaving her daughter for an unknown period of time. None.

Women in plain dresses made their way up and down the stairs, some with mops and buckets, all with their heads bowed. None of the women were talking to each other.

Margaret said scornfully, "So, what are you still standing there for? Come along. The classes will start in a minute or two." She walked off and Rachel followed her slowly, her mind only on Emily and Keith.

They walked upstairs, down the corridor, and into the large classroom that Rachel had seen the last time she was here. She immediately glanced at the blackboard, but this time it was wiped clean. "Sit right here." Margaret pointed at the middle seat in the front row.

Rachel sat down and turned around. The class was empty except for a woman who sat at the back, staring out the window. Rachel frowned. The young woman looked familiar, but not in the way the other women in this place did. Most of the women here looked familiar because the town was small. Most people were acquainted or knew about each other. But she was sure she didn't only know of the woman at the back. She knew her well. And then it dawned on her. She had been Rachel and Taylor's childhood playmate. She and her parents and siblings lived near the house they'd grown up in when they'd arrived in Fallow Creek. When their mother and stepfather moved them away to another part of the community, they'd lost touch with her. Later on, Rachel saw her around town once in a while, but by then they had grown apart.

Margaret glared at Rachel and walked out of the

class.

Rachel turned around again and said, "Lily! Lily Hunter!"

The woman turned to Rachel and stared at her for a short moment. And then her eyes lit up. "Rachel! Stubborn little Rachel!"

Rachel laughed and said, "Come on, Lily, I was never as stubborn as you."

They met in the middle of the class and hugged. "I haven't seen you in years," Lily said to her. "I heard you married Mike Cadwell."

They went to sit together on Rachel's table. She said, "I have seen you a few times around, but always through the window of the car." Rachel grinned. "I heard you refused every suitor that came your way and you're still single. That is a scandal in Fallow Creek!"

"That is why I was brought here," Lily said, looking around.

The class began to fill up quickly as women walked in and took their seats. Lily looked at Rachel and said, "I'm so glad that you are here. I feel like we will get along as well as we did when we were kids. We will talk after class." She looked around and whispered, "But let me warn you about the classes. You have to guard your heart against them because..." She stopped talking when a woman in her late fifties with a stern face and an imposing stature walked into the class. "We will talk later," she said quickly and then went to take her seat at the back of the class.

When the lectures began, Rachel immediately understood what Lily had been trying to warn her about. They were made to recite over and over again scriptures and quotations that were twisted and taken out of context, made to fit into the terrible doctrine of absolute submission. Because Rachel was seated in front, she could not escape reciting the scriptures and then the stupid quotations that were written by some dead elder in the past. Quotations completely against everything Rachel believed in now. The stern tutor focused on Rachel as she told them to recite the words, "I will submit completely to my husband and the elders of Fallow Creek and obey them in everything, no matter what. For they are God's voice on the earth to me." Rachel said the words, but rejected them in her heart. She knew she had to pretend to submit to the brainwashing, at least for now, if she wanted to leave this place quickly and see Emily again.

After the horrendous class was over, Lily walked up to her and Rachel shifted slightly so Lily could sit next to her.

"How was the class?" Lily made a face.

Rachel laughed and shook her head. "Awful."

"This is just the beginning," Lily said. "I've been here for about a week and the classes go on and on. In fifteen or twenty minutes, another tutor will be back for more 'mind renewal' classes. Before the next one comes, I want to know what brought you here."

Eager to share with someone who was sympathetic to her, she told Lily everything in as few words as she could, starting with her attempt to run away the first time, then leaving Fallow Creek with Mike, and then being kidnapped and brought back here. Finally, she told her about the pain of being separated from her daughter and Keith.

There were tears in her eyes when she finished. It had been difficult to talk about Keith, about his death. And yet she had told Lily everything.

Lily shook her head slowly and placed her hand on Rachel's back. "I'm so sorry, Rachel," she said. "I hate this place. Actually, I did not mind Fallow Creek so much until the pressure rose to marry me off. I did not want to get married and, just like you, I felt like if I ever did get married, it would be to someone I loved. I kept refusing everyone, especially because most of the people who wanted to marry me were already married. Finally, my parents got tired and decided that I needed to come here so I would change my mind about marriage."

"One of the reasons I left Mike was because I gradually began to feel that God was displeased that I was married to someone who already had a wife."

"Actually, no true marriage takes place once someone has a wife. This is the United States. It's illegal as well as immoral."

Rachel nodded. "I know that. And that was why I left. Mike tried to tell me that I belonged to him, but I told him I didn't. And then when I met Keith and fell in love with him, I wanted to be with him." She pressed her lips together as sadness overtook her again.

Lily said, "I wish we could escape from this place, but there is no way out. Trust me, I have tried."

Rachel gave her a sad smile. She was sure Lily had tried. She remembered the headstrong child Lily had been, forever going left when her parents or an older relative told her to go right.

"I cannot imagine how you feel now," Lily said.

"I thought I was suffering here, but to think that someone you love was taken away from you so violently, and now you've been separated from your baby. I don't know if I would be able to go on if it were me."

Rachel said, "I am barely surviving. The only thing that keeps me going is the hope of being reunited with Emily one day. Because of that, I have to submit to whatever brainwashing is going on in these classes so I can quickly see her again."

"I don't think we have much choice about the brainwashing thing," Lily said. "Nobody leaves this place without having their minds broken and becoming totally subjugated. Soon we will be like most of the women here — completely compliant."

Another tutor walked in, a petite woman with an angry expression. Lily stood up and went back to her seat while Rachel's mind went around and around what Lily had said. Soon, her mind and will would be broken, but then she would be able to leave this place and see Emily again. But that would also mean living as Mike's wife again. She was growing in her relationship with God and the thought of being under Mike's control again repulsed her. And yet she had no other choice.

TWENTY

Keith woke up to pitch darkness again. He reached out and switched on the table light beside him. He was still attached to the IV pole. He took a deep breath and began to remove the IV tube from his arm. He could not lie in this bed in hospital when Rachel was most likely in danger. He had to find her.

He sat up on the bed and slowly put his legs down on the floor as he recalled how he'd fallen the last time he'd tried to stand. Slowly, he rose from the bed but found that his legs still could not hold him up. He fell back and groaned.

"Lord, please help me," he muttered and slowly rose again, this time holding onto the table beside him. His legs were shaky, even holding the table. He frowned. What on earth was wrong with his legs? His arm was bandaged and still throbbed, but he ignored the pain.

He looked down at himself and sighed. He was still wearing the hospital gown. He looked around the room but couldn't find his clothes or his phone.

Still, he had to leave this hospital and find Rachel, even if it meant he would leave in his hospital gown.

He began to walk unsteadily, holding on first to the bedside table, and then to the bathroom door, and then leaning his hand on the wall. He paused briefly to catch his breath and leaned his back against the wall, panting and tired. He felt as though he had just done a hundred-meter sprint instead of only walking a few feet away from his bed.

He kept asking the Lord for help as he walked slowly toward the door, still leaning on the wall. He took a deep breath again and then stood at the entrance to the room, panting and groaning.

What are you doing, Keith? You are in no state to leave the hospital.

He ignored the voice in his mind and pressed his lips together, determined to leave. And then his heart sank as he stepped out of the room and into the hallway leading to the hospital entrance. It was a very long hallway and nurses walked up and down it. Anytime soon, one of them would ask why he was out of his bed and make him go back. And he knew there was no way he could make it down the long hallway in his state.

He ducked behind his room door when one of the nurses that had attended to him that morning began to approach. He heaved a sigh of relief when she turned left and he faced the hallway again. *Keith, what are you going to do now?* he thought, frustrated.

He thought about crawling down the corridor and then chuckled in spite of himself. *What a stupid idea.* Feeling hopeless, he began to turn back into his room to try to figure out what to do. Maybe he could convince the doctor to let him leave the hospital, even if for a short time. But he knew that would probably not work.

He saw Jenny walking down the hallway toward him and his heart soared. He could not contain his relief and called out to her, "Jenny!"

She stared at him as he stood there in the hallway, half-naked, and then hurried over. "What on earth, Pastor Keith!" She looked him over and shook her head. "What are you doing out of bed and in the hallway? I know Dr. Kingston hasn't discharged you. And you are too weak to be out of your bed."

He waved her concerns away and said urgently, "You have to help me, Jenny."

She nodded and then put her arm around his waist, clearly to lead him back into his room and onto his bed. He shook his head weakly and said to her, "No, Jenny. Not back to my bed."

She arched her eyebrows, staring quizzically at him. "Then where?"

"My legs feel heavy," he said to her. "I don't know what is wrong with them… but I need to get out of this hospital. Rachel might be in danger. I need to help her."

"No." Jenny shook her head. "You cannot leave the hospital now. Look at you."

He shrugged and asked her to bring a wheelchair for him.

"You're kidding, Pastor Keith," she said, gazing at him as though he had gone mad. "I am not getting you a wheelchair. And besides, where am I supposed to get one?"

"This is a hospital, Jenny. Look around. You will find one somewhere."

"I can't..."

He cut in, "Please, Jenny." He looked into her eyes. "I meant it when I said Rachel might be in danger. I won't be able to live with myself if she really is and I did nothing to help."

"Then maybe I should call the police. They will handle it."

"Call the police, Jenny, but I need to get to Rachel now... before it's too late." Jenny said nothing and Keith put his hand on her shoulder. "Time is running out." He sighed. "Get me a wheelchair!"

Jenny stared at him for a long moment and then nodded. "Okay, wait here. I will go and find you a wheelchair. But this is insane."

She began to walk away and he called out to her, "Please get me something to put on as well."

She raised her eyebrows and said, "Where am I supposed to find something for you to wear?" She left without waiting for an answer.

Another nurse approached and he ducked again before she could see him. He kept praying and hoping that Jenny would find a wheelchair for him and that somehow he would be able to leave the hospital unnoticed.

Five minutes later, Jenny appeared with a wheelchair. Gratitude filled his heart and he whispered, "Thank you, Lord."

"I had to steal this, Pastor," she said accusingly.

"Thank you, Jenny. And you did not steal it. You borrowed it. You will return it as soon as possible." She handed him a white robe, and he raised his brows. "A doctor's robe?"

She shrugged. "Would you rather walk around half-naked?"

"Point taken," he muttered, snatching the robe and yanking it over his trembling arms.

He sat in the wheelchair after putting the robe on, and she began to wheel him down the hallway. He knew they looked out of place, but he kept praying that no one would stop them.

Nurses and attendants walked by, staring at them, but none stopped them. Keith continued to pray as they passed the reception desk and then the waiting area. His heart thudded as they neared the entrance to the hospital. He could almost touch the door. They would make it out.

His mind went to Rachel again, and he began to run through his mind how he was going to find her. They reached the door and he exhaled in relief. Just as they were about to exit the hospital, Dr. Kingston walked through the door, almost bumping into them. Keith's heart sank to his feet. "Oh, Lord, please help me!"

The doctor stared at him in astonishment and then shook his head slowly. He hurried over and scolded Jenny for aiding Keith in his harebrained plan to escape the hospital, when he was clearly in no state to leave.

"Doctor, I really need to go," Keith pleaded. "I promise I will be back soon."

Dr. Kingston did not seem to be listening. He took hold of Keith's wheelchair and began to wheel him down the corridor again, while Keith complained bitterly. Two nurses walked behind them and Jenny beside him.

Dr. Kingston wheeled Keith into his room again, and he and the nurses carried Keith back into his bed. Keith pleaded, but they did not listen.

"You will be released when you are strong and well enough," the doctor said.

Keith tried to rise, but the nurses held him down. When Doctor Kingston picked up a syringe, Keith pleaded again, and then groaned when the doctor stuck the needle into his arm. Gradually, he began to feel sleepy and though he fought the sleep, he couldn't resist it.

"I'm so sorry, Rachel," he whispered, and then fell into a deep sleep.

TWENTY-ONE

In just a few days, Rachel had attended the mind renewal classes way too many times to count. She hated the classes, hated having to recite the nonsense that the tutors were mentally feeding them. The desperation and despair that had clung to her when she first came here had only increased, combined now with hopelessness.

She looked up at the tutor who was droning on about submitting to the elders in the town. If only she was not sitting in front of the class. Margaret had placed her where every tutor could see her clearly and where she was forced to repeat every word the tutors made them say. She shut her eyes briefly and opened them again as the tutor asked them to repeat the scripture that she had just quoted. Rachel recited the scripture mechanically while her mind traveled once more to Keith. She could not believe he was gone. Ever since Mike had told her about Keith's death, she had not stopped mourning him. She could not erase from her mind the picture she had seen of him lying lifeless in the grass. Tears welled up in her eyes, but she blinked them back.

A large part of her had died along with Keith. It would have been all of her if not for Emily. Unfortunately, the price for being reunited with Emily in the future did not just include swallowing the ungodly doctrines they were being constantly fed here; it also included going back to Mike as his wife. She felt sick to her stomach at the thought. She had been regularly studying her Bible, more than she had ever done in her life. Because of that, her relationship with God had grown tremendously. The thought of going back to live in sin with Mike left her with a constant stomach ache. She had been praying for deliverance and a miracle, but it didn't seem the Lord was willing to answer her.

The tiring class ended and the tutor left. Rachel turned around. When her eyes found Lily's, she smiled. Lily was the only person who made the stay in the House bearable. They had only a few minutes to talk before the next tutor came in to fill their minds with nonsense.

Lily came and sat next to Rachel. They immediately started to talk about their hopes and plans for the future, as they always did in between the grueling classes.

"I knew I never wanted to get married, especially in Fallow Creek, but everything you have told me about your life with Mike makes me even more determined not to. Unless I actually fall in love with someone. And I doubt that will happen in Fallow Creek," Lily said.

Soon, as they always did, they began to talk about escaping from the House and even from the town, though they knew there was no way out. Despite that fact, Rachel still felt a tiny gleam of hope enter her heart every time they talked about it. They were talking about the elder that had helped Rachel and Mike escape Fallow Creek when Lily tilted her face toward Rachel and asked, "What about your brother, Taylor? I remember that you were close when we were kids. He is quite influential in Fallow Creek. Maybe he could speak to the elders for you and see if they would agree to let you out of this place."

Rachel laughed harshly and shook her head. "Taylor is part of the system, Lily," she said. "He was present when the elders gave their verdict and sent me here. I begged him to help me, but he did not. Besides, Taylor and I have not been close in years. Since girls and boys grow up differently in this place, we gradually grew apart."

Lily lifted her brows and shook her head. "I liked Taylor when we were kids. He seemed different, but I guess people change." She narrowed her eyes, her expression thoughtful. "He has only one wife, doesn't he?"

"Yes, but I think he is planning on marrying another girl now."

"Who?" Lily asked with way too much interest in her voice.

Amused, Rachel searched Lily's eyes. She finally said, "I am not sure yet. Why, do you want to marry my brother?"

Lily rolled her eyes and looked away. "I'm not interested in getting married, Rachel. You know that. And even if I were, it will never be to someone who already has a wife. In spite of what these foolish people in Fallow Creek say, you cannot marry someone else when they are already married. It's against the law — the county's and God's."

Rachel nodded and said, "I remember telling Mike all that one day, but he just laughed and told me we married before God."

Lily sighed and said, "I still think that there is something different about your brother. I think if you can find a way to send a message to him and tell him how awful this place is, he might be able to help you get out of here."

"I don't think so," Rachel said.

"You haven't tried, Rachel. If I had a brother like Taylor, I would take advantage of it."

Rachel thought about what Lily had said briefly and then finally agreed that there was no harm in trying. "But how am I going to get a message to him? And even if he decides to help me, I doubt the elders will listen to him, no matter how influential he is."

"We will think of a way for you to send a message to Taylor. I heard of a woman about eight years ago who was sent here but was able to get a message out somehow and ask the elders for a fair hearing."

Rachel lifted her brows in surprise. "Really?" she asked, hope rising within her. "And did they agree to give her a fair hearing?"

"Yes, they did," Lily said. "But the hearing did not go in her favor. Still, it's worth a try."

Rachel's hope evaporated and she sighed loudly. "There is no use, Lily. It is not going to work."

"You never know until you have tried. What do you have to lose?"

A tutor entered the class and Lily immediately

stood up. "We will talk later," she whispered in Rachel's ear and quickly went to her seat.

It took everything in Rachel to pay attention to what the tutor was saying. She knew it was important to listen so she could recite the tutor's words correctly and not jeopardize her chance to leave the House, but her mind was preoccupied with what Lily had said.

When the classes thankfully ended at about nine in the evening, the time all the classes usually ended, Rachel stood up and turned around, waiting for Lily. They left the classroom together and walked slowly on their way to their assigned rooms. Usually, they could only talk in between classes or when they were outside cleaning the windows, which was part of their daily chores. The walk from the class to their rooms was short, and no one was allowed to loiter in the hallway or go to other people's rooms.

An idea had been nagging at the back of Rachel's mind during class, and now she said to Lily, "I think I have an idea on how to get a written message to my brother."

"You do?" Lily asked.

"Yes. You know that squad guard who is always staring at me whenever we go outside?"

"The one who looks like an oaf?"

Rachel giggled. "Yes, that one."

"He doesn't stare at you, Rachel. He gapes. He doesn't have enough sense to know that if Margaret ever sees him, he would be in trouble for ogling a married woman."

Rachel couldn't help laughing and then she said, "I will write a message and give it to that guard to help me send it to Taylor."

"What if he refuses?"

"I will just find a way to convince him to help me."

They were standing in front of Lily's room now and Lily lifted her brows while a smile played on her lips. "Rachel, what do you plan to do?"

"Nothing unseemly."

The hallway had emptied of people now, but they went on talking. "You have to be careful, Rachel. If it goes wrong and that guard reports you, you know what will happen."

"It won't go wrong."

Lily said, "I hope Taylor agrees to help you."

Rachel gasped as Margaret began to walk down the hallway toward them. "Margaret is coming, Lily. And she looks unhappy."

Lily said, "She always looks unhappy."

They both laughed and Rachel hurried away while Lily entered her room.

Rachel entered her own room and found that her roommate had already turned all the lights off. She sat on her bed a few inches away from her roommate's and turned on the small table lamp beside her. She reached into her purse and took out the notebook and pen which had been given to her the first day in the House for writing down notes in the classes. Opening the notebook, she stared at the blank page before her for a brief moment and began to write.

She wrote down everything she had said to Taylor the day she had been brought to the Restoration House and then added some other things she hadn't told him because Mike and the elders had been there — things Mike had done to her. She asked him to send a message to the elders telling them that she wanted a fair hearing. She reminded him that even though she was a woman, she had rights, just as men did. Finally, she reminded him of what he had said to her when they were children, before they came to Fallow Creek.

You said that even though I was a girl and younger than you, I was your best friend.

She finished writing and signed the letter with: *your dearest sister, Rachel.* She folded the letter carefully, took a small brown envelope out of her purse, and put the letter in it. She considered waiting until the next day to search for the guard Lily had referred to as an oaf, but she changed her mind. Nighttime was the best time to give him the message. They would easily be seen during the day. She had to be careful, though, that no one saw her with him tonight. If she could get out of the house without being seen by Margaret, she would be able to talk to the guard without anyone else seeing them.

She stood up from her bed and went to the door. Looking this way and that, she stepped into the hallway when she saw it was empty. The guard usually patrolled the front of the building at night. She had looked out of the bathroom window once, and when he saw her, he had given her a smile that turned her stomach.

Are you sure it's safe to approach that guard? she asked herself as she made her way soundlessly down the hallway. It could go badly for different reasons. If Margaret saw her, she would be in trouble. If another guard saw her with the oaf, she would be in trouble. If the oaf decided to report her or, worse, take advantage of her, she would be in big trouble.

She tiptoed down the stairs, looking around to make sure Margaret was nowhere in sight. At the bottom of the stairs, she paused and listened for any sound that would indicate that someone was near. When she heard nothing, she went to the front door, opened it, and stepped out of the house.

She immediately came face-to-face with the oaf guard. He arched his brows and gazed at her in surprise. She noticed the rifle in his right hand, resting at his side, and swallowed. Gathering herself together, she took a deep breath and forced herself to calmly walk toward him.

He did not seem bothered or troubled that she was outside this late, only surprised. She got to him and he looked down at her, towering over her.

She forced herself to smile brightly at him. "Hey, can you do me a favor?"

The expression on his face turned suspicious.

She showed him the letter in her hand. "I just want you to help me send a message to my brother, Taylor Dalton. You know him, right?"

He nodded slowly but said nothing to her.

"Will you help me send it?"

"I can't," he said, gazing into her eyes. His eyes traveled down to her lips and then to her chest.

She placed her hand on his arm so he would look at her face again and asked, "What is your name?"

"James," he said.

"James, please. It's just a letter to my brother. I miss him and I want to know that he's doing well."

The guard smiled, looking at her hand on his

arm, and she quickly removed it. His smile widened and turned lewd. "And what will you give me if I send the letter to your brother?"

Her heart began to pound. She knew exactly what he was asking for but, she forced herself to smile and asked, "What do you want?" She prayed he would be too ashamed to actually say it.

He looked around and then put his hand on her waist.

She wanted to slap him, but she moved away slightly so his hand fell off. Still smiling, she thrust the letter into his hand and said, "It's late. We will talk tomorrow." She backed away quickly and hurried into the house.

She leaned against the door, shut her eyes, and took a deep breath. Relief ran through her veins and then her eyes flew open when she heard footsteps approaching. She flew up the stairs and into her room. Closing the door quietly, she sighed and whispered, "Thank you, Lord."

She had done what she could. Hopefully, Taylor would agree to ask the elders to give her a fair hearing. "Lord, please let Taylor agree to speak to the elders on my behalf. And please give me favor with them," she whispered.

She shed her gown, put on her pajamas, and fell into bed. For the first time since she'd come, she fell asleep quickly.

TWENTY-TWO

The next morning, from up in her room, Rachel watched the guard, James, through the window. He was talking to another guard, and she waited impatiently for him to finish so she could catch his eye. Surely, Taylor had given him a message for her.

When he finally looked up at her, she discreetly mouthed, "Do you have a message for me?"

He shook his head and turned away.

Her heart sank. Taylor had not given him a message for her, which meant he had decided not to help her. She sighed sadly. Still, she would have to find a way to talk to the guard soon and find out what Taylor's reaction had been when he got her message.

In between classes, as they usually did, she and Lily talked in whispers. She told Lily about what had happened when she'd given the note to James. Lily cut in when she told her about how he had put his hand on her waist and smiled lewdly at her.

"Are you sure it's safe to approach this guard again?" Lily asked. "What if he does something worse next time you talk to him?"

Rachel said, "Which brings me to the next part of my story. This morning, I asked the guard if Taylor had given him any message for me and he…"

Lily cut in again. "Wait, Rachel. How did you ask him? Did you walk up to him in the open?"

"Of course not." Rachel shook her head. "I was in my room. I caught his eye and mouthed the words. Taylor didn't give him any message for me, but I plan to find out what Taylor's reaction was when James gave him my letter."

"No, Rachel." Lily shook her head slowly. "You're not going to meet this guard anymore. You know he wants something from you that you cannot give him. Asking him for a favor again might make him think you owe him. What will happen if he forces himself on you? You won't be able to complain to anyone for obvious reasons."

"But I have to go and find out, Lily."

"Then I will go with you," Lily said.

Rachel said nothing. Apart from the possibility of being assaulted by the guard, there were risks involved with loitering around alone at night. Those risks were multiplied when there was more than one person. Still, Lily was right. The risks involved with going to meet the guard alone at night were way worse.

"So, it is settled, Rachel. I will go with you."

Rachel sighed and nodded.

***

While the tutor was writing on the blackboard, Margaret appeared at the door of the classroom.

She turned her scowl on Rachel and told her a car was outside the house waiting to take her somewhere. The tutor turned around and shot Margaret an angry look, but Margaret ignored her. Rachel turned around, gave Lily a small smile, and then followed Margaret out of the class.

Margaret said nothing as they walked down the stairs, clearly sullen. Rachel was grateful to God for the woman's silence. Outside the house, Rachel climbed into a red jeep. She was alone in the car except for the driver. She asked the man where exactly they were going, but he said nothing to her. As he drove, she looked out the window, curious about where he was taking her, and then as they approached the community hall, her heart began to pound.

The driver parked in front of the hall and she got out of the car. She looked up at the hall and it immediately dawned on her why she was here. Taylor had succeeded in reaching out to the elders and convincing them to give her a fair hearing, and he had done so very quickly. She took a deep breath as anxiety pressed in on her and then murmured, "Go in, Rachel. This is your chance."

She made her way up the stairs to the entrance of the hall, her hands damp and her stomach queasy.

Before she opened the large mahogany door into the community hall, she prayed briefly, asking the Lord for favor and for wisdom to know what to say when she stood before the elders. Lily had told her that this sort of thing had only happened once in recent memory, and then it had been unsuccessful. She prayed that her case would be different. If she was successful, the best scenario would be that they would grant her what she wanted, which was to be able to leave Fallow Creek with her daughter. She would not stop Mike from visiting Emily any time he wanted since he was her father, but she was going to plead that Emily was better off with her mother at this time, since she was still a baby. She could not comprehend going back to live with Mike, but if today did not go in her favor, she would have to. She finally pushed the large doors open and entered the hall.

Taylor had been commissioned to rebuild this hall some years ago, as he had done to many other large buildings in town. The community hall had been a much smaller building until then. By the time Taylor was given the contract to reconstruct the building, it had become dilapidated because it was the oldest building in the town. She looked at the shiny marble floors and the large stone pillars, the high ceilings and wide windows. Taylor had outdone himself here. She made her way to the front of the hall where a row of five elders sat. She swallowed when she saw Dennis Hamilton, the spiritual leader of Fallow Creek, sitting with them. She had never spoken or had to deal with him before. Apart from the elders, no one else was in the hall.

None of the elders said anything for a long while as she stood before them, trying to steel her rapidly beating heart. Finally, Dennis Hamilton, who sat in the middle of the group, said, "Let us start." He uttered a brief prayer and then declared that it was time to start the hearing.

Rachel stood before them as they talked about her request for the hearing, which was very rare.

One of the elders told her that they had decided to hear her out because it felt like the right thing to do. They told her that Taylor, her brother, had briefed them on what exactly she wanted, and then told her to repeat and elaborate on her request.

She exhaled and gathered herself together, and then she began to tell them about her life with Mike. She knew they would see little wrong with what Mike had done to her. These men mostly ran their homes and had the same kind of characters as Mike. As for what he'd done to Keith, there was no point telling them about it because they would do nothing. She had vowed that if she ever got out of Fallow Creek, Mike would pay for his actions.

As she spoke, she began to feel increasingly hopeless. The men had nonchalant looks on their faces. Why had she believed she would ever stand a chance of convincing them to let her follow her own path? They were looking at her with derision. The only reason they were seated here allowing her to speak, she was sure, was because of their constant self-righteous need to feel as though they were just men; and, of course, because of Taylor's influence.

Despite her misgivings, she continued to speak. When she brought up the Bible story about the daughters of Zelophehad who had been granted their father's estate after they pleaded their case before Moses, most of the men scowled deeply. The part of the Bible that supported women taking control of their own destiny was clearly not popular with them.

She finally asked that she be allowed to leave the community in peace to make her own way and be allowed to take her daughter with her.

The elders began to murmur and then one of them said, "You want to take a child away from her father?"

"No, I want my baby to have a chance to grow up with her mother, which will not happen if I continue to stay in that Restoration House. And no matter where I go, her father is allowed to visit her." She sighed exasperatedly. "I don't know how long I am expected to stay in that house. My baby needs me. I still breastfeed…"

Rayford Young cut in. "You brought this on yourself. The length of your stay will be decided on by us."

Rachel did not reply. There was no need. She could see the way the case was going to go from the expressions on their faces and their words. Still, she prayed and held onto hope that, somehow, the Lord would intervene on her behalf.

Another elder, Blake Stone, called out Mike's name and Rachel sucked in her breath. She wasn't ready to see him, though she had known he would be here today.

Mike walked in and was asked to state his own case. He began to speak, but she tuned him out. She could already guess what he was going to say. His words would be full of accusations levied against her. She'd cheated on him as his wife. She did not submit to him as she should have done.

Her stomach churned with anger. He believed she was his wife, while she knew it was not so. They were neither married in the sight of the law or of God. The look on the men's faces told her everything she needed to know about how this case would turn out if the Lord did not intervene.

After Mike finished levying his accusations against her, they called Taylor out.

Taylor appeared from the back door and stood beside her. He turned to give her an encouraging smile and then turned to the elders again.

"You were the one who brought this case to us, Mr. Dalton," Dennis Hamilton said, "but I don't know what you were thinking. Your sister's request goes against everything we believe to be God's will."

Taylor said, "I brought her request to you all because even though this has not happened before, I think it's right for everyone to be heard, no matter who they are. Everyone has a right to defend themselves and to state their case."

Blake Stone nodded and said, "That is why we agreed to meet and hear her out."

"Then at least consider her request. Surely you cannot blame her for wanting to speak out against a man who she has accused of being cruel and whom she now despises."

Mike spoke up, "Ask her why she despises me. She has been committing adultery and now wants to take my child away."

Rachel cringed at the accusation and said, "What he accuses me of is not true. I have never slept with another man... and even if I did —" Her anger flared as she remembered what Mike had done to Keith, but she pressed it down. "Even if I did sleep with another man, it would not be adultery, because I am not married to Mike!"

Cries of protests broke out among the elders and Mike raged at her. Her words had clearly infuriated them, but she had to state the truth. Without a doubt, to them, this was really what this case was about. Judging a woman whose actions threatened to destabilize the way of life here.

Taylor turned to look at her and shook his head. He whispered, "You should not have said that."

She did not reply.

The commotion died down and Dennis Hamilton said in a loud voice, "Wait outside, Rachel... and you too, Taylor. We will discuss the case amongst ourselves and then make a decision."

She walked out of the hall with Taylor and then groaned once they were outside.

"You should not have said what you did, Rachel," Taylor said, gazing puzzlingly at her.

"I said the truth," Rachel answered.

Taylor continued to stare at her. He looked baffled. After a long moment, he said, "Who has been filling your head with false ideas?"

"God," she said boldly. "And they are certainly not false."

He looked taken aback. For a full minute, he said nothing as he scrutinized her face. Finally, he said, "God told you that you are not married to Mike? That you should commit adultery?"

"I did not commit adultery!" she said angrily. "And yes, God did tell me that I'm not married to Mike. And you know I am not, if you're going to be truthful with yourself, Taylor. You need to give up the lies that this place has filled you and everyone's head with. You were not like this before we came here. We believed..."

"Stop it!" Taylor said. "This is all wrong, Rachel. You are wrong."

"I am right and you know it," she said to him.

"No... no, you are not!"

She opened her mouth to insist that she was right, but the doors opened. Mike stood at the door, glaring at her and Taylor. "They want you both now," he said coldly, and then walked back into the hall.

Rachel entered the hall with Taylor, and they both stood in front of the elders.

"We have great respect for you, Taylor Dalton," Dennis Hamilton said. "That is why we agreed to hear your sister out. However, we will not tolerate any ideas or doctrines that threaten our way of life here."

Rachel's emotions roiled. *This is it, Lord.* They were about to give their decision. Her future relied on what they said.

"This is our decision," the spiritual leader continued. "We will show that we can be merciful in spite of the flagrant disregard for our laws and way of life here. Rachel, we have decided that in order for you to be able to leave the Restoration House and see your daughter, you will have to agree to remain with your husband and submit yourself completely to him as a wife should." He stared intently at her; his eyes hard. "However, if that is not to your liking, then you can leave Fallow Creek forever... but without your daughter. You will have twenty-four hours to pray and make your decision."

She widened her eyes in horror. She had to go back and live with Mike as his wife if she wanted to see Emily again? And if she didn't want to go back to him, which she didn't, she would have to leave

Fallow Creek and never see Emily again? She could choose to leave Fallow Creek and fight for Emily on the outside, but Mike had all the resources to make sure she didn't win. And now that the whole community was involved, their combined resources would guarantee that.

She could not speak, but Taylor protested on her behalf. "The ruling is way too harsh," he said as the elders started to rise from their seats, clearly done with the hearing. "Please don't banish her from Fallow Creek. At least let her be able to stay with me while Mike tries to win her heart back so she can see her daughter regularly."

The elders did not answer. They began to leave the hall and Rachel screamed. "No, I cannot go back to Mike."

"Then you can forget about Emily," Mike said with a sneer.

She ignored him and faced the elders, who were already at the door. "I cannot leave my daughter here," she said in desperation.

No one answered her. The elders all left the hall and Mike came and stood before her. "I am ready to take you back, Rachel, in spite of your betrayal. Remember that Emily needs you now when you make your decision."

She glared at him and suddenly could not control herself anymore. She slapped him hard and then raised her hand to slap him again.

Taylor held her back and Mike narrowed his eyes. "It's your decision, Rachel," he said in a voice as hard as stone. He walked away, and she watched him walk out of the hall, her heart heavy.

"I'm sorry, Rachel," Taylor said, looking at her

sympathetically.

She stared at the wall behind him, her heart aching. When she had considered the worst outcome of this case, she had thought it would be the elders insisting that she remained in the Restoration House. At least there she would not be far from Emily and she could go on trying to figure out a way to be with her daughter that did not include being with Mike. Now she was being forced to either leave Fallow Creek altogether without Emily or go back to Mike. She fell into her brother's arms and began to cry. The impossibility of her situation and the burden of the decision she had to make weighed heavily on her.

"I cannot go back to Mike!" she cried. But she already knew it was probably the decision she had to make. Emily was still a nursing baby who needed her mother. And Rachel could not even bear the thought of being permanently separated from her. And yet, how could she go back to Mike knowing it would be a sin before God? And she loathed him.

Taylor held her tightly. After a while, he said, "You have no choice, Rachel. Obviously as a mother you know you cannot leave your daughter at this time, no matter what Mike may have done to you."

Her brother was right, and yet he did not understand the dire situation she was in. To him, it was just a case of going back to a difficult marriage. But to her, it was something much worse.

She pulled away from him. "Mike killed the man I loved," she said.

"The man you loved?"

"Taylor, forget about that. I just told you Mike killed someone."

"Are you sure?"

She told him everything.

He looked up thoughtfully and said, "From what you said, I think it was an accident."

Speechless, Rachel looked at him for a long time and then shook her head sadly. There was no use trying to say more.

He gave her a sad smile. "I will try to talk to Mike and make sure he treats you well when you return to him,"

She did not answer.

"I have to go, Rachel. I will talk to you later."

She folded her arms as Taylor walked out of the hall, and then she began to walk out with unsteady legs. Outside, she got into the Jeep that had brought her here. She stared out of the window in sorrow as the driver drove her back to the Restoration House.

As soon as they reached the house, she entered and started to climb the stairs, hoping she could go straight to her room without attending any more classes today. She had to pray and ask for wisdom.

Margaret was at the top of the stairs with her hands propped on her waist. When Rachel tried to head toward her room, Margaret said, "You are going straight to your class now."

"I have to go to my room and pray," she said to Margaret.

Margaret scowled at her and opened her mouth to speak again, but Rachel cut her off. "The elders told me to take twenty-four hours to pray and make a decision," she said. She stared at Margaret, daring her to oppose the elders' order.

Margaret's face was red and she seemed to tremble with anger, but she did not stop Rachel as she walked past and headed in the direction of her room.

Once in her room, Rachel fell on her knees beside her bed. Thankfully, her roommate was still in class. She began to pray, asking the Lord for wisdom, but she knew deep down in her heart what her decision had to be. She had no choice in the matter. She had to go back to Mike or she would never see Emily again; at least, not in the near future.

The reality of her situation crashed in on her and she could not pray any longer. She sat on the floor and stared at the wall in front of her. *Why, Lord? Why?* She wiped away the tears slipping down her cheeks with her sleeve and then picked up her Bible from the table beside her bed. She casually opened it and her eyes fell on the words of Jesus in red letters. She began to read the words in the Book of Luke out loud, and fear and panic gripped her. Still, she went on reading.

"If any man come to me and hate not his father and mother, and wife, and children…" she stopped and swallowed a sob, and then continued, "…and brothers, and sisters, yes, and his own life, he cannot be my disciple."

When she finished reading, she bowed her head in sorrow and then looked up at the ceiling. "Lord, you cannot ask me to. I cannot leave Emily." But she already knew from the scripture what the Lord was asking her to do.

"I can't!" She stood up and paced the room. This was not right, and yet to go back to Mike and continue to live as his wife would be a sin against God. But how could the Lord ask her to leave her baby?

She looked at her Bible again and then stood up and stepped away from it. She shook her head as she wrestled with God's word in her heart. How could she leave Emily with Mike? And yet she would be willfully disobeying the Lord if she went back. She would be violating her conscience every day. If she knew Mike would leave her alone, it would be no problem. But she knew him. She didn't even want to think about what she would have to bear living with him. Still, she would bear it all for her daughter.

She went and picked up her Bible from the floor again. She opened it, hoping to find something different than what she had just read. Instead, she opened up a scripture that haunted her while slightly comforting her at the same time. She read the scripture again and again and then finally read it out loud. "For them that honor me I will honor, and they that despise me shall be lightly esteemed."

She closed her Bible and sat on her bed, thinking. She could ignore everything she had just read, but then she had promised the Lord she would obey Him in all things. What would her relationship with the Lord be like if she went back to Mike? What kind of life would she have after that?

"Emily," she cried. But the Lord had said He would honor those who honored Him. She meditated on the words once again, drawing comfort from them. She would obey the Lord, as difficult as it was, and believe He would honor her and ultimately bring her daughter back to her.

She sighed wearily, finally fully understanding what the scripture meant that said Christians were to take up their cross and follow the Lord.

Her heart was heavy and yet she had great hope. A supernatural peace had also settled in her heart in spite of the difficult decision she had finally come to.

She whispered, "Lord, I will honor you and leave everything to follow you. But I believe that you will bring Emily back to me one day." She hoped that day would be sooner rather than later.

She sighed again and once more felt like breaking down as she remembered all she had lost — Keith, and now Emily. She gathered herself together, however, as there was no point breaking down now.

The only consolation she had, if it even was consolation, was that she could leave Fallow Creek and go back to Destiny, the town she had come to love, especially because of Keith. As painful as thinking about him was, she smiled. He would be happy about her decision to live in Destiny if he was here.

She stood up and went to get the notebook and a pen from her purse. She knew exactly what to do to honor him and help the people of Destiny, the people he had loved when he was alive.

She began to write a long letter to Taylor. She would see him again tomorrow when she appeared before the elders to tell them her decision, but she was sure she would not be able to spend enough time with him to tell him everything she wanted before they sent her out of the town. The letter would have to do.

After she finished, she waited for the mind renewal classes to be over and then left her room. She found Lily heading to her own room and told her everything that had happened, and then she asked her friend to deliver the letter to the guard for her, as she wasn't in the mood for his leery attentions today. "Tell the oaf it's from me. Hopefully, he doesn't have designs on you as well," Rachel said as Lily willingly took the letter.

"I know how to handle him if he tries anything."

Rachel smiled. She was sure Lily did. After they talked briefly and hugged, Rachel went back to her room and sat on the bed again. She prayed about the letter she had written to Taylor, asking the Lord once more for favor with her brother. She ended the prayer and then stretched out on her bed and closed her eyes to go to sleep. It was all in Taylor's hands now... and the Lord's.

TWENTY-THREE

The sun was high in the sky when Rachel arrived in Destiny. Since she had been allowed to take nothing of hers from Mike's house, she had no luggage. That did not bother her. What bothered her was that she had not even been allowed to say goodbye to Emily.

Taylor had thankfully bought her an air ticket or she would not have had any money to make the journey to Destiny. He had also transferred some money into a bank account for her and given her a debit card. She had been overwhelmed with gratitude and had thanked him profusely, but he'd ignored her words, his eyes ablaze with anger.

"Do you realize what you are doing, Rachel?" he had asked her. "When will I get to see you again?"

She smiled sadly at him. They had grown apart in the last ten or so years, but her present trials had drawn them close again. She said to him, "You can come and visit me in Destiny anytime, Taylor. They respect you here, so I am pretty sure they will let you out to play once in a while." She smiled to let him know she was joking, but he did not smile back. Instead, he stared at her for what seemed like an eternity and then the anger melted off his face. He reached out and gathered her in a tight hug.

She sighed as she remembered the final hearing and how the elders had reacted when she'd told them what her decision was. When they gave her a little time to speak with Taylor before bundling her away, she had been surprised. She asked him if he'd received her letter and he nodded. When he reached into his pocket and handed her a check, relief had flooded her. He had also made her some promises that she was tremendously grateful for.

Mike had been sullen throughout the hearing, but she'd ignored him. She had focused on her brother. Apart from Taylor and Emily, and perhaps Olivia's kids, she would miss nothing in Fallow Creek. She had many bad memories of this place.

She walked through the streets of Destiny, taking in the familiar sights and sounds. Wiping her brow with a small handkerchief, she slowly began to make her way to the town hall. Her heart ached. Everything and everyone reminded her of Keith. Unsurprisingly, the town had changed very little. A large part of the town was still in ruins.

Keith had begun to put plans in place to rebuild Destiny, and despite the fact that she'd only been away for a short time, she was sure there would have been some changes to the look of the town if Keith were still alive.

Tears blinded her as she walked, but she refused to let them spill down her cheeks. As painful as remembering Keith was, she was not here to mourn him, at least not yet. She was first of all here to do what she knew he would have wanted.

She got to the town hall, a little smaller than the one in Fallow Creek, but somewhat similar. Walking up the stairs, she smiled in greeting at a few people who turned to look at her. Inside, she walked up to the mayor's secretary and was pointed in the direction of his office. Even though Destiny was slightly bigger than Fallow Creek, the red tape there was absent here. She was grateful for that, as she had no appointment with the mayor.

She climbed up a flight of stairs and walked down the hallway. She stopped in front of the last office. The door was open and she could see Mayor Winston behind his desk, his eyes on his computer. He looked up when she knocked and then beamed. "Come in," he said.

Rachel walked in and sat across from the mayor. After she introduced herself, Mayor Winston nodded. "Yes, I remember someone telling me about a family that moved into that old abandoned house. Everyone was surprised when you all moved out within a few weeks of coming here."

"It's a long story," she said.

He leaned forward, threading his fingers together on his desk. "So what can I do for you?"

A sob rose within her as she once again remembered Keith. She took a deep breath and got a hold of her emotions. She smiled at the mayor and handed him the check Taylor had written for the town on her request. It was what the content of the letter she had sent to him a few days ago was about. She'd told him about the devastation in Destiny and asked if he would help. He'd graciously done so, giving her a check for much more than she could ever have hoped for.

Mayor Winston looked at the check and then blinked rapidly. His mouth fell open and he looked up at her. "This is for two hundred thousand dollars."

She gave him a sad smile. "It's from a generous donor to help rebuild the town."

He nodded and smiled from ear to ear. "Thank you so much," he said as he looked at her. "This will definitely go a long way toward rebuilding our precious Destiny."

She told him about Taylor's generous offer to also send some of his builders and equipment to help rebuild Destiny, as he had a construction company.

The mayor looked overcome with emotions. "How can I possibly thank you and your brother?"

Rachel smiled and then stood up. The mayor held out his hand and she shook it.

She left the mayor's office with a mixture of emotions. She was happy to give something that would help the town greatly, but sad because Keith would have been so happy if he were alive. "For you, Keith," she said as she stood on the steps of the town hall.

She began to make her way to Eric and Paula's. Hopefully, they'd not been too worried about her sudden disappearance and would let her stay in their house until she could decide where exactly to go. She still had to leave Destiny in order to find a job and be financially independent, even if she did not know when she would see Emily again. Being in Destiny again had given her a renewed determination. She would fight for Emily, no matter how hard or long the process might be.

She began to walk by Keith's store, and at first

she wanted to cross to the other side because of how much it reminded her of him and the sorrow that brought her. But instead of avoiding the store, she stopped in front of it and tried to look inside. The blinds were drawn and she could hardly see anything.

She walked on, but rather than take the straight road to Eric and Paula's, she turned left and walked to Keith's house. She stood in front of his door and let the sorrow that came over her swallow her up. She would have sat on the ground sobbing if not for the fact that she was outside. She tried to open the door, but it was locked, just as she'd guessed it would be.

She cried out, "Oh, Keith. Why did I ever come into your life?" He would still be alive if not for her.

And then a new determination entered her heart and she knew she would fight to see Mike punished for what he had done.

She stayed in front of Keith's house for a little longer and then she moved on. A short while later, she got to Paula and Eric's and knocked on the door. She waited, but no one came to the door. She knocked again and again, and then sat on the front steps and closed her eyes. Tears fell down her cheeks, but she immediately wiped them away.

She felt bone tired and then drowsy. She hadn't slept well last night. She sighed and rested her forehead on her knees, her eyes closed. She felt herself drifting away and then jerked awake when someone yelled her name.

"Rachel!" Paula hurried over to her and they fell into each other's arms. When they separated, Paula looked her over and said, "Where have you been,

Rachel?"

"I was kidnapped."

Paula's jaw dropped. "Kidnapped? By whom?"

"It's a long story, Paula. I really don't feel like talking about it right now."

Paula nodded and wrapped her hands around Rachel's waist. She opened the front door and they walked in together. "Eric and I were so worried," she said. "You disappeared and we kept looking everywhere for you. We became even more worried when Pastor Keith told us..."

"Wait!" Rachel stared at Paula in confusion. "Keith? When did you speak with Keith?"

Paula frowned. "What is wrong, Rachel? You look like you've just seen a ghost."

"Paula! Tell me. When did you speak with Keith?"

"Just this morning. You didn't know? Keith had an accident, but he is recovering. He wanted..."

Rachel screamed and grabbed Paula's hand. "What are you saying, Paula? I thought Keith was dead!"

Paula shook her head. "No, he is not! I saw him this morning in the hospital. He hasn't been able to leave his bed for some time because he has a fractured leg and arm and was very weak. However, his bones are healing and he is getting stronger."

Rachel listened with her heart racing. She slowly sat down on the couch, her feet unable to carry her anymore. Paula sat beside her. "Who told you Keith was dead?"

Rachel stared into Paula's eyes disbelievingly. "You're telling me that Keith is alive?"

"Yes. He is."

Joy, relief, and a feeling she had no words for

except that it was the best feeling she had ever had flooded her soul. She sprang up from the couch and raced out of the door.

"Where are you going, Rachel?"

She said over her shoulder, "To see Keith! To see the man I love!"

"Do you even know the way to the hospital?" Paula called out.

"Let's go, then," Rachel yelled joyfully.

Paula ran up to her, and Rachel grabbed her hand. She ran as fast as she could, holding on to Paula, laughing with joy, not caring about the people who turned around to stare at her. All she cared about was seeing Keith and holding him. She'd dreamt of being in his arms and kissing him so many times in the last few days. Always, she woke up in tears, because she'd thought she would never see him again. Now she couldn't wait to see him, to actually hold him, and kiss him. Nothing else mattered more at this moment.

TWENTY-FOUR

Keith held onto the bedpost of his hospital bed as once again he tried to stand up straight. He finally pulled himself up from the bed and slowly let go of the bedpost, praying he would be able to stand on his own. He did and rejoiced. Now, he had to try to walk out of the room. But first, he needed to put his clothes on. Jenny had helped him find his clothes. They had been in a hidden corner of the small wardrobe in the room.

He imagined himself walking out of the room, down the long hallway, and out of the hospital, and then going on his quest to find Rachel. He would not let the doctor stop him this time.

After he had put on his clothes, he rested for a minute. He put one foot in front of the other and then groaned in pain. He moaned, "Rachel, where are you?" He knew without a doubt that something was wrong. If she was safe, she would have come to see him in the hospital. When Paula came this morning to visit him, he had asked her over and over again if she had seen Rachel, but Paula had ignored his questions. Even Jenny, who was usually eager to please, had looked away without answering when he'd asked about Rachel.

He got to the door of his room, groaning in pain. His legs could not carry him any farther. He leaned against the door and exhaled, trying to catch his breath. Shutting his eyes, he moaned in distress when Rachel's face clearly appeared in his mind.

"Keith, oh Keith!"

He sucked in his breath sharply. He was now imagining her voice calling his name. He felt like weeping. What had happened to her?

Someone touched his cheeks and he felt soft lips on his. His eyes flew open, and he stared into Rachel's eyes. She stepped back slightly and he blinked, wondering if he was imagining her. "Rachel?" He took hold of her hands and said slowly, "You're really here?"

She nodded, tears streaming down her face.

He looked her over. "You're safe, Rachel. I've missed you so much."

She pressed her lips together and fell into his arms.

He wrapped his arms around her, hugging her fiercely, and kissed her.

They kissed fiercely and passionately, their tears mingling together, his heart beating wildly with joy and love for her. When Rachel drew back slightly, he touched her cheeks at the same time as she touched his.

"I cannot believe you're alive," she said softly and kissed him again. She planted kisses on his forehead, his cheeks, and his chin and then her lips found his once more. Time seemed to stand still as they kissed and held each other tightly. Finally, Rachel stepped back again and laughed, her face radiant with joy.

"I love you so much," he said, kissing her hair. "When I thought something bad had happened to you, I thought I was going to die of heartache."

"I didn't know if I could go on living when I thought you were dead," she said.

He stared at her in surprise. "You thought I was dead?"

"Yes. Mike showed me a picture of you lying in the grass, looking lifeless. He told me you were dead."

Keith shook with rage. "That wicked man." He told her how he had been followed by an SUV when he was driving to Eric and Paula's to see her. "The car hit me from behind, and I lost control and crashed into a tree. I fell unconscious and woke up in the hospital hours later. Some kind people walking by saw my car and found me some distance away and brought me here."

Rachel covered her mouth. "If not for Emily, I know I would have given up completely when Mike told me you were dead." She flung her arms around his neck and pressed her body to his. "I cannot believe you are here, Keith, after believing you were dead for days." She kissed him again. "I am never letting you go."

He laughed. "Well, we cannot stand here forever, kissing."

"Why not?" She gave him a lopsided smile.

He smiled back and asked if she could help him back to bed. His leg was already aching from standing for too long. After they sat side by side on the edge of the bed, he took her hand and said, "Tell me everything that happened."

Rachel wove her fingers through his and began to tell him how she had been kidnapped and had woken up in Fallow Creek. She told him about being separated from her daughter and taken to the Restoration House, about the brainwashing that went on there, about Lily, her childhood friend who she'd gotten along with, and then how she had sent a letter to Taylor asking for a fair hearing before the elders.

As she talked, Keith's heart grew heavier and heavier for her. She had gone through so much. He raised their joined hands and kissed the back of her hand.

She smiled at him and went on. She told him about the hearing and then finally about the elders' final ruling. She bit her lip, her voice choked with emotion, as she said, "They asked me to choose between going back to Mike and to Emily, or leaving the town and never seeing Emily again. But for me, the choice was between going back to live in sin with Mike, thereby disobeying God, or leaving the town in order to obey God, but leaving my daughter behind." She shut her eyes as tears ran down her cheeks. He put his arm around her and drew her to him. He rubbed her back, trying to comfort her.

She pulled back slightly after some time and then continued talking. "I went back to that Restoration House already knowing the difficult decision I was going to make. As much as I loathed Mike and did not want to continue to live in sin with him, I felt like I had no choice because of my daughter."

Keith listened as she talked about praying and then opening up her Bible. Her eyes were overwhelmingly sad as she quoted the scripture that she'd read.

"I knew without a doubt that the Lord was asking me to follow Him in spite of what I would lose, which was having my daughter with me."

She told him about the other scripture that she had read, which had given her a little bit of comfort. "Because of that scripture, I knew without a doubt that I would see Emily again, no matter how long it took. Now that I see you are alive, I see the wisdom of God. I will have you by my side no matter how hard things will be in the future, and that is extremely comforting."

Keith ran his hand down her back, his heart breaking over and over again for her. The decision she had made was one no mother should ever be forced to make. "I'm so sorry, Rachel," he said. "It might all be hard for you now, but I believe you will see Emily soon. We will fight Mike with all we have."

Rachel nodded. "Mike will not go unpunished." Pain and anger shone through her eyes and he understood how she felt. He hugged her to him again, and then remembered what he'd planned to ask her some days ago, before the accident.

She pulled his head down and kissed him slowly.

He drew back from her, eager to ask her if she would spend the rest of her life with him, but she wrapped her arms around him and leaned in to kiss him again.

"Wait, Rachel," he said, pulling away from her. "I have something important to ask you."

She stared quizzically at him. "What is it?"

His pulse raced as put his hand in his left jeans pocket. The engagement ring wasn't there anymore. He stuck his hand in the right pocket. It wasn't there, either.

Rachel stared at him with an amused smile. "What is it, Keith?"

He slowly stood up from the bed and Rachel immediately stood and put her arm around him. His heart began to race with worry and he forced himself to calm down. Maybe it had fallen out in the wardrobe.

He began to walk to the wardrobe on the other side of the room, Rachel's arm around him, steadying him. *Lord, please help me find it.* He opened the wardrobe, praying he would find it, and then heaved a sigh of relief when he saw the small blue box lying on the wardrobe floor. He asked Rachel to close her eyes so she would not see the box.

Rachel laughed. "Why?"

"Trust me, Rachel. Just close your eyes."

She did, and he slowly picked up the box, ignoring the pain that shot though his arm. He put it in his pocket and then told her she could open her eyes. She smiled, looking at him suspiciously. "What are you hiding from me, Keith?" she asked.

He shrugged and she led him back to the bed. When he sat again, she said, "Okay. What is it, Keith? What do you want to ask me?"

He could see from her eyes that she'd probably guessed what he was up to. There was no need to delay any further. He brought out the box from his pocket. He considered kneeling but knew he would not be able to manage. He felt slightly disappointed at the fact, but he quickly brushed it away when Rachel smiled at him. He might not be able to kneel and propose to her, but the fact that she was here and he could finally ask her to marry him was all that mattered.

"So, Rachel Dalton," he took her hand, "the truth is that I fell in love with you the very first day I saw you. But I thought you were married, so I tried to bury my feelings. But I could not get you out of my mind. When I finally found out that you were single, I let my feelings show, and you can imagine how much joy I felt when you told me you loved me too."

Her eyes were soft as she looked at him. She touched his cheeks and said, "I love you with all my heart, Keith. Sometimes I feel like my heart will explode with just how much I love you."

He chuckled and went on. "I love everything about you. I wake up every day thinking about you and go to bed dreaming about you. I want you to be with me always." He brought the box out of his pocket and opened it. She covered her mouth with her hand and tears welled up in her eyes.

He held the box out to her and said, "Will you marry me, Rachel? Will you make me the happiest man in this world?"

She flung her arms around him and pressed him tightly to her. She kissed him and whispered, "Yes, Keith. I will marry you."

He grinned as his heart soared with joy.

She hugged him again and he drew back and slipped his grandmother's ring on her finger. He kissed the ring, and then turned around when he heard people clapping and cheering. He grinned at Paula, the doctor, and nurses who were standing at the door. Ann, one of the nurses who had come in every day to give him his medicine, said, "Finally, our pastor is getting married!"

Keith laughed. He kissed Rachel again and then searched her eyes while she searched his. After the cheering and clapping subsided, he said to her, "I have one more thing to ask you."

"What is it, Keith?"

"I want us to get married as soon as possible so you can move into my house. Then we can start the process of getting Emily back to you."

She nodded eagerly as her eyes lit up. "There is nothing I want more than to marry you." He hugged her and she said, "I have something to tell you, too." She told him about the letter she had sent to her brother and her request. And then she told him about the check she had given the mayor from her brother. "When I thought you were dead, I knew I had to do something to remember you by. Something you would want more than anything else in the world." She smiled at him. "And that is to rebuild the town you love."

He couldn't believe what she'd just told him. "Two hundred thousand dollars, Rachel! But your brother doesn't even know Destiny."

She smiled at him. "It's the answer to all your prayers, Keith. And also, Taylor owns a construction company and he promised to send equipment and builders... practically everything we need to rebuild the town."

Keith shook his head in wonder and then silently whispered a prayer of gratitude to God. "I am completely overwhelmed, Rachel. Thank you so much. Thank you for the money to rebuild our town." For a brief moment, his mind was consumed with thoughts on the best ways to use the money, and then he brushed it all aside and focused on Rachel, more precious than all the money in the world. She had suffered so much and given up so much to come here. He would protect her until his dying day. "No matter how long it takes, Rachel, I promise you, we will get Emily."

She smiled at him. "I hope so, Keith. For now, though, I have you and the Lord, and I am content."

She took his hand and he beamed, overwhelmed with his love for her. "Can we pray?" he asked, and she nodded.

They bowed their heads, their hands joined together, and Keith thanked the Lord for bringing Rachel back to him and asked that the Lord would give them strength for the long battle ahead. And then, with a smile, he asked the Lord to bless their future union and that they would always put Him first, no matter what.

He ended the prayer and reached out to caress her cheek, marveling at how gracious the Lord was to him. She was everything he had ever prayed for. The road ahead would not be easy, but she was right. As long as they had each other and the Lord, everything would work out eventually.

A LOOK AT:
THE PATH TO DESTINY

A STORY OF FORGIVING THOSE WHO HAVE DONE WRONG AND BRINGING LIGHT TO THE DARKNESS – THE DESTINY SERIES IS CHRISTIAN ROMANCE, SUSPENSE AND INTRIGUE AT ITS BEST.

Newlyweds Keith and Rachel are basking in their newfound love, rebuilding their lives and the small town of Destiny. It all seems idyllic except the sorrow over Emily, Rachel's absent infant daughter who has been separated from her mother by an obsessive father. Rachel's first husband Mike Caldwell is a town elder of a small polygamist community, Fallow Creek where Emily is being kept and where Rachel had lived. Having Emily, escaping Fallow Creek and discovering herself in Destiny led Rachel to Keith.

With a closer connection to God than she has ever felt before Rachel receives a calling, by the Lord to go with Keith to Fallow Creek and to bring the word of God there… a light in the darkness. Rachel felt the Lord speak to her, telling her to forgive those who had wronged her and to follow his plan.

COMING JUNE 2020

ABOUT THE AUTHOR

Like the characters in her stories, Emma Easter juggles a range of identities.

In the low-income community where she works, Easter is known as a family medicine physician who treats patients of all ages and backgrounds.

College friends see her as an accomplished musician, having studied and mastered five classical instruments—but behind closed doors, she's just as comfortable rocking an air guitar to Creed. And when she isn't giving her heart, soul, and sanity to her three young children she's indulging in her most secret identity of all: meeting new characters, crafting fresh plots, and exploring every corner of her imagination.

Across all these different roles, one cohesive thread has tied everything together: her faith and love of Jesus Christ.

Find more great titles by Emma Easter and Christian Kindle News at https://christiankindlenews.com/our-authors/emma-easter/